The BURNING ZONE

MICHAEL ANSON'S

The BURNING ZONE

An Apothecary Greene Procedure

PAGE D'OR
MMXIX

Page d'Or is an imprint of Prosperity Education Limited
Registered offices: 58 Sherlock Close, Cambridge CB3 0HP,
United Kingdom

First published 2019
Reprinted in 2020

Whilst based around the historical fact of Edward Wightman's judicial
burning in Lichfield, *The Burning Zone* is a work of fiction as is its
portrayal of characters/descendants of the victim's family.

A catalogue record for this book is available from the British Library

ISBN: 978-1-9161297-1-9

Designed by Steph Thelwell
Typeset in Caslon Antique by Noel Robson
Cover designed by ORP Cambridge

For further information visit: www.pagedor.co.uk

Ad infinitum et ultra.

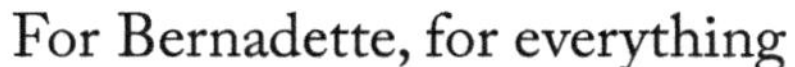

For Bernadette, for everything

Richard Greene (1716–1793): surgeon, apothecary and proprietor of a museum that attracted the notice of the antiquary and the curious of every denomination. Reproduced from Stebbing Shaw, *History and Antiquities of Staffordshire*, Vol.1 (London, 1798).

One of two surviving engravings of Richard Greene's Museum, Lichfield, published in *The Gentleman's Magazine* of 1788.

A

PARTICULAR, AND DESCRIPTIVE

CATALOGUE

OF THE

CURIOSITIES,

NATURAL AND *ARTIFICIAL,*

IN THE

𝕷𝖎𝖈𝖍𝖋𝖎𝖊𝖑𝖉 𝕸𝖚𝖘𝖊𝖚𝖒.

COLLECTED

(IN THE SPACE OF FORTY-SIX YEARS;)

BY

RICHARD GREENE.

THE THIRD EDITION.

LICHFIELD:

PRINTED, AND SOLD, BY JOHN JACKSON.

MDCCLXXXVI.

(PRICE ONE SHILLING).

The title page of Greene's third and final catalogue. 1786. © The Samuel Johnson Birthplace Museum, Lichfield.

Adapted from Spede's map of Lichfield in 1610. A city virtually unchanged in the mid-18th century. Reproduced with permission from the National Monuments Record Archives.

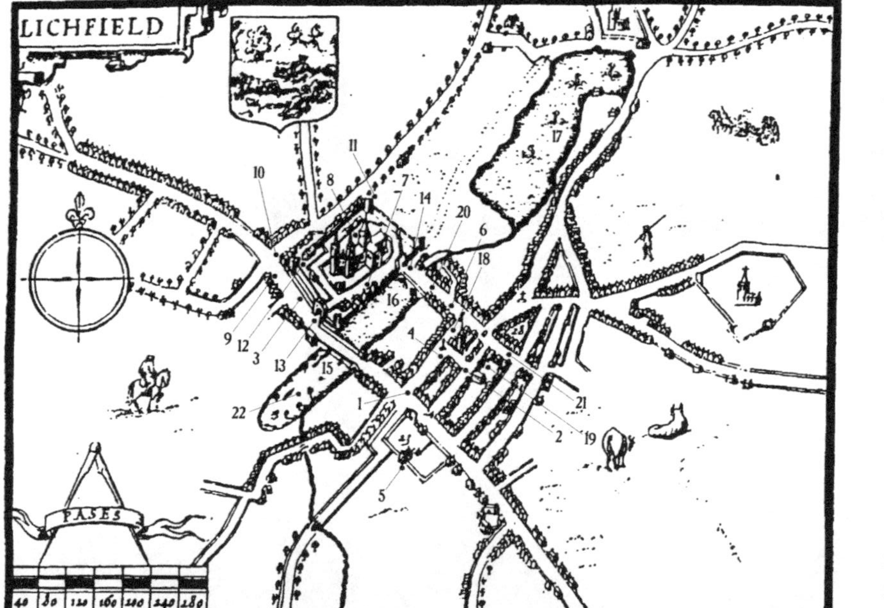

1 Richard Greene's Apothecary
2 The Ashmole/Blomefield House
3 Erasmus Darwin's House
4 Samuel Johnson's House
5 The Friary. Michael Rawlins
6 Richard Neille's House
7 The Prebendary House
8 The Bishop's Palace
9 Doctor Milley's Hospital
10 The North-West Tower
11 The Bishop's Tower
12 Vicars Close
13 The West Gate
14 The South Gate
15 The Vivarium
16 Minster Pool
17 Stow Pool
18 The Market Place
19 The Guildhall
20 The Dam
21 Greenhill

Loyal and Ancient City

Spede's map of the City of Lichfield from the early part of the 17th century portrays an inconsiderable market town located beside a trio of large meres that separate its small quadrangle of streets from a Cathedral church set within a heavily fortified Close. It was the latter – the medieval walls, moats and two formidable gates – in addition to the singularly strategic location of the little city itself, that brought down upon it the three devastating Civil War sieges that were to utterly wreck 'this great fortress'.

By 1646 the Cathedral church was a roofless shell, its great steeple brought down by parliamentary artillery, its principal defences wrecked by the first use of explosive mines in Britain. So comprehensive was its ruin that wholesale demolition was considered by the Commonwealth parliament in the aftermath of the war. Its future was only finally guaranteed by The Restoration of Charles the Second, when Elias Ashmole – himself a native Lichfeldian, educated at the Cathedral School – led the petitioners for the resurrection of the great building at the heart of 'This Loyal and Ancient City'.

By the middle of the 18th century, its fortunes restored, and now a bustling agricultural and coaching nexus for the East Midlands, its renown as a cultural beacon had spread further still. What one of its most famous sons, the great lexicographer Doctor Samuel Johnson, described as 'a City of Philosophers' would, in fact, produce equally famous sons and a renowned daughter – from within its small ambit. Poetess Anna Seward – 'The Swan of Lichfield' – the precociously accomplished daughter of Canon

Residentiary Seward, presided over the City's formidable literary scene as hostess of her father's grace-and-favour residence, the superbly rebuilt Bishop's Palace within The Close. Her paean to Cook's *Voyages* of discovery was the first, prescient, public recognition of their historic importance.

Seward's equally formidable mentor, Doctor Erasmus Darwin, one of his era's most admired proponents of the natural sciences, provided a ready focus for the Midland's renowned Lunar Society – the intellectual power-house for the region's 'coming men' – the likes of Matthew Boulton, Josiah Wedgwood and Thomas Baskerville. Not a hundred yards from Darwin's stately house beside the ruins of The Close's West Gate was the birthplace of the celebrated actor-manager David Garrick, later the doyen of the London stage, whose reputation would bring even the great theatrical diva of her age, Mrs Sarah Siddons, to perform to rapturous audiences at the City's Guildhall.

Not least, in terms of his inestimable contribution to Lichfield's cultural and intellectual life over half a century, though most certainly the least likely to occupy a uniquely stellar role in the city's fame, was an Apothecary named Richard Greene. Awarded an honorary doctorate in Medicine from the University of St Andrews for his outstanding services to that profession, Greene was, in addition, one of the leading antiquarians and pioneering museum curators of eighteenth-century Britain. In an Age of Enlightenment characterised by a small and select number of aristocratic aesthetes and collectors whose deep pockets and Grand Tours swelled the private collections that adorned their great houses, Richard Greene's Museum, in rooms above his Apothecary shop and accommodation in Lichfield's Saddler Street, were open to all for the price of a few pence admission.

From its beginnings in 1740, when Greene and his wife Theodosia opened their new premises, until its closure on Greene's demise some 50 years later, the collections grew to the extent that several full-page illustrations in *The Gentleman's Magazine* of the

1780's feature the unique assemblage of antiquities, curiosities, arms and armour, clocks, printed ephemera and, most particularly natural history, that had drawn tens of thousands of spellbound visitors over the decades. Greene himself would become a regular and most eclectic contributor to the *Magazine*, encouraged by its sometime editor, his cousin, Samuel Johnson. That Doctor, born less than a hundred yards away from the famous stained-glass windows that would later attract myriad customers through The Apothecary doors, famously commented – admiringly if somewhat ambiguously: "Sir, I would rather have embarked upon the building of a Man-of-War, than undertake such a project."

The astonishing variety and not least, the scholarly identification of the huge collection is preserved in prized copies of the three ever-expanding guide books produced by their curator between 1746 and 1786, still to be found in Lichfield's Johnson Birthplace Museum and in the Salt Library, Stafford.

Just as Richard and Theodosia Greene provide both *The Burning Zone* and the companion volumes *The Bishop's Grimoire* and *The Ashmole Box* with their intriguing central characters, so too do the magnificently eccentric catalogue entries provide a verbatim header to each chapter of the novels.

(1)

Lichfield, Staffordshire

April 1787

The grey-green eyes turned briefly, appraisingly, to the small vase raised on books beside the table easel; then, a glance across to an aging china palette, its sheen crazed with hairlines of spent pigment.

The tiny brush dipped, darting, into a smear of Norwich Madder and with deft certainty lined a stalk and its swag of leaf in a single, almost languid, motion.

With a small sigh of release the elderly figure leaned back, the better to regard the sinuous dance of the red-lined stem, its long curve joined now to a luxuriant droop of trumpet blooms.

"*Rhododendron nudiflorum*, raised as a seedling from Azalea Pontica and native to the state of Carolina in the Americas." The quick hand signed off its task with a pencilled inscription at the foot of the page; the quiet enunciation that accompanied it passing quite unheeded by her absorbed companion. He sat against the casement in the first ebbing of the afternoon light, ordered papers spread across the table at his side.

She watched, a smile touching pale lips, fine creases crinkling around her eyes, as the small man leaned ever-closer to his text, his pen – poised – weaving small arabesques above the lines. For an instant, as the head ducked towards another page, sunlight caught the shadow of old scars and puckered skin across his brow, a glimpse of livid striations across his hand's back.

For that same instant a flicker of shadow seemed to cross the woman's plump, good-natured face: *A far distant black wing, beating, against the dying light.*

She stood to stretch her aching back before leaving the room in a rustle of skirts. The sound of the scratching pen remained, an awkward counterpoint to the measured rhythm of the long clock, cased in shadow by the stairs. The busy ink-stained fingers were no strangers to death. In fact, its bright essence, its dark residues and tongue-twisting taxonomies had been the very stuff of their owner's lifework. Scratching absently at his nose, the fingers left yet another blue-black smudge upon the unremarkable face. The small sigh of satisfaction that escaped him was now the only sound to punctuate the perfect ticking meter, as first one and then another of the black printed proof leaves passed muster and joined the stack at his well-patched elbow.

ITEM:

Several calculi; one in particular taken from the stomach of an old horse, belonging to Mr Heath of Tamworth; it weighed five pounds; upon sawing it through the middle, a nail, above two inches long, was found to be the nucleus; one half of the above stone was given to Sir Ashton Lever's Museum.

Several hours had passed unnoticed as the final typographic errors were excised from the close-set pages, though scarcely a line had been scanned without some memory of acquisition flashing past the mind's eye.

ITEM:

In a clear spirit, Fingers, with their tendons torn off by violence.

Across a jumble of roofs to the west, the last of the sunset sank in a half-hearted dance, colours playing unnoticed across the few un-cluttered spaces on the wall behind the absorbed figure – pools of light drawing a soft glow from the polished mahogany of the display cases and the adzed boards of the old oak floor; a pearlescent shimmer from the glassed cabinets and a dull acknowledgement from the blades, the firelocks and armour, whose display occupied the passage wall to the stairs.

ITEM:

Two fine specimens of the Hauberk or Chain Mail, each ring
of which receives four others, and is drilled and riveted; the one
has the Cap and Coat, the other the same, with the addition
of trousers; as nothing of the like sort is to be seen in The
Tower of London, these are extremely curious and valuable.

With the onset of twilight, the elderly figure stood, gingerly
stretching his aching shoulders and thinking only now to call for
candles; a thought prompted by the piercing ache behind tired
eyes that only the black poppy pills could relieve anymore. No,
he would need a clear head for the dissection at Darwin's in the
morning. He contented himself with a final glance around the
dimming cornucopia of the upstairs rooms. The proofreading of
the dedication would have to wait until the body business was
done. Not least, it would provide blessed respite for a nose subjected to the hours spent in that worthy gentleman's cellar lair poring
over a rapidly aging cadaver.

As the sound of his light tread receded, downstairs to the realm
of supper and familiar comforts, a vagrant draught stirred the topmost of the small smudged sheets on the trestle top. Eighty-four
leaves, mute testament to a lifetime of scholarly passion, dimming
now with the flow of night through the casement leads:

A particular and descriptive catalogue of the Curiosities,
natural and artificial, in the Lichfield Museum, collected
(in the space of forty-six years) by Richard Greene.
3rd Edition. Lichfield MDCCLXXXVI.
Printed and sold by John Jackson.
Price one shilling.

Unheeded on that night of small satisfactions, another sheet lay
close by, in the security of a double-locked drawer. A sheet on
which, almost thirty years earlier, a far younger man had pains-

takingly recorded a newly found epitaph; his drawing of a grave-stone inscribed with a barely legible inscription. Ancient words that had opened a portal into a world of waking nightmare; a lichened memorial that had brought him face to face with a calculating and murderous evil.

Its memory, three decades on, still had the power to visit his unquiet hours. For tonight, though, the unravelling of those labyrinthine coils must remain an *anticipation*, to be embarked upon in Mr Apothecary Greene's own good time; the old gentleman by this time being engaged below upon his second pork chop.

(2)

ITEM:

On the mantle tree over the fireplace: a goldfinch,
a cat with a Mouse in her mouth. An Hedge
Hog, with her young ones. Two leverets.

The hanging had been at Stafford; the corpse of the wife murderer, Stebbing, being then carted to Lichfield by prior arrangement and with all despatch. It had arrived at the house by the old cathedral moat at much the same time that Richard Greene was taking to his bed. During the night it lay in rigorous isolation, close to the Doctor's well stocked wine cellar, and a deal too close to the kitchen – if his housekeeper was to be believed.

For all that he had set out with a spring in his step on a bright and crisp morning, as the Darwin house approached, the Apothecary – if pressed – might have admitted more to the sense of professional obligation rather than to any great affection for the bombastic owner of the grand house whose steps rose before him. They'd rubbed along well enough over twenty years and certainly shared a score of enthusiasms and pursuits in common, but *affection*? That, now, would be another thing altogether.

A mutual respect had made their association more than simply tolerable, and within the close-knit proprieties of Cathedral society, social niceties smoothed their occasional wrinkles to a well-pressed civility. The Apothecary had long suspected, though, that his own not inconsiderable commercial acumen – evidenced by a thriving retail trade in creams, pastes and nostrums sold as far afield as Liverpool – was perhaps the cause of a certain resentment on the part of his old acquaintance; a hint that *trade* would never sit quite at ease with the ecclesiastical *sensibilities* and professional *gravitas* that were Doctor Darwin's constant neighbours.

The congregation from the morning's first service was leaving The Close as Greene arrived at the house by the West Gate, doffing his hat in the chilly morning air as a number of greetings were called his way. Having clambered the imposing staircase with its fussy wrought-iron chinoiserie, he was admitted before the jingle of the doorbell had died away. As he handed his topcoat and hat to a dull-liveried servant the huge figure of Erasmus Darwin seemed suddenly to fill the hall with its presence: "Ah, Greene! Capital, c-c-capital!" The stutter brought a strange vulnerability to his grossly obese host's welcome.

"I did assure you of my small services if business permitted, Erasmus," the newcomer said quietly.

"Ah, *business*! Yes, y'd-d-did indeed!" He rubbed a bulbous nose, squinting down at his visitor. "We'll take a glass before we begin, I b-believe. It's no damn' warmer than usual, down below. I regret, though, even that's not stopped the b-brute from ripening. A fellow of foul disposition and fouler habits yet, so I'm t-t-told – but he'll serve us well enough, don't y'think?"

Thinking in any detail about what the morning held in store for him was something that Richard Greene was attempting to avoid as he sipped the scalding beer and gratefully inhaled the heady spices. He gazed, instead, around the airy room in which they stood.

"You have not yet seen the beneficence of Miss Seward's gift to the Museum, Doctor," he said to his host. "Such treasures from The South Seas are scarcely to be believed."

"You'll forgive me for not sharing your t-t-taste for native f-f-feathers and f-flummeries Greene, though I grant you that Cook's discoveries reveal our grasp of the world's wonders to be little m-m-more than childlike in its paucity and its p-p-presumption. But, God's *Teeth*, man, can you really cram so much as another m-m-*mollusc* into that Magpie's nest of yours?"

Greene laughed easily in response. "Why, we shall simply have to move into the second-best bedroom if other such benefices and bequests come my way. Samwell is a man of our calling, after all, and I doubt that the Captain's own surgeon would scour Otaheite and then take the trouble to burden his vessel – or the ever-generous Miss Seward – with anything less than remarkable."

"We shall agree to d-d-differ," boomed Darwin, with a genially dismissive wave of a fat-fingered hand, "as is often our way." A smile touched his thick lips as he clasped an enveloping arm about the Apothecary's shoulders. "But now to filleting and p-pickling, Richard, before we exhaust ourselves in chatter."

They descended from the stone-flagged hall into the cellar, led by a growing stench every bit as noisome as Greene had supposed. An unwelcome memory of chops rose unbidden. He would never get used to the bouquet of imminent putrefaction, he reminded himself for the thousandth time, though now was a little late in life to review one's calling.

He looked across at the blue-tinged corpse, splayed, stark and graceless, beneath the candle lamps. He was suddenly aware of his own creaking frame and its ever-more transparent skin whose liver-spots and scaly creases kept him bound together. He longed, then, to be back with his fine catalogue and its tang of inks and fresh paper.

Erasmus Darwin took a deep breath before bearing down with the cranial saw, just above the blank eyes that stared from the grotesquely skewed head. "You'll d-dine with me when we're done here?" he enquired.

At his host's insistence, a manservant had been instructed to light the Apothecary on his short walk home. As was customary in the Darwin household, dinner was served at precisely two in the afternoon, Richard Greene's inventiveness having briefly failed him in the quick-witted provision of an adequate excuse to avoid the invitation.

They had dined alone in the weak light of an increasingly blustery afternoon, and in the absence of the Doctor's wife and their enthusiastically extended family, Darwin's quicksilver mind kept his retiring guest entranced through the seemingly endless courses which came and went from the table.

The two men shared a passion for Botany and the natural sciences, and once Darwin's sardonic and irritable lapses could be ignored, Greene found the stoop-shouldered grotesque at the head of the table impossible to dislike. The fact that one could rarely slip a word – even edgeways – into his host's flow of erudition, reminded the listener all-too readily of his own cousin, Johnson. And although that estimable Doctor spent ever-fewer months back in this, his native city in his later years, pity the unfortunate hostess who endured *both* that pair of bear-like intellects caged simultaneously in her salon.

When, around eight, the slight figure was finally released from his host's bravura monologue, Greene's head was reeling with the deliberations of the Lunar Society, the improvement of carriage chassis, the incidence of physical deformity in the criminal cranium and a sight more Madeira than he would have chosen. Indeed, whilst the Doctor preached a very proper diet of moderation and abstinence to his patients, his own practice – at his ever-generous table – was largely at odds with his theory.

"M-m-my man will light you safe to home, G-Greene," his bibulous host had insisted, waving aside the Apothecary's half-hearted protestation before retreating unsteadily into the dimly lit hall.

As the two men left the lee of The Close walls, a cruel breeze cut through felt and worsted as they hurried across the *Vivarium* bridge; the surface of the marshy pools to left and right beginning to cloud with ice, half seen in the wildly guttering flame of the torchlight.

It was just as they had negotiated the broken cobblestones by The George Inn – prey to coach wheels without number – that Greene's attendant slipped on the treacherous surface, arms flung wide as his feet skidded from under him. With a shocked cry, Greene flinched back from the flailing torch, its heat searing his cheek and eye, sparks showering down upon his shoulder and the acrid reek of his own burnt hair fouling his nostrils.

In the bare instants before the cursing servant could regain his footing, a long-suppressed phantasm of pure terror gripped Greene. His eyes filled with the after-image of *other* flames, *other* blistering memories he had so carefully banished. And there, too, *oh Christ* – no more than a few score yards away – was The Friary, half glimpsed through streaming eyes across a frost-white Green. No lights shone from the ancient pile that crouched behind its high dark walls, but it was there that it had all begun.

There, on a spring day in a sunlit garden thirty years ago, where he had unwittingly placed a first foot onto the first rung on that demonic ladder; there where the damnable inscription had been uncovered, to fasten, leech-like, onto innocent curiosity.

For a momentary eternity he stood transfixed, frozen, by the appalling potency of his memories whilst Darwin's man tugged with mounting alarm at the Apothecary's unresponsive arm: "Sir? *Please*, Mr Greene, Sir? Are you *hurt*, Sir? Forgive my clumsiness I beg you, Sir?"

For those slipped seconds, though, the unseeing, unhearing object of his entreaties was beyond all reach; back in the place where nightmares bloom.

(3)

In the shallow case against the wainscot: an ancient crucifix of bone with, still attached, sundry beads of its rosarie. Likely of mendicant Greyfriars origin, whose grant of *liberum sepultum* assured that those buried in their cemetery or in the habit of their order would be secure from the attack of evil spirits.

17thApril, 1746. On that bright afternoon, as the desperate remnants of Bonnie Charlie's highlanders were being hunted with dogs and bayoneted in the budding heather for miles around Culloden Moor, Richard Greene was taking a bowl of tea in Mr Rawlins' parlour and discussing the cultivation of musk roses.

Scarcely four months earlier, within the self-same oak-panelled walls, the Duke, now busily earning the title of *Butcher*, had also taken tea in the briefly commandeered house. On that day, though, the talk had been of a *tactical* rather than horticultural nature, as Cumberland and his senior staff had discussed a strategy to hold the ever-nearing army of the Scottish Pretender at Derby. Today, though, heedless of the old room's echoes, or of far-off events, the young Mr Greene had been summoned to record a discovery.

It lay propped against the kitchen garden gate, still glistening from the bucketsful of water employed to sluice the heavy loam from its surface, and after social niceties had been briefly observed, his aged host had hurried him out of doors, hobbling ahead through the warrenous house.

"It's a grave slab, most certainly," agreed the Apothecary, peering closely at the inscription which ran around the edges of the slab, framing a deeply incised cross.

Pointing at its decorated head: "A *cross fleurie*, I believe a herald would call it," he added, turning to his host; a spare elderly man, stooped attentively at his side.

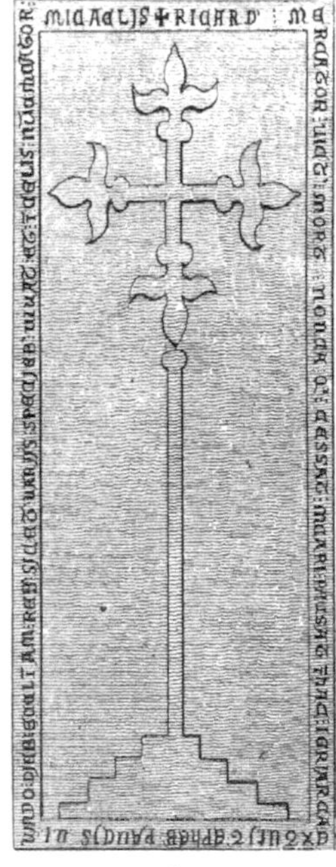

Writing rapidly in a precise hand he copied the archaic letterforms. After pausing to brush off the worst of the remaining mud, Greene continued: "I fear my Latin is not of such an off-the-cuff variety that will permit anything approaching an immediate translation. I can say that it is a memorial to one 'Richard the Merchant' and that there is mention of his generosity to the Church, but the rest must await assistance from a lexicon, and as much inspiration – and patience – as I can muster."

The elderly face creased in quiet appreciation of the younger man's modest disclaimer, as he went on: "Surely one of the Reverent Gentlemen of The Close could oblige with far greater facility than mine?"

"Most likely, Mr Greene," responded Michael Rawlins, drily, "but to be quite frank – and knowing of your interest in all things pertaining to our ancient City – I felt that your drafting skills and, shall we say, your *discretion*, might spare me from the effusions of those learned gentlemen and their particular enthusiasm for my sherry wine. I do get so weary of being talked *at*, if you will permit me such unchristian candour?"

Nothing, in fact, could have surprised the Apothecary more than the request, delivered just past opening time, that he attend upon this, the reclusive owner of The Friary. The messenger, a boy with an alarmingly swollen cheek, stood by, fidgeting miserably, as Greene squinted at the note – only as a postscript reading:

The boy would appear to have a gumboil; if it may be relieved for sixpence, kindly proceed.

He had met Rawlins only twice, when – on both occasions – the elderly man had happened upon him out sketching. His work had been politely admired and several suggestions regarding curiosities tucked away in the city's nether courts and alleyways had been made by the sparse figure, with brisk economy. Not now wishing to overstay what he sensed to be a somewhat finite welcome, the Apothecary completed his observations in the well-tended garden and promised to relay the translated text as soon as it was complete.

"I shall look forward to it, Mr Greene." The bony head in its sparse wig bobbed once as the massively studded door in the garden wall was closing.

"It is not every day one comes upon tombstones in one's tulip bed."

That it was to be more than two months before a raw-scarred and alarmingly gaunt young man would be able to return with the task complete entered neither head on that spring day in Holy Week.

Richard Greene was spared the knowledge that a season in Hell awaited him.

(4)

In a drawer within the Bureau, marked A: Twenty-one specimens
of small writing hardly legible without a glass, amongst
which the Creed, Lord's Prayer and Ten Commandments,
in the compass of half a guinea. Some writing by Matthew
Buckinger, born without hands and feet, in Germany 1674.

18ᵗʰ April, 1746. The following day being Easter Saturday, there
was a brisk trade in the costly powdered pigments which the
Apothecary stocked. Like camphor for mid-winter, blue-bags for
the wasp days of August and, today, paints for eggs, much of the
shop's business ebbed and flowed with the currents of the year: the
trick being, as the Shrewsbury apprentice-master had reiterated
with numbing regularity, to *foresee* in order to *flourish.*

The shop in Saddler Street had been established little more
than for a half-dozen years and was indeed flourishing. Its proprietor set out on his rounds leaving a competent assistant, his own
apprentice, and a keen-eyed wife to preside over the toothpaste
manufactory newly set up in the garden potting shed.

Although there had been no time for a leisurely scrutiny of the
notes and drawing made the previous afternoon, a small scheme
was hatching in his head as he returned from his last patient, in
The Close.

He had crossed The Millrace and was passing between the high
old houses in Dam Street as the attractive stratagem formed. *Why
not? Why not, indeed? A careful redrawing of the grave slab with
its gothic inscription nicely rendered, accompanied by a succinct and
scholarly observation on its antiquity and sense. After all, had Cousin*

Johnson not invited a contribution to 'The Gentleman's Magazine' on several occasions? This would neatly fit the bill.

The scream took a second – several seconds – to fully punctuate his reverie, and he had to jolt his attention back to the moment to properly register its source.

"Fire! Fire! Oh God help us – he's still abed and helpless!" A distraught figure burst from a porchway behind the Apothecary, her mob-cap flying from dishevelled hair as she rushed towards him. Greene reached out instinctively, but she stopped and screamed again, a dreadful ululating wail, as she pointed up. As if conjured by her hand, a great gout of black smoke burst from beneath the eaves of the house she had fled. She stifled another wail with blackened hands pressed to her mouth as Richard Greene grabbed her by shawled shoulders.

"Your Master? *Quick,* girl, is it your Master in there? Mr Neille? Old Mr Neille?"

Though not one of his patients, the Apothecary knew the stiff and proper occupant of the house to be a retired man of means, one of the City's racing fraternity, not long arrived from the North.

"Yessir," gulped the terrified girl, "Oh God, for pity's sake don't let him burn."

By now, all within earshot – a dozen or more – were running towards the wild-eyed girl, but before any could approach for further explanation, Greene pushed the maid to one side and launched himself into the darkened entrance to the high house.

Already, an acrid skein of smoke roiled down from above, fogging the hallway and the narrow stairs, all but choking Greene in his first unguarded breath. He knew from bitter experience that every second counted in the confines of these tinder-dry dwellings – crammed with the horsehair, lathes and wattles which partitioned their age-old wooden frames. Without hesitation he dragged off his neckerchief and, pressing to his nose and mouth, ran for the stairs.

As he breasted the first landing the sound of crackling seemed to fill the air above, and dense smoke billowed about him as he flung open the nearest door. An upstairs parlour, quite empty, met his streaming eyes as he crouched ever lower to avoid the suffocating fumes.

A muffled crash from the floor above jerked his attention away from the mocking emptiness, and he knew with awful certainty that his goal lay at the heart of the conflagration that was now roaring on the top storey. As he stumbled towards the stairs a shower of huge sparks cascaded down the stairwell and onto the landing, flames leaping in response from the thick Turkey carpet at his feet.

Pausing only to haul his moleskin coat off and over his bent head, Greene ploughed up the remaining flight into a wall of heat that snatched the air from his lungs. Even as he approached the nearest bedchamber door he knew he was too late – as the sound of exploding glass cracked out through the all-enveloping roar.

He flinched violently back from the appalling heat, an arm bent hopelessly across his face as he fought towards the planked door. Ducking to one side, he kicked with all his might, cowering back from the flaring gust that belched from the blazing room.

As his half-blinded eyes caught a glimpse of what the chamber held, a window into Perdition itself opened to the reeling man. Spread-eagled upon a blazing tester, arms and legs lashed to its posts, a hideously blistered figure writhed in the last extremities of agony on a bed of flame. In the instant of vision that remained to Greene, his quailing mind registered one last, abominable, comprehension: a bloody void framed a silent scream beneath melting eyes, *in a mouth possessed of no tongue.* Even before the realisation could numb his very soul, a concussive blackness smashed down upon the Apothecary's barely protected head and he stumbled, fell and tumbled like a cast-off bundle of smouldering rags down the staircase. Above, an incandescent gale raged across the collapsing ruin of roof and walls.

(5)

Close by the large bureau: The Pogge fish; a young stoat
taken in Shrewsbury 1740; a pea chicken with three legges;
large centipedes near seven inches long;an uncommon
spider taken in London; the short-winged Gryllus.

Sometimes, the flame-snakes would let him be and a great,
abiding calm flowed into the dark world. Then, though, just as he
sought rest in the fluffiest of the clouds, he would feel the wriggle
and scorch of the serpents' vile coils as they wrapped about his face
and tongue, slithering around fingers and legs to overwhelm him,
time and again. At other times a huge white face he seemed to
know, bent down from the clouds to brush the crawling fire from
his face and pour water, trickle by drop, into the place from which
his broken cries came.

The red film that lay across his sight was sometimes cooled by
a blackness laid upon him; he cried out as it was pulled away, foul
with red and yellow, and whimpered at the sting of light.

Then, in some inconceivable future, the looming face briefly
became a wife who called his name. He saw, for an instant, the
sudden flash of pure light enter the grey-green eyes, before he
retreated, gasping, into the place where the snakes couldn't come.
It was a beginning, though, thought the trembling woman, eyes
closed with gratitude in a face near-transparent with exhaustion.

As days became weeks and the first bandages were cautiously removed, quiet reason crept back into Richard Greene's eyes. As
swellings responded to his own balms and lotions, weeping burns

dried and crusted whilst the flesh re-made itself on hands and arms, face, neck and shoulders.

Though his lips began to lose their split-bladder pout and the juices of his mouth and nose regained their flow, he could not trust himself to speak; for speech meant words and he had no other word than *murder*, and again – *murder*.

Then, a voice, Theodosia's voice, was saying insistently: "Richard! Richard my dear! It is your dream again, no more, no more! It is past! You are at home and safe with me, Husband. Open your eyes. Your eyes, my dear! There is a friend here to help you mend."

With childlike obedience he allowed the familiar room to fill his sight, though it, in turn, seemed suddenly filled by a youthful face already running to fat.

"Splendid! Remarkable in every way!" it boomed.

The city's most recently arrived doctor – thus, the city's most immediately *summonable* professional newcomer – bent low over him, dimming all the new-found light as he stared intently into the Apothecary's unblinking eyes.

"You are returned to us safe if not yet altogether sound, as yet, my dear fellow," said young Doctor Ablett, rising to a stoop-shouldered stance.

"I am assured by one and all that you were quite the Paladin plunging into that inferno with no thought for your own safety! The City's been a-buzz with little else for weeks!"

"*Weeks?*" whispered a spectral voice through half-healed lips. "*How could…?*"

"We feared you lost, my dear," enjoined a second voice as his wife appeared at the Doctor's shoulder. "You have scarcely regained consciousness these four weeks past." As the bandage-swathed figure tried to come to terms with the chasm that had opened in his life, a great onrush of tiredness swept through him and sleep claimed every atom of his wounded mind and body.

"Regular applications of honey balm, a mild purgative, and as much fresh fruit and chopped liver he can be induced to swallow,

Mrs Greene. We'll have him back to his fossils and orreries in no time, now."

The physician smiled expansively at the ashen woman, her eyes smudged with sleeplessness.

"Time and rest will be the healers now, dear lady." He glanced back at the comatose patient: "He'll be scarred on his brow, I fear, though the beam that felled him could have been the death-blow for a lesser spirit. Still, the cranium suffered no permanent damage which I could discern, so that quick-witted brain of his will be delighting us all for many years to come, I trust."

Theodosia Greene gave a wan smile of acknowledgement and expressed her thanks, once again, as the ungainly figure crammed itself down the narrow stairs. How could this bumptious man – or anyone – know the helpless agony of watching her husband struggling in the coils of a nightmare so dreadful it had seemed to sap his very *essence* during the days and nights of her seemingly endless vigil?

Now, an unspoken prayer of gratitude and two of the black opium pills were all the exhausted woman could manage before she slumped asleep by the parlour fire.

The crackle and dance of the flames filled the quiet room, though neither seen nor heard by the oblivious occupants of number forty Saddler Street.

ITEM:

In the lobby at the stairhead: An iron bridle for a Scold; it is so contrived as to fit any kind of head, an aperture for the mouth, and a flap of iron for pressing down the tongue.

The evening of 23rd December, 1773. For the third time in her life, Theodosia Greene watched aghast as an injured husband was returned to her; though this time, at least, he did so on his own legs rather than as the ghastly apparition rushed through the streets from the Dam Street fire, or, mere months later, as a frozen, half-drowned scarecrow, in that terrible Winter of '46.

To the heartfelt relief of Erasmus Darwin's servant, Apothecary Greene had seemed sufficiently recovered to be supported the few remaining steps to the multi-coloured glass of the window in Saddler Street that proclaimed his shop, with home and museum on the floors above.

After brandy had been administered to her husband by his agitated and indignant wife, Darwin's man was sent off with a mixture of admonition and tight-lipped reassurance in equal measure. Her *Old Curiosity* was safely home and that, when all had been said and done, was what truly mattered to the mistress of the Greene household.

The shop to which the object of her affections descended on the following morning – much restored, and at first glance, little the worse for his experience – was a paradigm of order and bustle. The fragrance of the countless herbs and essences that had passed through the well-worn mortars of brass and stone suffused the low-ceilinged premises. Jars of blue-lettered porcelain stood in ranks beneath japanned canisters of barks, berries and leaves, those beside the dark, ribbed poison bottles and all, cheek by label, precisely arrayed with the flasks of oils and acids; the whole, forming a hand-labelled lexicon of impenetrable ciphers to the casual eye.

A small consulting room led from the side of the counter, where matters of an intimate nature could be examined behind the privacy of a closed door. Here also – though screened from squeamish eyes – were the well-scoured tabletop and stone sink, the boxed and graded blades and implements of the surgeon's trade. For *trade* it was deemed to be in the prickly order of things that governed status and determined *ton* and station in the county's salons and parlours.

To be a *Physician*, such as his erstwhile host – with one of Thomas Baskerville's nicely cut plates to announce the fact – denoted a *University* man: one whose demeanour, in most cases, could be relied upon whether at one's *soiree* or at one's sick-bed. Thus, *Sheriff* Greene of 1758, *Bailiff* Greene of just the previous year, and *Alderman* Greene of many years standing (whilst being an eminently respectable and indeed *laudable* personage in City society) would never pass through the invisible portal of *Quality* if such civic basilisks as the Honourable Mrs Seppel and Lady Ethelhampton had their way. If Richard Greene had cared one *jot*, one single *iota* about such censures and prohibitions, then he might have chosen to *display* the Honorary Doctorate of Medicine awarded, some years earlier, by the University of St. Andrews: a foundation so venerable and ancient that even the Honourable Mrs Seppel may have been given pause for reflection. Rather than seeking the approbation of such very *judgemental* eyes, the Apothecary had chosen, instead, to privately relish the great privilege of its bestowal *for outstanding contributions to the Natural Sciences.*

He revelled in the prosaic role of Surgeon Apothecary and the affection and gratitude of the generality of his fellow citizens. Indeed, most things about the unassuming man tended to be *quiet*

– from his self-effacing scholarship to his unquestioned excellence as a druggist and medical practitioner.

Many years earlier, whilst still serving his apprenticeship in Shrewsbury, the twenty-one-year-old Greene had been visiting Lichfield with half an eye to his future, when tragedy struck the household of his uncle, Michael Johnson. *Could it truly be close on forty years ago?* he had asked himself only days earlier, on passing the corner bookshop. There, those many years back, in the flat light of one awful morning, he had helped to cut down, and then to lay out, the contorted body of his poor bewildered cousin, Nathaniel. The pallid, withdrawn youth, apparently overwhelmed by the departure of his adored brother, Samuel, for London, had done away with himself by means of a halter knotted to the stairs in the tall corner house by the Marketplace.

None outside the family would ever know the truth of Nat's passing, and the apprentice Apothecary who had so carefully arranged the linen stock about the wealed neck had learned a lesson in discretion, that day in 1737; one which he would never forget. Indeed, it was just such prudence which today, in the year of Grace, 1773, provided a constant stream of custom to the shop in Saddler Street – both behind the closed door of the little back room and across the well-scrubbed counter.

After a morning spent in the laying on of comfrey to a blackened haematoma, the lancing of sundry pustules, the splinting of a broken toe and a local call to pronounce upon a bloody stool, the small man barely suppressed a groan of frustration when he was called away from bread and bacon to attend upon a father and small daughter waiting for him below in the shop.

He smiled, questioningly, at first the solemn child with a box clasped to her chest, and then at the diffident parent worrying a coarse hat between large work-worn hands.

"She's brung 'er kitten, Mister Greene, on account of 'ow she reckons you'll want un fer yer Moosean, like. Worth a bob or two, mebbe?"

"Indeed?" responded the Apothecary with a warm smile for the child. "And why might that be, my dear?"

"'Cos e's got two 'eads, Sir," replied the child, reaching for the lid with grubby fingers.

With Christmas Eve no more than a day away, the afternoon saw a brisk trade in tobacco and seasonal spices, and a multitude of the cane-sugar sweetmeats from the counter jars, whilst in the scullery Theodosia Greene oversaw the final blending of the fortified tonic wine whose vapours, alone, made the head swim. There would be a brisk trade, filling all the holiday orders for the Apothecary's 'cure-all' (as she privately called it), lest supplies should dwindle over the festive closure and a plethora of aches and niggles return to lower a thirsty patient's spirits. Satisfied that the laudanum tincture had been added drop by careful drop, precisely to her husband's instructions, she left a perspiring maid to the stirring.

Another light fall of snow around four o'clock heralded the early closure of the street's shops, as folk hurried home in the chill twilight. It was, thus, an hour or so earlier than usual this evening, that Richard Greene managed to return to the world of wonder above the household domain. To his considerable satisfaction he was joined there by his wife, briskly setting up her easel and laying out the watercolour tablets in their china cups.

"I shall keep you company for as long as my eyes can bear your twilight, Richard. Though the torment you inflict upon your *own* sight is more than you would tolerate in a patient. There are times when you are quite beyond me, Mr Greene. Are you nearly done?"

"Don't fuss, Theodosia. You know it only serves to make you fretful." He looked up, with a crooked smile that could still caress the best place in her heart. "Are you still working from your summer sketches, or shall I fetch *Johnson* for you?" he said, nodding as he spoke towards a small bookcase grudgingly squeezed between the ever-encroaching cabinets of display. The wood-blocked illustrations to Gerard's great 'Herbal' were her frequent touchstone, though as she may have discreetly admitted, her own *scratchings* and *splodgings* – as she habitually referred to her delicate plant and flower studies – did possess a certain *liveliness* that was sometimes to be found lacking in Johnson's emendation to the majestic original.

"Yes, to the first, and thank you, no, to the second, my dear," She bent towards a small wicker basket at her foot. "The teazels have dried quite perfectly though might they not be more at home in a manual for Fullers and wool-weavers than on the pages of our *Pharmacopeia?*"

"Not if the estimable Dioscorides is to believed," he replied, with an enigmatic finality that she knew marked the end of chatter. They both had work to do, he had tacitly announced, though she knew that with his nod to that most ancient source of the flower-painter's art, he embraced her, and his multitude of other passions, with infuriating even-handedness. Within two hours his labour of love was all but complete; the remaining pages kept back, the better to savour the glow of accomplishment radiant in their close-set lines:

*The great encrease of Articles since the publication of the last
Edition of my Catalogue, has induced me, for the accommodation of my numerous Visitors to compile a new one, much
more enlarged, and better arranged than the former. I entreat
permission to inscribe it to my illustrious and generous benefac-
tors, Sir Ashton Lever and Mr Pennant; the one immortalised
by his own matchless Museum, and the other by his various,
faithfull and splendid publication in Antiquities and Natural
History.
To the Public in general, and to my kind friends in particular,
I take this opportunity of returning my Thanks for their liberal
Patronage.
The limits of my Museum have lately been considerably extended, and this new descriptive arrangement of its contents will,*

I hope, be a plain and sufficient Guide when the inevitable
avocations of Business prevent my personal Attendance.
It may be necessary to add, that the MUSEUM is constantly
open to the inspection of the Public.
Richard Greene.
Museum in Saddler St
Lichfield. Dec 1st 1773.

With the accustomed street noises down below now muffled by the snowfall, his slow tread reverberated through the silent rooms as he paced through his ordered universe. Then, as countless times before, he paused by the little glassed box beneath the faux marble of Handel's bust. Not one of the twenty aching years since the lad's death had dulled the edge of the Apothecary's grief, and – even now – the memory of that Christmas birth still brought a tightness to his throat.

It was then, perhaps, with the indelible image of a little face pillowed for its final rest, its innocence and his own wracking impotence in the face of death, that a convulsive shudder ran through the old man's body. He knew, now, that once again his only choice was to confront the phantasm that had ambushed him so utterly the previous night. How else could he hope, finally, to scour away the images that had lain in wait for so long?

Hesitantly, with numbing reluctance, he let his memory edge back almost three decades into that terrible time; much as one might hope that the candle's flicker would penetrate the waiting infinity of darkness at the foot of the cellar stairs.

(7)

On the wall to the left hand of the Organ: Shoes, five inches and
a half from the Toe to the Heel, worn by the celebrated Dwarf,
Count Boruwlaski, a native of Poland, aged 47, whose height
measured 3 feet and 3 inches; He was shewn at the Three Crowns
in Litchfield at which time he paid a visit to the Museum.

Mid-May, 1746. Once he had regained the use of wasted muscles,
it seemed, to all his legion well-wishers, that Richard Greene was
making a salutary recovery. Within the space of little more than a
month, he was regularly to be seen about his business for several
hours a day, though no-one thought to comment that his increasingly regular outings led him as far away from the blackened gap
in Dam Street as he could contrive. Equally, none would begin to
imagine the adamantine power of will that kept at bay the memory of what it had contained.

He had come to realise, within days of regaining his feet, that
whilst every man, woman and child in the little city knew of what
they insisted on calling his *selfless courage* and *Christian gallantry*,
not a living soul amongst them even suspected that the immo-
lation of the late Richard Neille had been anything more than a
tragic accident.

With mute incredulity he managed to meet every platitude
and truism uttered about the old man's death by a populace who
seemed more curious as to why the Lord Bishop *in person* should
have officiated at the funeral than why a vigorous – albeit elderly
– man had been unable to save *himself* in the moments before the
fire took hold.

Some deep, absolute, imperative of silence was dictated to the Apothecary by an instinct he had come to trust above all else. He knew now, with utter certainty, that even were he to blurt out the substance of his appalling witness to murder, there remained no wisp of evidence to support it.

Enquiries made throughout his acquaintances had established, firstly, that the victim's coffin was interred with no more than a scooping of the jumbled ashes remaining from the building's molten collapse; secondly, that old Mr Neille's distraught serving-girl had returned from her market errands only moments before the fire had revealed itself. Her employer had been left abed, with a touch of gout, to await — she thought — either a visit from his physician later that morning, or, at least, the delivery of some medicament or other. Only housekeepers were privy to such confidences, she had sniffed, "and 'er were miles away when the Master needed 'un."

The girl had sworn on oath at the Coroner's inquest, Theodosia reported, that she had been out for scarcely more than a quarter of an hour, on account of the housekeeper's absence at a family christening in Walsall. The girl had returned, expecting, she tearfully insisted, to admit the anticipated visitor at the appointed time. Then, though, everything was horribly forestalled by the conflagration that met her a moment after her arrival. She insisted that there had been no reply to the frantic appeals shouted upstairs.

Both she and, as it transpired, the Coroner, had rapidly concluded that the poor old gentleman had been overcome by suffocation and was already unconscious by the time the alarm had been raised. The simple fact that not one of the city's small coterie of doctors had materialised at the Dam Street house – either then or later – seemed to have gone unremarked. One, old Halliday, had since died of a broken neck, in a drunken fall from his horse out at Wall. Another, James, the *bête noire* of the Apothecary's professional life, was taking the waters at Bath and was not expected to return until August. The remainder, to a man, disclaimed any knowledge of the deceased. Who then, had been expected that morning? Apparently, none but the Apothecary thought the question worth the asking. Even the newly unemployed housekeeper professed complete ignorance of the identity of her late employer's physician: "There was never really any call for one, Mrs Greene: he was always the most sprightly old Gent. Never so much as a snuffle in all the months I...." She dissolved in tears. The Apothecary's wife had extricated herself from the maudlin company as soon as decency permitted, leaving the bereft woman to return to her gin.

Stern admonitions against domestic negligence and the perennial threat of civic fire had been broadcast from the Bench, before adjournment. A verdict of Death by Misadventure was recorded and a coffin half-full of ash buried, with considerable pomp, the next day.

"Apparently," the Apothecary's wife later confided, "the poor old man was a descendant of one of the Bishops of Lichfield, way back before The Rebellion, in King James' time."

Richard Greene nodded, absently, as he peered at the notes he had made in what now seemed to be another lifetime. "The clergy have always well looked-after their own, my dear. It is to set an example of familial duty for us all, I believe."

Theodosia Greene smiled to herself: her husband's perceptions remained unblunted by his experience. Her relief was to be short-lived.

She had left him surrounded by discarded leaves torn from his jotting book, as version after version of an attempted translation of The Friary epigraph was rejected.

"Surely it can be little more than the usual pious homilies?" she had ventured, as yet another balled-up page had landed on the rug.

"In part, yes; I'm sure you are right," he'd replied, "though there's a form of words – some compressed and versey trick to it – that I seem to be missing entirely. I begin to fear it's beyond my very earthbound skills; much as I warned Mr Rawlins."

Knowing only too well that Mr Greene was much given to snorts, grunts, and a particularly vexing toneless whistle when lost in thought, she had paid little heed to the sharp intake of breath heard from the frowning man as she left to order supper.

She had closed the door and shivered as she entered the passage; the draughts in the old house seeming to confound even the most ingenious remedy. As she re-entered the parlour moments later, she bent to retrieve her sewing basket, and it was only as she was straightening that she caught sight of her husband. He sat rigid, shaking, with sweat glistening on a deathly white brow and the raw lividity of the scar which disfigured it. A sheet of his translation, scored with scratchings-out was clenched, white-knuckled, in a trembling hand.

"Merciful *Heavens*, Richard, what has happened? *Richard*, can you hear me?"

Gradually, as if awakening from a palsied stupor, her husband responded to her. A rouge-red spot flowed back into his colourless cheeks and his eyes began to lose the vacant, mesmerised fixity which had so frightened the woman now crouched at his knee.

"It is a rhyme of sorts," Richard Greene said, in a small, wondering voice, "though it seemed at first to be some frightful joke at my expense."

"*Joke? At your expense?* Richard, what can you mean? The inscription is centuries old – you told me that yourself."

"Indeed it is, my dear, though now that its … *meter*" – he had seemed to search for the word – "can be discerned, it has a … *pertinence* that is so unexpected as to be quite shocking to me." He rallied himself visibly and, vainly attempting to form a smile, continued: "Forgive me for frightening you, I was simply … *abashed* … at what I read. It is nothing more than foolishness, rest assured."

Wordlessly, she took the sheet from his unresisting fingers and with a puzzled frown looked at the first paragraph of the decipherment, the other lines being scored through with impatient strokes.

Richard the Merchant here extended lies
Death like a step-dame gladly closed his eyes
Happy he rests beneath this sacred stone
No more to trade beyond The Burning Zone

Looking up from the words she saw a look of such desolation, such imploring solitude in her husband's eyes, that she hurled the page aside and gathered him in her arms. Between his sobs, his shoulders convulsing against her bosom, she heard muffled words almost coughed into the warmth of her embrace.

"I can *hear* him, still, Theodosia. *Hear* him, though he had no voice. I know it is madness."

"Of *course* you can, my dear, of course. It is only to be expected. Your hurts will take time to mend; you must be patient. These dark fancies *will* pass, my dear, we have the good doctor's word on that. You are overwrought and confused by your labours; I blame myself entirely."

With that he was led to bed. As his aching head sunk into the bolster, he prayed, as he had never prayed in his life, that tonight – at least – he would be spared the dream of a black figure mounting his stairs. A figure bearing a bag of blades and rope and tinder.

(8)

ITEM:

In the center, beneath the WIND DIAL: A Picture;
which being viewed from one corner of the room
represents a clergyman in his canonical dress; from the
opposite corner, a Dutch Fishmonger in his shop.

The Apothecary's welcome at The Friary's studded door verged so close to the fulsome that Greene wondered whether his unnaturally genial host was entirely sober. It was only when he was led into the imposing library that he was able to identify old Mr Rawlins' behaviour as relief rather than intoxication. There, seated in a crimson and black tableau were two of those particular ecclesiastical gentlemen mentioned with such unchristian candour on his previous visit. There, too, as if to confirm the memory, stood a much-depleted decanter and drained glasses eloquently displayed on the tabletop before them.

Greene knew them both, naturally enough, and they rose with practised condescension to take his hand in soft, pale fingers, and to enquire, most solicitously, after his health. The fact that no such enquiries had reached him during long, housebound weeks of his convalescence was not lost on the small man as he joined them around the table.

"Mr Rawlins has been apprising us of his intriguing *excavation*," intoned the Reverend Mr Archdeacon Smallbrook, through pursed, bloodless lips that lent his words a fussy sibilance. "Though one must admit that the merest *whisper* of a discovery had already penetrated even our old walls, in The Close. Such is the village-like society of our little City."

Blithely ignoring the stiletto-thrust of reproof, their elderly host most pointedly filled a brimming stem-glass for Richard Greene without reference to the other glasses close by him on the table. With the merest raising of an eyebrow, the silk-coated figure known to the Apothecary as the Cathedral Librarian indicated that the omission had not passed unnoticed. Since arriving in Lichfield, Richard Greene had frequently delved into the book-stacks and over-loaded shelves of the Chapter House, though he had found this curator's predecessor far more to his taste than the florid, self-regarding figure of Theophilus Pomlett, who now addressed him:

"Does your own presence indicate a successful *essay* at interpretation, may one enquire, Mr Greene? For I believe Mr Rawlins sought your, ah, *expertise*, some *considerable* time ago, now?"

Greene felt a flush of annoyance, heightened by embarrassment rising above his collar. He nodded, politely, towards the watching figure of their host.

"Indeed, Mr Pomlett, you are correct on both counts. Although I did," he paused, regaining his composure, "in my defence, stress to this gentleman that my small talents could not begin to match the erudition so readily available within The Close, he still chose to honour me with his confidence."

"Heavens above, Smallbrook," the voice of Michael Rawlins interposed. "You seem so *bent* upon scouring away the last vestiges of antiquity from our poor old Cathedral I could imagine nothing of less interest to you than *another* tombstone. You've an embarrassment of them already, it would seem – in the light of the wholesale clearances upon which you are so busily engaged."

"Sir, Sir, you do me the *gravest* injustice," returned the Canon Residentiary, the smile on his sharp features reaching no further than his mouth. "My disposals and refurbishments are no more and no less than the attempts of a humble *Steward*, a servant of The Lord, to restore His house from the depredations of Civil Strife. Indeed, Mr Greene," he turned, patronisingly, to the silent listener, "your own *Collection of Curiosities* is now the repository of a number of the poor old scraps we have so reluctantly excised from the damaged fabric."

Nodding, straight faced, the Apothecary acknowledged the fact, and said to their host: "The Museum has certainly benefited from the Archdeacon's bounty, Mr Rawlins, with a number of his *poor old scraps* serving as valued and most poignant reminders of the former glories of the Cathedral. You must visit the garden behind my house, gentlemen, I have installed there some singular sculptural relics considered surplus to Cathedral requirements, but which delight my visitors."

The Reverend Smallbrook could detect no trace of irony in the Apothecary's face and was forced to respond with a shrug of modest disclaimer. He was, however, completely unprepared for Greene's next remark.

"It is fortuitous that you have raised the matter of *relics*, Sir, as you may be able to set my mind at rest concerning the fate of the Pipe Organ which was once, I am led to believe, one of the glories of our Cathedral? The account I have received of its present whereabouts can not, surely, be anything more than a malicious jest?"

The Canon Residentiary abandoned all pretence of good humour, glaring – suddenly flushed – at his interrogator. "I can scarcely be held responsible for the actions of billeted soldiery, Mr Greene. Their oafish depredations are the responsibility of their senior officers, if not, indeed, of his Grace the Duke of Cumberland, *himself*. No blame can be laid with the Dean and Chapter!"

"Then it *is* true that Cumberland's men were permitted to use the organ-pipes as firewood! The pipes of an instrument so venerable that Bishop Hackett had it removed from the body of the Church for safekeeping and restoration?"

"Though I am *mystified* by your concern, Mr Greene, you will, I believe, find that Dean Penny has passed the carcase of the sad old thing onto Alcock, our excellent Organist. Why, even *he* perceives it to be the anachronism it has, alas, become!"

"Apparently now employing it as a *clothes-press*, so I am informed," responded Greene, evenly.

"I do not make the domestic arrangements of Cathedral *functionaries* my concern, Sir," replied the Canon with icy formality.

"Then let us return to what still lies in my kitchen garden, Gentlemen," interposed Rawlins, making his first – and only – attempt at defusing the encoded altercation he was so enjoying.

"These gentlemen have produced *several* most elegant transliterations in the space of little more than … two or three hours at this table, Mr Greene." His gaze, scarcely concealing its mischievousness, never left the Apothecary.

"How, I wonder, will they compare with your own? You have brought your rendition with you, I trust?"

"I have Mr Rawlins, though shamefully overdue as the Reverend Pomlett reminded us all. I pray that you will excuse me, Sir, Gentlemen? I shall leave my poor effort with you as I am suddenly reminded that I must not over-stretch my recuperative powers. I shall be gratified to hear your opinion of my scrawl in due course, Mr Rawlins. Though, please, feel free to employ it for the amusement of these gentlemen." This, said so disingenuously that all assembled sprang to their feet, as the small man made his departure; the room seeming suddenly empty at his leaving.

It became rapidly apparent to the visitors from The Close that, whilst their host was still determinedly ignoring their empty glasses, neither was he displaying the least intention of sharing the Apothecary's text. The richly coated figures fidgeted awhile in the void left by Greene's departure, before scooping coat tails out from beneath well-breeched posteriors and making their own farewells.

"There is, assuredly, a *degree* of polish which might be applied to these *spontaneous* efforts of an afternoon, Mr Rawlins," effused the Canon, "but I believe we may speak with some confidence of the intentions of our Tudor scribe." He nodded to himself, as if convinced by his own authority. "We would hazard a guess of your grave-slab's origin as being in that most awesomely omened of years, fifteen hundred and thirty-nine; our claustral records indicating a significant benefice by one, *Richard Dyott, Merchant*. It was made scarcely months before the Dissolution from which you, subsequently, have so significantly benefited, Mr Rawlins." The Archdeacon gestured about him, lily-white palm spread and raised heavenwards, gesturing at the fabric of the ancient building around them.

"I can assure you, Gentlemen, that I count my blessings on a regular basis," said their taciturn host.

"Just as we, perforce, must count the hours, Sir," responded the Archdeacon, rising on spindly haunches. "We shall leave our *scribblings*," he pouted in a manner most unbecoming to the geography of a gaunt face, "in the hope that they may, at least, *hold their own* with the earnest rendition of our worthy Apothecary."

As the door closed behind the departing clergy, a profound silence seemed to flow back into the ancient building. After pouring a measure of brandy wine, the successor to generations of long-departed Abbots settled comfortably into their erstwhile parlour to savour the fruits of the day.

(9)

ITEM:

Within the bureau drawer marked B: a great number of ancient
DEEDS and **EVIDENCES** amongst which may be found:
A warrant, directed to the Headborough of Hendon for
impressing twenty horses and carts for the use of the Pretender.
Dated at Leek, 3d December 1745. Signed James Urquart.

Had the Apothecary been informed that a piece of green cheese
had fallen from the Moon into his onion bed, he could have hardly been more surprised. Old Michael Rawlins *here?* In the *shop* and
asking most civilly for a moment or so of Mr Greene's time, if he
would be so obliging?

The Friary's hermit-like owner could well afford to indulge
both his taste for seclusion and his *particularity* – as polite society
would have it – so his appearance in the closing minutes of business was of seismic significance to the amazed shopkeeper.

"Forgive me for such visitation, unannounced, Mr Greene.
I thought to catch you open the better to diminish my intrusion
upon your family hours." His sharp features scanned the orderly
shop and seemed to penetrate the less-orderly comforts of the
floor above.

"You are most welcome, Mr Rawlins," said Greene with artless
simplicity. "Will you do me the honour of taking a cordial with
us? It is our custom at about this hour."

"I should be delighted," replied the old man, now alone with
Greene in the dimming premises. "Lead on, pray."

"To say that your rendition of those antique words is *superi-
or* would be something of an understatement, Sir," said Michael

Rawlins as soon as social niceties had been performed. They were left, now, to *men's business* by a wife of practised discretion, though not before their visitor had revealed an urbane and engaging face normally denied to public gaze. Noting the floral samplers and watercolours that adorned the panelled parlour, he had commented knowledgably about the flower painting of the renowned Elizabeth Blackwell before prettily complimenting Theodosia on her own study, newly hung above the mantle; unnoticed, as yet, by her husband.

"Even without its cartouche, I should have known it instantly as *Rosa Semperflorens,* Mrs Greene. Your lightness of touch and, if I may make so bold, your acuity of eye does entire justice to a bloom of deceptive simplicity. I shall be honoured if you would choose to record one of my musk roses." Blushing with pleasure, she replied: "Mr Rawlins, you have me reddening like some silly girl! I am unused to having such praise lavished upon my efforts. You are most kind, Sir, and I shall look forward to just such an opportunity. My husband has told me all about your lovely gardens – praise *indeed* that he saw past the antiquity you discovered there. I fear that, for Richard, flowers remain a distant scent and a means of keeping a chattering wife occupied."

"In that case, perhaps you will permit me the pleasure of sharing the estimable Mrs Blackwell's *Curious Herbal* with both you and Mr Greene. Appositely, it is a remarkable collaboration between husband and wife; his, the text, hers, half a thousand cuts – *of the most useful plants which are now used in the practice of Physic* – as I seem to recall it." Seeing the nearly imperceptible look flashed between man and wife, he stopped short, his face creasing into folds of abashed amusement. "Oh, forgive a greying numbskull! Are you not both the *very* couple yourselves! You must know it like I know my own backhand!"

"We do, most certainly, Mr Rawlins, though our tattered copy would not do to be seen in company with your own, I fear." Seeing a mote of embarrassment lingering in the elderly face, she continued: "It is, after all, the sharing of one's enthusiasms that is the greatest pleasure. Now, though, if you will excuse me, I shall leave you gentlemen to yours."

At Rawlin's compliment, made as soon as the two men were alone, Greene had shrugged modestly, before replying: "I found little of comfort in it, if the truth be told, Mr Rawlins." And then, it was as if the words would no longer be constrained.

"Once past the paean, I came upon a form of words which, shall we say, thrust themselves upon me in a most discomfiting manner." As he watched concern grow in the old man's face, Greene hurriedly finished: "I know it to be utter nonsense that words on an age-old stone should so disturb me. If, indeed... ," he added weakly, "my paltry rendition is even half-correct."

"On that point let me offer you assurance, Mr Greene, the comparison between the literal context of your translation and the decidedly earthbound versions volunteered by our reverend friends tally with precision. It is, however, the *character* of your interpretation that, I believe, captures the very essence of the inscription. Of that I am certain. But, if one might enquire, how, exactly...?"

"...My discomfiture – my ... *unease* I suppose I must call it – is less to do with any original sense, or purpose that the inscription was intended to record, but more to do with the *coincidence* of the words; their *mirroring...* ," he unconsciously touched his brow, "of my own recent misadventure."

The spare figure of Michael Rawlins seemed, momentarily, to retreat within itself. Then he returned, locking the Apothecary with what Greene realised was one of the clearest, most penetrating, gaze he had ever encountered.

"Lichfield has a taste for burning, Mr Greene," he said quietly, "as you have found to your cost."

"I am a man of business and have ever been so," Michael Rawlins stated bluntly.

"So, Mr Greene, you have sat in a parlour whose grace and

antiquity I have purchased, and suffered an ecclesiastical visitation in a library I can well afford to stock but am little qualified to enjoy." He forestalled the Apothecary's polite demurral with the impatient wave of a liver-spotted hand.

"Brass works and gun-proofing in Birmingham, long ago guaranteed my fortune, Mr Greene, though they afford scant satisfaction in my declining years. What you made of those old, dead words convinces me of the existence of another world, another sphere of life itself, to which I have had scant access. That you are a poet, Sir, is beyond question. You have brought that cold stone to life in a way I would not have believed possible. I have come, in part, to thank you for it Mr Greene, you've opened a door for me." The sombreness of Michael Rawlin's face seemed all at odds with the generosity of his sentiment, and the words *in part* hung, somehow, in the air between them, though neither could prevent a sense of immense gratification sweeping through the small man. To cover his embarrassment, he hurriedly refilled their spent glasses before turning back to the visitor who was now gazing in apparent abstraction around the well-used room.

Hesitant, now, he said: "You mentioned *a taste*, Mr Rawlins. That Lichfield has ... *a taste*. I fail, quite, to follow your... ," he tailed off lamely.

After a long silence, Rawlins spoke. "Whilst the treasure trove of the Classics is denied to me by a lack of scholarship, I have made it my business – and my pleasure – to assemble works of geography and topography so that my mind's eye can transport me to where my feet have never trodden. Also, having the good fortune to inhabit an ancient Franciscan foundation, has given me an appetite for the story of our City and our County. It is to some of the sorrier episodes of that story that I alluded."

"Indeed, Mr Rawlins, I am intrigued; pray continue," murmured Greene.

"Scarcely a dozen years after the interment of our merchant, *Richard...* ," a brief smile ghosted across the lined features, "...

and the Dissolution of all England's religious houses, Mary Tudor burnt her mark upon Lichfield. Three souls perished at the stake in the Marketplace. Yards, only, from where Michael Johnson's establishment now stands, down on the corner."

The Apothecary nodded, absorbed by Rawlins account. "If that misguided Lady had sought to drive a final nail into the coffin of English Catholicism, she could hardly have done so to greater effect," he commented. "She provided so many awful examples of the Spanish way with dissent, that she unwittingly paved the way for her sister, Elizabeth. I knew nothing, though, of the Lichfield burnings you mention."

Obviously pleased by Greene's engagement, the elderly man held up a bony, long-fingered hand and enumerated the names of John Hayward, John Goreway, and the last of the trio, Joyce Lewis of Mancetter, who perished in flames scarcely months before the death of their persecutor.

"And that was the end of the whole ghastly business, with the death of Mary, herself?" enquired Greene.

"Oh no, Sir, far from it, I regret to say." Seeing the question in the Apothecary's eyes, he continued: "No, we were spared the vileness which Elizabeth visited upon the Jesuits and the Recusants of her reign, though more by chance than by judgement, if one studies Fox's grisly record of martyrdom across the land."

"Why *then*, Mr Rawlins? For surely the abomination of public Burnings persisted no closer to our own times?"

"Close enough, Mr Greene, close enough. Indeed, on that score, Lichfield has been stained with the blackest taint of all, for it was in that self-same Marketplace that the last burning in all of England took place. A poor demented Anabaptist who thought himself The Messiah, sent to the flames by a Bishop's court."

"The Bishop of *Lichfield?*" interposed Greene.

"Aye, and a Consistory Court so intent on fawning upon King James' every fear and fancy that they were prepared to commit judicial murder in his name."

"When was this exactly?" Greene enquired, endeavouring to cast his mind back into the early reaches of the previous century.

"Around the year Sixteen ten, or twelve, if my memory serves me, although of one fact I can be certain. As if the craven wickedness of their action was insufficient, the Court's sentence was carried out in Holy Week."

A sudden, shroud-like silence seemed to descend on the parlour, broken only by the distant sounds from the kitchen below.

"On which *day* of Holy Week," asked Richard Greene in a hoarse whisper he scarcely recognised as his own. His eyes fixed, unblinking, upon the Apothecary, the elderly man replied: "On Easter Saturday, Mr Greene; on the particular orders of the Bishop. *The Very Reverend Richard Neille.*"

The eyes of the two men seemed to lock, as they stared out over the abyss that had opened at their feet. Then, seeing the look of blank horror spread across the Apothecary's face, his elderly visitor said quietly: "No, Mr Greene. I give no credence to coincidence either, even if it be one as devilish as this. If it will not distress you unduly, perhaps you might wish to recount your own recent encounter with The Dark Angel?"

Sensing the small man's reluctance, Rawlins leaned across and placed a hand, awkwardly, upon the Apothecary's arm: "I fear that much may depend upon it."

10

ITEM:

Beside the Orrery: a machine for explaining the circulation
of the Blood, by means of a coloured Spirit in glass
contorted tubes, invented by Signor Nicodemi of Florence.
Amphisbaena or double-headed Snake, falsely so called.
A very ancient Cross Bow for killing mice.

It had been close to midnight when the two men finally parted company. Richard Greene had insisted on lighting his visitor
home, and they walked the short distance to The Friary walls, both
lost in their thoughts.

Before crossing the darkened garden to his front door, Michael
Rawlins said:

"I shall employ what remains of my good offices in The Close
to determine what I may concerning Bishop Neille and the heresy
trial. Records might still survive in the Cathedral Muniments, in
spite of the wreckage wrought by the fanatics during The Rebellion. I shall apprise you of my findings – if any – and, in the meantime, urge you to mention our enquiries to no-one."

He looked around, at the skyline of the sleeping city and
seemed about to speak again. Instead, he waved an abrupt farewell
and walked away into the dark bulk of his house.

In the days which followed, the Apothecary's waking hours were
almost swamped by one of those epidemics of feverish colds which
appeared like some Biblical scourge to strike down a great swathe
of the populace, with heed to neither age nor station. Both his
own wife and their shop-man Tillett, succumbed to its onslaught

and were packed off to their respective beds by an increasingly over-stretched Apothecary.

It came, then, as no surprise, to be called out – well past his solitary supper – to attend upon a stricken visitor to one of the grander residences in The Close. Within the arcane usages of *Grace and Favour* that seemed to characterise Lichfield's ecclesiastical society, the actual *attendance* expected of the Prebendaries at any Cathedral function amounted to little more than the occasional ceremony of pomp and circumstance. At such times, those worthies might briefly process, gorgeous in their vestments and *gravitas*, prior to a lengthy dinner at The Palace, and thence, a well-earned retreat to the pressing pursuits of County Life in the surrounding shires.

So it was that the so-called Prebendary Houses had long been a lucrative source of income to their absentee landlords, to be inhabited by those whose social aspirations made such accommodation *de rigueur*.

It was at just one such door that the Apothecary presented himself in the flickering light; a smoky flambeau dying in its wrought iron cresset above the grand porch.

He was admitted to the ample presence of the householder, a Mr Clarke, who immediately introduced him to a pale, intense-looking younger man sitting, broodingly, by the room's fire as Greene was ushered in.

"Mr Greene, forgive the lateness of the hour, I beg you: I should not have called on your services had my nephew's wife not been taken so very poorly."

The young man was introduced as Timothy Sharratt, "recently returned from the Americas to our unhealthy airs," his uncle lamented.

"My wife has been in poor health for several months past, due to most tragic bereavements. They seem to have entirely sapped her spirits," the young man explained earnestly. "I fear that she possesses scant reserves of strength, or spirit, to cope with this malady. I pray you can alleviate her condition for she refuses all sustenance in her few moments of lucidity."

Looking at the concern written upon both men's faces, Greene suspected that the summons had not come a moment too soon.

"May I enquire why you sought no earlier assistance, Mr Clarke?" asked Greene, thinking that he already knew the answer as the flush of embarrassment rose in the big man's face. "Well, I … Doctor Riddick normally attends upon my household, Mr Greene, but it would appear he has been called away to … some other…," he tailed off, gesturing, helplessly, with heavily ringed hands. "Please conduct me to your wife without further delay, Mr Sharratt."

The large blue and white bowl of pot-pourri at the stair-head did little to disguise the rank, sick-room fetor, its stench compounded by an oppressive airlessness. Without a backward glance, Greene said softly: "Please have both windows opened without delay," as he crossed the dimly lit room to the motionless occupant of its huge bed.

A thin, fine-boned face, framed with sweat-matted black hair, lay upon the bolster. Wheezing breaths, so light as to be almost inaudible, issued from slack lips in a face whose cheeks were livid with fever-heat.

"We must lower the lady's temperature immediately," said the Apothecary, reaching for a slight, limp wrist from below the heaped coverlets. "I shall require towels, flannels and copious fresh water."

"I shall send my housekeeper and her girl to you at once," came Clarke's voice from the door. "Timothy, it is best we leave Mr Greene to his business. There's nothing more for us to do here."

It was close on two hours later, before the Apothecary – his face lined with tiredness – descended to rejoin the waiting men, below.

"Well Sir, what's the prognostication?" blurted Clarke with strained geniality. "All's well, I trust!"

Before he could reply Greene caught the look of withering contempt in the young man's eyes, flashed at the bumbling figure of his uncle.

"Scarcely *well*, Sir; though a mite better than when I found her."

"Will she *live*, Greene!?" Sharratt burst out, obviously unable to contain himself any longer.

"Timothy! I hardly think....."

"*Will she live, Sir?*" he hissed, with a passion that had the corpulent Clarke flinching visibly from its lash. Unperturbed, the Apothecary replied evenly: "I believe so, Mr Sharratt, though your concern is in no way extravagant. She has been coaxed into swallowing near-to a full glass of sugar water, which is a beginning, at least. I have left instructions that she must be attended throughout the night in order that her fluid balances are restored. Her dehydration had come perilously close to damaging her vital functions beyond repair, Mr Sharratt. We must endeavour, now, to soothe such damage whist introducing only such medication as a severely weakened constitution can endure. Your housekeeper appears a most capable person, Mr Clarke," he continued, turning to the older man. "I have left her with a tincture and powders of my own preparation, to be administered with absolute precision." He glanced back at Sharratt. "The dosage, and its regularity, will be crucial in the coming days, Sir. Your wife's defences must be re-made with the greatest care."

The young man nodded, curtly, before replying: "I do not wish to sound ungracious, Mr Greene, but we must hope that *your* powders and potions are more efficacious – or at least, less injurious – than those my uncle has been insisting upon during my wife's illness." He glared openly at the now thoroughly abashed figure of Clarke.

"But James' Powders are known to be a *sovereign* remedy for all manner of complaints. Why, my own dear late wife employed them on every....."

"*James' Powders?*" interposed Greene, with a vehemence that shocked his listeners. "You administered that noxious *quackery* to a young woman already in a weakened state? Have you *no* sense, Sir? Are you unaware of the *infamous* reputation of that vile concoction? James is a living affront to the profession of Medicine! I have to tell you that it is a wonder your wife has survived at all, Mr Sharratt. Those powders are of a lethality scarcely to be imagined. *Kill or cure*, Gentlemen, that is the simplistic maxim of Doctor James, though his mistakes rarely enjoy the opportunity of redress."

"I protest, Greene!" Puffed the red-faced man. "As I was saying, before your tirade, my own late wife... ."

"I am neither your Physician nor an apologist for the legion shortcomings of the medical profession, Mr Clarke, so I have no knowledge of how your wife passed away. At risk of giving you grave offence, Sir, I would, however, suggest that if the unfortunate lady was one of the unnumbered and tragically innocent dupes of James' *Universal Panacea*, then her demise was, all-too-likely, a direct result of powders whose main constituent is a deadly poison."

"You go too far, Sir! How dare you impugn the honour and reputation of... ."

"...*The author of a lauded medical dictionary?*" Greene cut in, the sarcasm bristling from his words. "...*The son of a respected Lichfield family of medical men?* No, what I impugn, Mr Clarke, is the probity of a druggist whose nostrums are more suited to the purposes of the assassin. I cannot believe that Doctor Riddick would condone your endorsement of the Powders?"

The big man seemed, suddenly, to deflate like a pricked bladder, glancing, beseechingly, at his nephew, as he replied: "I was at my wits end, Mr Greene, and in the absence of Doctor Riddick did no more than a hundred in my place would have done!"

The Apothecary simply nodded, spent fury replaced by an aching weariness. "I shall return in the morning, and on a regular basis, until the lady is restored to health." With iron forebearance he did not add '*or until Doctor Riddick returns*'.

As he was shown out into the darkness of The Close, the immense mass of the Cathedral rose above him. He hesitated only for a moment before turning for the West Gate and the longer of the two ways home; the better to avoid Dam Street.

11

ITEM:

In the cases over the CLOSET DOOR; An Indian tomahawk,
maucassons, or Indian shoes, ornamented with human scalps,
tanned, with the hair preserved; two scalping knives, the
sheaths decorated with dyed Porcupine Quills, fringed
with tassels of tin and colour'd horse-hair; American
Rifleman's jacket, of coarse linen cloth, fringed.

In the week that followed Greene's visit to the Prebendary House,
he presided over the young woman's gradual return to stability. The
more he came to know Hepzibah Sharratt, the more he realised
the parlous state of health and mind which the fever had so avidly
fixed upon. Though for her to have survived the further onslaught
of the poisonous medication *at all* belied the elfin delicacy that
stole back into her features as they began to soften and fill with a
faint glow of returning health. *Here is a will-and-a-half,* thought
Richard Greene, looking down into the sleeping face. They had,
as yet, not formed any words for him, but he noticed that her lips
seemed to have taken on a little colour, parted slightly, exhaling
soft, easy breaths.

On the evening of the eighth day, with a gusty wind rattling
branches at the windows, he was leaving her bedside when a voice,
barely more than a whisper, followed him.

"*I am in your debt.*"

Even by the time he had crossed back to the bedside, she had
fallen back into a deep sleep. He left the bedroom and took to the
stairs with a new spring to his step.

In the days that followed he was to find her a withdrawn and diffident patient who would rarely meet his gaze or rise to his gentle questioning with anything but the barest response. It was, though, little short of two weeks after his first visit – with Doctor Riddick still taking the air in Derbyshire – that Greene was able to learn anything of what lay behind the young woman's solitary manner.

After that first occasion, Clarke usually managed to absent himself from the Apothecary's visits, though Timothy Sharratt became noticeably less sullen and brusque as his young wife passed out of immediate danger. It seemed to Greene that there was little warmth between the couple, conspicuously so on Hepzibah's part, though he often found her husband at the bedside when he arrived. As he was making to leave, he turned back to Sharratt – who had brought him to the door: "Would you object to a nerve-tonic prescription for your wife, Sir? She appears uncommonly forlorn and listless, for all the rallying of her *bodily* health."

Dismissing the maid who stood with Greene's coat, Sharratt waved the small man into the parlour in which their first encounter had occurred. "Will you take a glass with me Mr Greene," he enquired. Before the surprised Apothecary could respond, Sharratt had moved proprietorially towards his uncle's decanters.

"If it will please you, Sir. There is something more you wish to discuss concerning your wife's condition?"

"There is, Mr Greene," he let out a long sigh, "and I fear you've hit the nail squarely on its head when you talk of *condition*. With all due respect, though, I fear that its treatment lies far beyond the bounds of the *pharmacopaea*."

"You may well be correct, Sir, though unless I know more of its source, its beginnings, who is to say wherein a remedy might lie?"

"I intended no offence, Mr Greene, please believe me. I have not the slightest doubt that Hepzibah would be in her grave by now, had it not been for your intervention. I meant to say, rather, that she is somehow scarred in her mind by the dreadful fate of her mother and uncle."

Seeing the unspoken question in the Apothecary's eyes, he hurried on: "Of course, you could not know of it; their deaths occurred during last Winter in Western Pennsylvania, which is… ," he faltered momentarily, "…which *was*, our home."

He walked to the fireplace and prodded the small fire, unnecessarily, before turning back to his listener.

"You'll know, I'm sure, of the burgeoning and deadly rivalry between the French and our people on the eastern seaboard of The Americas, Mr Greene?"

Greene nodded, wordlessly, waiting for Sharratt to continue.

"This winter the French made their first overt moves against the Virginian Planters. They sent out an armed force down the Ohio River to mark out their territorial pretensions – whilst the Planters were engaged on much the same manoeuvre. France intends to raise a chain of forts down to the mouth of the Mississippi."

"And your people are *Virginians*? Forgive me, I am somewhat at sea, here."

"No, I am not explaining myself well, Mr Greene. My father-in-law, Blanchmayne, Isiah Blanchmayne, and his late brother, have been engaged in trade throughout the Middle Colonies for many years and I have been in his employ these five years past; ever since I married his daughter, in fact. My mother was a Clarke," he gestured around him at the plump interior, "the sister of my Uncle Billy." His expression caught between a grimace and a grin, continuing: "You have already made his acquaintance."

Seeing that the Apothecary was none the wiser, Sharratt shook his head, as if in exasperation with himself, and hurried on.

"The Blanchmaynes had business at the Fort that stands where the *Monongahela* and *Allegheny* rivers meet, and it was to that benighted place that my father-in-law foolishly permitted his wife to accompany them. His own brother, Ned, was dead set against it, but, if the truth be told, Mr Greene, the crusading zeal of my late mother-in-law was as unstoppable as a torrent in full spate.

She, somehow, convinced her husband that her Bible would be their sword and buckler, and that its blessed contents would be *as 'Manna and Nectar'* – her own words, Mr Greene – to the savages encamped around the joining of the rivers. How she prevailed upon her husband shall never be understood; but prevail, she did." He paused as a look of such anguish crossed his face that Greene took an involuntary step towards him, only to be halted by a peremptory hand.

"Unknown to the Garrison, the French had been covertly at work amongst the *Iroquois* tribes that winter and though, even now, no open state of war prevails, a murderous mood had been fomented among them."

He bent, again to the fire, before he could continue.

"My father-in-law barely escaped with his life when their party was ambushed some miles from its destination. His brother, Ned Blanchmayne, had been scouting ahead with the Wagon master, and the savages let them pass, apparently, before springing the trap. Ned's ... remains ... were discovered later – he'd been tortured to death, mutilated beyond recognition. Parry, the Wagon-master was never seen again. Mr Blanchmayne, *Isiah*, fought clear, with the two survivors of a dozen-strong party, though not before his wife had been dragged away by a dozen of the savages. They escaped as much by the vagaries of fate as by the blunderbusses they bore. Within hours he managed to return with garrison troops, desperate to pick up the savages' trail. They found Hepzibah's mother close to where poor Ned had been slaughtered." His voice faltered, cracked; he cleared his throat, continuing:

"It seems the savages had all taken their filthy pleasure with her, Mr Greene, one after another, before they disembowelled her. Her head had been taken as a trophy; her bible left within... ." He shook his head as if to clear it before continuing:

"In his distraction, in the desperation of his own guilt and grief, my father-in-law saw fit to describe the manner of the deaths – in every detail – to my wife and me, upon his eventual return. Hepzibah has neither smiled nor spoken a single word to her father since that day seven months ago."

"Even so, how could he bear to be parted from her, now, at such a time?" asked Greene, quietly.

"Parted? I fail to follow you, Mr Greene? It was he who brought us back to England. Here, to the only family to which he can now lay claim, albeit that it is mine."

"Then, *where…*?" began Greene in utter perplexity.

"In London, Sir, on shipping business, I believe, and to regularise his company affairs after the death of his brother. Though Ned was the eldest, I gather they shared the equity, more-or-less half and half as partners," interjected Sharratt.

"Her father left the day before my wife took ill. We have been unable to contact him, so he can have no idea of the state in which we have been. One thing that I do know with absolute certainty, Mr Greene, is that if he had lost Hepzibah, here, to the fever, it would have been more than even a man of his fortitude could bear. This family owes you more than one life, of that I can assure you."

Greene diffused the solemnity of the moment with his usual busy diffidence: "You appear to have a great deal of admiration for your father-in-law, Sir?"

The young man thought for a moment before responding: "I could never find it in myself to condone the foolhardiness that brought his family to such disaster, Mr Greene. I respect him, though, with all my heart – for his mastery of trade in that unforgiving land – and for the mettle he has shown in his determination to re-forge a life in the train of such horror."

He spread his hands, and asked, haltingly: "Do you begin, now, to understand the profundity of Hepzibah's melancholy, Mr Greene? If you know of a key to it – any way to loosen its grip upon her – then you will be returning a wife to me, Sir. For, in truth, I have none at this moment."

"I shall sleep on it, Mr Sharratt, as I find that the most elusive remedies often present themselves when least expected. Meanwhile," he turned in the doorway, "a stroll to take the air along the Deans Walk will be no bad thing for either of you. Assure your wife – if you will – that it is part of my prescription. Good night, Mr Sharratt."

The Apothecary left the red-brick house and stood awhile in the twilight, enjoying the clean tang of the night air. Although his mind was full of the horrors that had been recounted, his thoughts all seemed to return to the dark, almost violet, eyes in which that universe of damage resided. How might they look if only they could be touched with a smile? He turned, decisively, towards the South gate and Dam Street and hurried home.

(12)

ITEM:

On the right hand side the shellcase: the ancient Finger
Stocks from Beaudesert (the seat of the Right Hon.
The Earl of Uxbridge) a punishment formerly inflicted
by the Lord of Misrule on such servants as committed
misdemeanours at the time of keeping Christmas. A powder
Flask of Buffalo's horn on which is curiously engraved a
plan of the Havannah, Saratoga, New York & etc.

The Sabbath day that dawned offered little chance of rest. He
spent it, morning till dusk, filling the backlog of prescriptions and
attending to at least some of the myriad neglected tasks normally addressed by his still ailing staff. On the previous Wednesday,
Theodosia, unwisely, had insisted that she was fully recovered
from the wretched aches and biliousness that had kept her to her
bed for more than a week. After a morning spent in a vain and increasingly dejected attempt to bring some order back to the shop
and her home above, she had returned to her bed in floods of tears.
After finding her husband's museum coat in its accustomed place,
fallen and in its usual crumpled heap behind the closet door on
the upstairs landing, she had bent, angrily, to pick it up. "Oh drat
the man!" she had exclaimed, to no-one in particular, before an
all-too familiar wave of nausea swept across her. Richard had been
considerate, but, she decided, maddeningly matter-of-fact about
her illness, displaying particularly little sympathy for her miserable humour that morning.

"If I have told *one* of my patients that they must stay resting in
order to shake off this brute of a distemper, then I have told *two*

dozen! But does *one* of you take the slightest heed? What can I do to help those whose mulish intransigence is their own worst enemy!?"

"I am neither a mule nor one of your wretched patients, *Mr Greene*. I am, may Heaven help me, your *wife*! Why must I *remind* you of the fact?"

"Oh, Theodosia, I meant only… ," he responded, helplessly, but before he could express the doomed sentiment, she had pulled the coverlet over her head and retreated into angry sobs.

For the past ten days, whenever she emerged, wan, from her own purgatory, she had been forced to watch her husband's endless comings and goings with a mixture of concern and exasperation. In spite of his long, harrowing illness, he took precious little notice of his *own* advice, and was already so absorbed again, so *otherwise engaged* for every waking hour, that it seemed an eternity since either *she* had claimed his full attention, or – her pale lips puckered into a moue of annoyance – *he* had thought to bestow it. There always seemed to be time for the World and all its waifs, and space for every new oddity or wonder, but altogether *too little* of each for the spouse who, somehow, had to cope with it all. And if he told her, just once again, about the *remarkable* recovery of that American *Chit* in The Close whose treatment seemed to occupy so *much* of his precious time, then she may very well hurl one of his precious American tomahawks at him and see how he liked that!

When she woke to the distant peal of Evensong from the Cathedral, she had already decided: they would have a holiday.

She remembered with a start of satisfaction, that this coming Sunday being Whitsuntide, Monday would, of course, be Bower Day.

"And after that, a few days stay in Cheshire, with Richard," she had said out loud, to her self, startling the maid at her darning next door. '*A tonic for us both*', she thought, fondly anticipating those most superior Haberdashers and Mercers to be found around her sister's Knutsford home, and a houseful of children and laughter. She decided she would tell Richard that evening. *'He will be delighted'*, was her final thought before she drifted back to sleep.

There are times in life, the Apothecary knew, when only the most careful acquiescence will suffice, and this he had immediately recognised as one of them. He had managed not only to show a mite more pleasure than was strictly required, but also to enthuse at the prospect of spending several days – at least – away from everything that needed doing, added to the prospect of a houseful of children known to be at *a difficult age.*

This cheerful agreement to her plans, though slightly puzzling, appeared to work wonders for Theodosia's spirits. She rose on Thursday in time to poach a little fish for their supper, and on Friday accompanied her housekeeper on a keen-eyed trawl through the market. Saturday saw her returned to her usual bustling self, though her husband managed to insist upon early nights, the better to be on sparkling form for the holiday.

So, if the truth be told, when Richard Greene finally sank into his armchair after a solitary supper he was indeed looking forward to part of the holiday that lay ahead, even if that part extended little further than Bower Day.

On the Monday that follows the seventh Sunday after Easter, for as long as anyone cared to remember, the ancient Court of Array – a supposedly martial review of Men and Arms – had become a shambling, day-long procession of mirth and disorderliness. Though much frowned on by the more straitlaced citizens, its venerable antiquity guaranteed that year upon year it would roll and stumble along its tumultuous course, blithely immune to censure.

It was, however, still the done thing that at eight o'clock on this Monday morning, those same disapproving Worthies should be present for the marshalling and departure of the huge procession from the Marketplace.

It was of some small comfort to those sensitive souls that – for the most part – its participants at least *seemed* sober at that early hour.

The day-long procession was composed of Ward Men, Craft Companies and military units, accompanied by the Bailiffs, Dozeners, Town Clerk, Serjeants at Mace, Sheriff and Gaoler. Where once they had paraded the images of Patron Saints, now they made do with elaborate decorations of greenery and flowers, or garlanded puppets mimicking their bearers.

In recent times, to Greene's delight, there had been a burgeoning of *Automata* and creaky mechanical contrivances which rarely managed to survive the uphill transit to St Michael's churchyard. Their often-spectacular failure was met with unbounded hilarity by the rowdier element, much given to the firing of spontaneous volleys of gunshots over the rooftops. It had become a generally accepted fact – though one abhorred in polite society – that this day of license and tomfoolery now, invariably, stretched into the next, with a plethora of head-aching sufferers still plagued by the persistence of revellers unable to differentiate next day from previous night.

Foreknowledge of the impending chaos thus explained the brevity of the note from Michael Rawlins. Obviously left by Ablitt, the apprentice Apothecary, it was discovered propped against the Sharks' teeth on the Parlour mantle; left, apparently, for when Greene returned late from his Saturday rounds, though unnoticed till now.

Mr Greene, Though we shall, doubtless, rub shoulders at the Bower, I foresee little or no opportunity to conduct meaningful intercourse then or before. I shall despatch the substance of my recent enquiry to you shortly, when it is as complete as can be managed. Our discussion of its essence must await a quiet

moment some days hence when you have had time to consider it.
I am, Sir, your servant, M. Rawlins. The Friary, on Saturday

Such was his bone-weariness, Greene replaced the note on the mantelpiece and sought his bed. Tomorrow could look after itself.

(13)

On the left hand of the eastern **WINDOW**: two glasses,
which contain fluids of different specific gravities, which
being inverted pass through each other without mixing.

The day dawned with a blue sky of impeccable credentials; a light
breeze from the Southwest and the shop's barometer set at fair.
As he opened the bedchamber window and relished the freshness
of the morning, it seemed that the whole city was charged with
vigour; he could smell it in the air, he assured himself.

This was the day for ribbons and new bonnets, best cravats and
powdered periwigs – if one was to enter the social stakes of 'see
and be seen'. Though Richard Greene considered himself largely
immune from such conceits, his wife knew that there was a time
and a place when such things needed to be taken out of a husband's hands.

"No, Richard!" she exclaimed. "Not the yellow, it gives your gills
a distinctly liverish quality. The blue, surely. It will lend a nicely de-
fining line to your chin and is already much favoured this season."

Below them, the length of Saddler Street was already alive
with a one-way stream of townsfolk making for *The Array*. After
carefully locking the shop premises, the Apothecary followed Mrs
Greene into the jostling throng. First would come the convening
of a Court meeting in the Guildhall, whose immediate adjournment was the signal for the crowds to engulf the leafy bowers
erected on Greenhill. Then, after the calling of the names of all
householders of the City's twenty-one Wards by the Constables,
fines would be noted for any man found to be absent. Thus, with

official business decently and speedily enacted, the real business of the day could commence with huge quantities of free beef, cake and prunes served from the branch-decked stalls, all to be washed down with a matching volume of wine and the city's renowned ale.

The morning advanced in good-natured, ever-rising uproar, the parade eddying, surging, re-forming and false-starting under the weight of its own gargantuan unwieldiness, all compounded by the great press of onlookers and well-wishers who flowed in and out of its ranks to the utter distractions of would-be marshals.

At least half the crowd, it seemed to Theodosia Greene, wanted to greet her husband and pump his hand, the better to congratulate him on his return to health. It was from the midst of this welter of bonhomie that the Apothecary spied the elderly figure of Michael Rawlins.

The elderly man was seated amongst a group of city society, perched sedately on the grass verge outside the Honourable Mrs Seppel's fine new house on the hillside.

Needing to extract himself from a particularly tedious round of enquiries into his health in particular – and the state of medicine in general – being jointly conducted by the brothers Leggatt, he waved – as if in acknowledgement of the distant Rawlins – and made his excuses to the twin bores.

It was at much the same time that a hitherto recalcitrant Semaphore tableau grated, alarmingly, into life, from atop its flower-decked haywain: a row of carved, gaudily painted Redcoats groaning into motion with extended arms bearing flapping signal flags. The sudden combination of complaining mechanism, flailing extremities and flags snapping briskly in the breeze, proved too much for the nearest horses – a pair of huge old dray-mares that had been sharing companionable fodder at the roadside.

With nostrils flaring and great metal-shod hooves rearing above the thoroughly alarmed bystanders, mayhem piled upon mishap. From nowhere, a black-and-white dog darted from the crowd, snapping and snarling at the already-terrified horses.

With cries of alarm and warning, the operators of the signal station tumbled down from the heavy cart as it slewed and then toppled; one horse pulled down in the twisting trail, the other lunging away in a tangle of broken harness and wigwags. Apart from the scores of immediate bystanders who were either busy escaping from the pandemonium, or rushing to give assistance, the rest of the crowd saw only another hilarious mishap: quite simply, the stuff of which Bower Days were made.

In response to this unlooked-for diversion, the day's first ragged sputtering of gunshots erupted from the rear of the crowds, sending a multitude of rooks and pigeons into an aerial frenzy over the thousands of noisy heads.

Seeing that some order was being restored to the situation and determined – today of all days – not to become involved in the inevitable bruises and bloody noses, Greene pushed ahead towards the group where Rawlins sat. He saw, as he neared the Seppel house, that all but the elderly man had abandoned their chairs to gain a better view of the Semaphore's wreck.

The odd bang still reverberated around the houses on the hill as he approached, smiling suddenly to himself at the sight of his elderly acquaintance taking the opportunity for a brief nap in the temporary absence of his party. As the Apothecary mounted the verge, intent on making a rendezvous for later that day, the smile froze on his lips.

Suddenly he was running, his carefully positioned wig tumbling from his head as he scrambled the last yards to the sprawl of chairs around the picnic table. Michael Rawlins sat, slumped only slightly, his head sunk forward. The blossoming stain was scarcely visible against the burgundy brocade of his coat – where a bullet hole glistened, blackly, above his heart.

(14)

On some shelves next the ORGAN: a fragment of the Tusk of
an Elephant, found near eight feet below the surface of the Earth,
in the Parish of Alderminster, in the Lands of Thos. Partridge.
Esq. of Clopton, near Stratford on Avon, Warwickshire.

As the Apothecary bent towards the figure he knew to be stone
dead, the first scream erupted from behind his back as the laughing party returned to their refreshments. Before he even knew
what he was saying, he found himself shouting: "A ricochet! *Wild-
fire*! Those damned fools and their firearms have finally killed a
man!" As horrified faces pressed all around him, he whirled, arms
outstretched to hold them back.

"The Sheriff must be informed! How many more must be
killed or maimed before this idiocy is contained?" He recognised
several men among the pale, gaping, circle. "*Quickly*, friends! We
must remove poor Rawlins from the press. Help me."

Within moments, they had carried the stick-like corpse into
the flagged hall of the Seppel house, its ashen owner – in the
absence of her festive staff – frantically collecting towels, and a
sheet to cover the body, lying, now, with blood puddling about its
shoulders.

"How could this have *happened*, Mr Greene? How is such a
wound *possible* from...." The Honourable Lady's urgent questions
were forestalled by Greene's reply:

"Bullets have a life of their own, Madam; particularly those
fired, without regard, by frivolous fools."

As if to reinforce his words, another ragged crackle of fire sounded, distantly, through the half-open door.

"Depending on its angle of fire and the surface it strikes, a half-spent bullet can claim a life as readily as any other, Mrs Seppel." He looked down upon the shrouded body at his feet, intoning a silent prayer for forgiveness, when he added: "…as the tragic accident which has befallen this poor man attests."

At that moment a red-faced figure burst through the half-open door with the most perfunctory of knocks.

"*Sheriff!*" bristled the lady of the house, magically regaining her shaken composure, "*Hardly* before time, I think. I intend to see that the blame for this dreadful business shall be laid *wholly* at your door. Is this … this *Bacchanalia* … over which you preside, run so *utterly* beyond decent regulation that we should now expect corpses upon our floors? *Well,* Sir? What's to be *done* about it?"

Seeing the look of stricken incompetence spreading across the Sheriff's florid features, Greene bowed to the incensed lady before the unfortunate officer could even begin to splutter a response.

"I shall, of course, attest fully to the circumstances of this tragic accident, Mrs Seppel, though now I must regain my wife and make the necessary arrangements for the removal of Mr Rawlins."

He turned to the quivering, tongue-tied man still standing speechless at the sight of the draped corpse. "I shall arrange for the removal to be direct to my own surgery, if that will be acceptable, Sheriff? You will doubtless wish for a post-mortem record to be made before burial?"

"Just so, Mr Greene. Just so. We are all in your debt, once again, Sir. Oh *yes,* Sir! … *Such* promptitude, such a timely intervention. You are an example to us *all,* Sir!"

"Scarcely *timely,* I fear, Sheriff…" – from the corner of his eye Greene caught the Honourable Lady directing a look of withering disdain at the babbling officer – "…it being, unfortunately, *after* the event."

Again, a far-off tapping of gunfire sounded, as if on cue at a Guildhall melodrama.

The harried official gazed, helplessly, between the cadaver and the irate householder, as Richard Greene quietly made his farewells and walked out into the heedless festivities.

As he had expected, a knot of the curious remained outside the wrought-iron gate to the regimented garden; Mrs Seppel's erstwhile guests having departed in some haste, as soon as decency allowed. He pointedly ignored the stares and shouted enquiries as he made his way through.

It was as he cleared the fringes of the small crowd that he had a prickling sense of being closely observed. He paused, momentarily, to see, for the briefest instant – a tall, square-jawed man gazing at him with unblinking fixity from the corner of the houses at George Lane.

Something about the big man – his walnut-brown features visible beneath a low-pulled hat, a topcoat worn despite the clemency of the day – stopped the Apothecary in his tracks. In that instant, though, the figure was gone, seeming to duck away around the blind corner.

As Morris Men and a prancing motley of musicians flooded across his view, Greene knew it would be pointless to attempt to follow. He knew, also, that in the look of calculating fixity he had caught, there was a deal more than idle curiosity.

He stared up at those same houses at the corner of the lane, their blank windows facing across to the lawn where Michael Rawlins had met his death. As he looked, an unlatched window frame flashed as it swung in the sharp breeze, up high, in the attic gable of the corner house. A house undoubtedly emptied like most others in the festive City; a house whose un-regarded windows would provide a sniper's eyrie.

He knew, with a stab of urgency, that he must, somehow, gain entrance to The Friary – if it was not already too late.

Amongst the perfumed company of the Lichfield Ladies Box Club, Theodosia Greene – unaware of the tragedy which had been played out not a hundred yards away – caught a glimpse of her husband's wigless head bobbing like a dishevelled cork, as he breasted the flow of the seething crowd. Abruptly, the chitchat about that season's plans for functions to alleviate the plight of the Rural Poor lost all its savour for the staring woman. There seemed to be some desperate urgency to her husband's departure.

Leaving all the sounds of revelry behind, Richard Greene half-walked, half-ran the deserted length of Bore Street. His breath came in ragged gasps, with a searing sensation growing in his chest. He knew more than enough about the finite limits of recuperation and convalescence to realise that he was pushing himself dangerously past the limits of his scarcely restored strength.

Knowing, too, that the staff would, to a man, be abroad amongst the holidaymakers – leaving the old house unattended – Greene limped across the gardens towards the side entry by the stables. As he turned the corner, wheezing with effort, he saw to his utter dismay that he was, indeed, too late.

Glass from the broken door pane littered the cobbles and the door itself swung open to his hand. It took little more than a couple of wretched minutes in the silent, empty rooms, to see the jumbled disorder: drawers up-ended, their contents strewn across the faded carpets and, in the Library, whole shelves swept to the ground in the ferocity of the search.

Staring at the brutal violation of the home that Michael Rawlins had loved so well, the Apothecary had not the slightest doubt of what had been sought here. An upsurge of despair threatened to overwhelm him, as he realised that, without the *substance* of the enquiries that poor Rawlins had been about to share, then the murderous evil that now stalked even the daylight hours of the little city would remain unknowable and untouchable.

With a stab of sheer dread the Apothecary understood that now *he* – and he alone – knew of two mortal horrors at the heart his community.

He shuddered inwardly at the thought that his silence, his

dreadful *complicity*, meant that both were now regarded as accidents. As a party to two deaths that only he knew to be murders, the law would call him, quite simply, an accessory.

Hangmen were not known to deal in nuances.

Bile filled his mouth as he hurried away, silence and emptiness seeming to radiate like dark beacons at his retreating back.

ITEM:

Beneath the Birds in a Glass Case: Some anatomical
injected preparations, by Mr Thomas Webb Greene, while
a Pupil in Saint Thomas's Hospital. Viz: The kidneys
of the Human Body, the Heart of a Man, the heart of a
Woman, that of a child. A double Placenta, injected, the red
colour'd Wax represents the arteries, the yellow, the veins.

Theodosia Greene had returned hot, tired and not a little disen-
chanted with a husband whose unexplained absence from her side
had been repeatedly commented upon throughout an increasingly
tedious day. The fact that she had returned only to find him en-
grossed in a sheaf of stained yellow pages spread across her dining
table did little to improve her temper.

A pent-up flood of annoyance was well on its way to becoming
a tirade, when the man – as if oblivious to all she was saying –
stood up, and taking her hands in his, said quietly: "You cannot
have heard, my dear. Poor Rawlins has been shot dead. A tragic
accident that I was only seconds away from witnessing. There was
much to which I was required to attend – not least being the reception of his body, down below. It has been most trying, all in all."

"*Dead?*" she whispered. "Old Mr Rawlins? Who was in this
very room only…?" Tears sprang to her eyes. "Oh, Richard, forgive me for an empty-headed witterer. For sure, there are rumours
galore of a *wounding*, an accidental shooting, but *this*..? Oh, Dear
Lord, what a blight upon the day. So your disappearance…?"

"…was concerned with another aspect of this bad business
altogether," said Greene evenly. "I knew that I had to seek out

some most valuable documents poor Rawlins had promised to me in the note which came on Saturday."

She looked puzzled.

"You must still have been indisposed when it arrived. I found it propped on the mantelpiece only yesterday," continued Greene.

Her husband's face creased into even deeper concern: "It will soon be common knowledge, I regret to tell you, that The Friary was burgled in Rawlins' absence." He watched the look of pained disbelief spreading across his wife's face, and hurriedly continued: "Some blackguard simply took the opportunity of cracking one of the city's grander houses, guessing it to be empty."

Theodosia looked in perplexity at the strewn pages on the table: "So these are not what you went seeking? Papers of such obvious value that they were filched by *a sneak-thief*?"

"No, my dear, quite the opposite, for these are the *very* ones I sought, though I must explain! I left The Friary empty-handed and quite perturbed by what I had come across, believing that these," he indicated the sheets, "had indeed been scooped up in the general pillaging which seems to have occurred. Imagine, then, my amazement at finding them *here*! Safe, sound and tidily packaged: left leaning against the passage door!"

This, in fact, had been just how the bewildered Greene had found them as he made his distracted way to the rear entrance to the premises.

"I can only imagine that whomsoever of The Friary servants was charged with their delivery, found us gone from home. Like the rest of Lichfield, he would have been pleasure-bent and unwilling to return with the parcel undelivered. Providence has played a pretty hand in this, and no mistake."

Still puzzled, she reached for the nearest sheet. Holding the small, stained page to the fading light, she read:

...and stands accused of other cursed Opinions belched by the instinct of Satan. The aforesaid Crimes, Heresies and other

detestable Blasphemies and Error, stubbornly and perti-
naciously, knowingly, maliciously and with a hardened Heart,
published defended and dispersed. He shall be adjudged as a
diseased Sheep of the Flock of Our Lord.
We, James, as a Zealot of Justice and a Defender of the Catholic
Faith, shall root out and extirpate and punish with condign
punishment such heretical error as ought to be burnt with fire.

With a sudden shudder, Theodosia Greene dropped the sheet back onto the table. "What a *ghastly* thing! Why should you be so concerned about it, Richard? What is it?"

"An ancient sentence of death, my dear, signed by King James the First.… "

He made to reach another stained fragment from the strewn table top, continuing:

"…but I fear there is even worse, besides, amidst Old Rawlins' notes."

"Oh *Husband!*" she said, the anger in her tone forestalled him. "There are times when your passion for such grubby curiosities is beyond even *me*. I have sore feet, an aching head, and now with this wicked news, a pressing need for my bed. I *entreat* you to join me there without delay. There *surely* must be another time and place for such grisly mementoes, Richard. Your humour seems to have become increasingly morbid of late. *Desist*, for Pity's sake, tonight at least!"

With her features set in a mask of ill-temper, Mrs Greene swept from the room, leaving her husband to stare at the scatter of pages.

"An ancient death sentence, indeed… ," he said, into the silence of her departure, moving once more to pick up that other tattered page. He studied its ruined script for long moments before adding, as if to himself: "…though one, I fear, whose lethality is far from spent."

(16)

In the MUSEUM on the ceiling: claws of a large lobster, 14 inches in circumference, a large fungus or Puff Ball, found in a field at Wall; it measures twelve inches in diameter and weighs little more than four ounce; a very ancient woman's Hat, of split cane, nearly two feet in diameter, the stomach of an Old Lion: when first inflated, it contained nineteen pints of Water.

For all his studiously cultivated professional detachment, the autopsy Greene performed in the early hours of the next morning was an experience he would gladly have foregone.

Deprived of all that Greene had found so engaging – and surprising – in their all-too brief acquaintance, the husk of old Michael Rawlins was little short of grotesque in death. An Adam's apple protruded like some tumorous carbuncle from the scrawny neck, the emaciation of old age mocking the eye with skeletal ribs and scarecrow shoulders, a little pot belly, hard, above the gawky splay of hips, a penis and its flaccid sac shrivelled between stick legs, toenails thick, discoloured horn.

The Apothecary's first incision, his scalpel releasing a pent-up fetor into the curtained recess, revealed the ball – so acute had been its angle of entry – above the heart, close to the left armpit. It lodged now, low in the sternum, glistening black amidst the splintered bone and the mangled tissue of its travel. He retrieved it with forceps, letting it fall into the slipware basin at his elbow. In his mind's eye he saw again the position of the slumped body, the placing of its chair, the height and angle of that blank, open window, caught by the breeze. Their conjunction was precise, unarguable. He noted with care the damage to ventricle, septum, rib and lung, the slate filling with his neat script. With a sigh of relief he completed his sewing and with infinite gentleness sponged away the residues of his unhappy task before covering the body in fresh, coarse linen, lightly fastened about neck, waist and ankles. It would be collected at nine, to be prepared for burial up at St. Michael's the following morning. Not a moment too soon, thought Greene, gratefully throwing open the consulting-room window, savouring the freshness of the morning air as it filled the orderly room with its blessed scents.

In the absence of either family or close friends of the deceased, it was only after the funeral that Greene could make the time for the less pressing demands of his own business.

He had found himself, by default, the agent for the funeral arrangements and, to his amazement, to have been nominated in Rawlins' recently revised Will as executor for the disposal of the estate. "There is an arrangement of a fifty-guinea emolument for the discharge of this onerous responsibility," Rawlins' solicitor had ponderously informed him, upon breaking the news to the morose Apothecary. "It would appear that m'client developed a high regard for your … ah … *probity* … and … ah … *discretion* – I believe *those* were his words – in the last months of his life. You will also learn of the bequest of a number of items, curiosities for your … ah … *collection*."

With a disdainful sniff, he continued: "As I had the honour to be his *previous* nominee, and remain – at least – *joint* trustee, with *your own good self*, there will be a number of business matters with which you will doubtless wish to deal without delay. I shall have the necessary papers delivered here to your … ah … *shop* without delay. Good day, Mr Greene."

With that terse farewell, Cardew Chapman, man at law, made his departure, leaving Richard Greene in no doubt of his bruised sensibilities. Pondering – though only briefly – on the vanities and vexations of the human condition, the small man packed his black leather satchel and set out on his neglected rounds.

In a day of surprises, he was met with a smile by Timothy Sharratt as he was shown into the Morning Room of the Prebendary House.

"Your arrival is most timely, Sir," beamed the young man. "I believe we may expect company that will gladden your heart as it has gladdened my own." He looked past the Apothecary to a slight figure crossing the hall towards the open door. Greene turned, and with a small smile disguising a sudden welter of emotions, bowed. "Mrs Sharratt, your servant. I am delighted to see you so obviously recovered."

Piercing eyes, set in a face framed with jet-black ringlets, met his and held them. A slim, long-fingered hand was extended towards him.

"I believe I am indebted to you, Sir, though I fear I have few memories of your intervention." Small, full lips, roseate against the perfect whiteness of her skin pronounced the words in a face devoid of expression.

"*Hepzi*! For heaven's sake, without Mr Greene's... ."

"You have indeed been gravely ill, Madam," the Apothecary interjected, cutting through Timothy Sharratt's obvious embarrassment. He continued, graciously:

"Your return to health is thus all-the-more gratifying. You will permit me?" He raised a slim unresisting wrist between thumb and fingers and measured its pulse against his pocket watch.

"Indeed! Most satisfactory!" he said, quite oblivious to the silence that had descended on the room. "And now, Sir... ," he turned to the young woman's husband, "...a judicious balance of red meat, fresh fruit and a modicum of exercise will ensure that this Lady's recovery is ... maintained." His pause was so slight as to pass unnoticed.

Opening a bag that suddenly seemed a strident black against

the room's limewashed wainscot, he removed two stoppered phials. "An iron tonic for the fortification of the blood, and a mild sedative to ensure restful sleep; these should now suffice to complete your physical recovery, Mrs Sharratt."

Did her eyes sharpen, just for an instant, at the word *physical*? he wondered later. Though, in thinking back, thoughts of the lips and those dark ringlets seemed, somehow, to cloud his memory. He closed his bag and straightened.

"I need detain you no longer," he said to the still-discomfited man and his blankly expressionless young wife.

Before either could reply, the sound of a coach reining in, with the slamming of doors and the scrunching of feet on the gravel path, carried through to them.

Although Hepzibah Sharratt's face remained completely still, her husband exclaimed: "Why, what fortunate timing, Greene. You shall now meet my father-in-law! We have been expecting his return from London by the hour. My uncle's coach will have collected him from the Birmingham Mail."

With that, the front door was opened upon a tall, thickset man, immediately greeted by the effusive form of William Clarke who had materialised from discreet invisibility in the Parlour.

"You are most welcome back, my dear fellow," effused the corpulent householder as the newcomer was helped from his coat. "I trust our affairs have prospered?"

Sharratt strode forward with his hand extended. "Father Blanchmayne, your return is as timely as it is welcome. You will wish to meet our visitor, Apothecary Greene: we owe him more than you can know."

"You say so, Tim? Then I'll not doubt a word of it," said the hard-muscled man, now fully revealed in the play of afternoon sunlight through the white-painted casements in the hall. He walked, smiling questioningly, towards Richard Greene, offering a bronzed, spatulate hand.

"Isiah Blanchmayne, Mr Greene. I am obviously in your debt,

Sir, and shall be pleased to know of its extent."

As Richard Greene took the rough, dry hand in his, he found himself looking into extraordinary blue eyes, unblinking eyes, set in a square-jawed face whose skin was tanned to the colour of walnuts.

"Had it not been for Mr Greene's services, I fear your daughter would not have been here to greet you, Sir," cut in young Sharratt's voice.

Still holding Greene's hand in a rigid grip, the big man turned to acknowledge Hepzibah, who stood beside the fireplace, her eyes cast down.

"Then that is a debt whose repayment I am unlikely to manage, Mr Greene, try as I shall. I cannot begin to imagine what has transpired in my absence."

He finally released the Apothecary's numb hand and strode towards his daughter. "How about a welcome for your Pa?" he boomed, taking her stiff shoulders in his hands and pulling her unresponsive body into a smothering embrace.

Alone amongst the room's occupants, Richard Greene saw the look of utter desolation in the young woman's eyes as she met his, her slim body rigid, frozen, in the bear-like hug.

"You'll take some refreshment with us, Mr Greene?" bumbled William Clarke, now the soul of affability.

"Thank you, but no," replied Greene, attempting to maintain a composure he did not feel. "You will all have much to discuss at such a home-coming; and I have business to which I must attend."

"Then I shall make it my business to attend on you, Sir, as soon as may be," interposed Blanchmayne with heavy-handed courtesy.

The Apothecary made his farewells, catching – momentarily – the unblinking blue eyes fixed upon him.

As he came to the road outside, the driver of the Brougham was still lifting down travelling valises from the dust-grimed vehicle.

"Has Mr Blanchmayne come all the way from London?" he asked, with easy informality.

"No Sir, I do believe he's been in Birmingham a week or so. I heard his account being settled at the Star, and that was for a sight more than a bed and a breakfast."

Greene nodded to the garrulous coachman and walked briskly away, dismissing, as pure imagination, the eyes he felt following his departure. On a whim, he turned back, up towards the Bishop's Palace, rather than make his departure through the South Gate. Following the orderly avenue of trees, he walked the length of the great Cathedral church on the slope below him. He paused for several moments staring up at the newly restored steeple, its immense stone shaft soaring from the battlemented tower, its quarry-bright ashlar in stark contrast to the stained and blackened fabric of the church itself: a scarred and patched reminder of The Great Rebellion. He peered, then, within its deepening shadow, to where the Library stood, faint lights a dull gleam behind its green-glassed leads. It was from here, with 'the few remaining good offices' of Theophilus Pomlett, that Michael Rawlins had assembled the stained, dog-eared scraps of testament whose substance now haunted the Apothecary's waking hours. One by one, page upon drab page, they swirled back in a vile cotillion; the dry, legalistic horror of neatly penned words, composed as a rationale for death by burning; the sentence deliberated with such judicial relish by the Bishop's court – the Consistory which had convened in all its sanctimonious panoply in the Chapter House at the foot of this well-trimmed lawn. A Court whose members – each of their names – had been retrieved by Michael Rawlins only three days before his murder; with the list, though, had come another.

With a sense of urgency that seemed to grow with every limping step, it was to this single sheet that the Apothecary now hurried home. Written in Rawlins' own spidery hand it had revealed – line by line – a catalogue of nightmare.

Richard Greene knew now, beyond any doubt, that a pitiless vengeance was being exacted from beyond the grave – another grave that had held only ashes.

17

ITEM:

Over the Fireplace: A vertical Anemoscope, or Wind Dial, neatly ornamented with painting, carving and gilding. Within the circle (which contains the thirty two points of the Compass) is seen a landscape on one side, the view of an old Abbey in Ruins, on the other, a view of the Sea, some ships topped by waves.

It was in the dates that the appalling symmetry lay: together, forming a vista of cruelty so far-extended over the years as to be rendered invisible – unless its pattern was discerned – or even dreamt of.

Rawlins' recovery of the Consistory roll-call had, in itself, been remarkable, not least for the fact that the Library was only now, a century on, emerging from the wreckage and spoliation of most of its treasures – one of the uncounted victims of sieges and storms that had ripped through the Cathedral church and Close in the years of civil war.

There they had been, listed in a ragged, broken-backed volume stained by soot and rain, the men who sat in judgement on the Anabaptist, Edward Wightman. Names and titles dutifully re-corded, the letter of the Law observed in its every starched nicety: Eight officers appointed to ensure utmost rigour and orthodoxy in its every deliberation.

The Apothecary had been unaware that Rawlins must then have plundered the Guildhall archive, parish registers, or wherever the dismal events of death are to be found, set down.

It was here, though, when all those strands were gathered in, that the wickedness – and its appalling pattern – was revealed:

*Chancellor of the Diocese: Midgeley, Thos. Died Lich. April 22nd
1614*
Clerk to the Chapter: Everley, Wm. Died Lich. May 29th 1619
*Most Reverend Archdeacon Barnard, Mw. Died Yoxhall, nr
Lich April 19th 1624*
*Canon Residentiary the Rev. Partridge, Thos. Died Lich. April
15th 1629*
*The Very Reverend Wemyss, Nathan. Died Tatenhill, nr Lich
April 17th 1634*

Had there been a blinding instant of illumination or hour upon hour of seeking something, *anything?* Greene wondered numbly.

Somehow, though, Rawlins had perceived the blasphemous motif, the demonic symmetry that lay concealed: Every man had died on the Saturday of Holy Week, on whatever date it fell in that year; *each man somehow consumed by fire.*

With ice in his heart, the Apothecary had read on:

*Thomas Midgeley… 'whilst in the act, it is supposed, of endeav-
ouring to save the Stallion Redmark from a conflagration at
Boothall, his demesne'.*
*William Everley… 'of grievous mischance with lamp-oil which
claimed his family entire'.*
*Matthew Barnard, late of Pipe Hill… 'adjudged dead by light-
ning strike, found seared unto death, with his dogs'.*
*Thomas Partridge… 'whilst taking tobacco, in a coat of waxed
stuff. Lingered in great distress and died'.*
*Nathan Wemyss… 'found fallen from a sudden palsy, in his
private chamber, in part most grievously consumed at his own
grate'.*

1614 to 1634: Twenty devilishly ordered years, each of five deaths four years apart; just sufficiently far – with the ebb and flow of lives – to obscure the design. What though of those other three?

Rawlins' scratchy penmanship seemed to blur and waver to the Apothecary's aching eyes.

On the much-decayed court record, water stains blossomed in smears and mists of ink, each successive line dissolving into ragged, sooty fog. Rawlins had striven – and all-but succeeded – to transcribe each completely:

William Laud   Impeache he House of Common
*   1641   executed by behead 645.*

From Bishop's chaplain to Archbishop and arraigned Traitor in thirty-odd years, thought Greene, immediately recognising the loathed name from his schooling. One, though, that had become so far-removed from the City of Lichfield, so *elevated*, that the infernal retribution doubtlessly planned for it must have been *deferred* until it was too late. Laud, by then, being in transit to a Golgotha of his own making.

Though, next, the all-too-familiar name of Bishop Richard Neille had come close to obliteration on the filthy page: 'eille' stood out from a grimy crevasse slashed into the sheet. Rawlins' notes had far more to say about that righteous judge:

Though subsequently Archbishop of York, described as: 'The Bench of the most servile justices that ever disgraced the Law Courts'. No Bishop in history moved as often and left such ignominy in his wake. Consecrated Rochester 1608, Lichfield 1610 though holding Deanery of Westminster, Lincoln 1614, Durham 1617, Winchester 1628, York 1632.
This appointment caused such universal outrage it prompted O. Cromwell's maiden speech in The Commons. Only Neille's death in 1640 saved him from Laud's fate on the Scaffold.

And more besides, thought Greene, grimly: he knew all too well what would have followed.

By whatever means, Richard Neille, burner of heretics, had escaped his intended fate and died a peaceful death at the great age of 78. Once again, thought Greene ruefully, one of those gilded mediocrities insulated – *preserved* – in life by preferment and privilege. In death, though, the malign hand had followed him, somehow crossing even that last dread Borderland to strike where once it had failed. The Bishop's namesake, Mr Dick Neille of Dam Street, sportsman and gentleman of means, grandson at many removes, had died in his stead:

...by fire; the day being the Saturday before Easter, in Holy Week.

That this obscenity had occurred close on a century and a half after the original barbarous judgement added such a dimension of calculated and unrelenting malevolence to the sum of horror spread before him that for one quaking moment the tired reader imagined he might be consumed by the words alone.

With sick certainty the Apothecary knew that only one remained for the roster of vengeance to be finally filled. He thought his aching head might burst as he tried in vain to focus on the last vestige of what survived on the ruined page.

The melted script swam and blurred, giving up no more than the letters *...olome... bb.. .f.. roxa...*

He rose abruptly, knocking the candle stand to the floor, hands pressed to his temples as a red mist flooded his vision. The room seeming to lurch around him, he swayed and would have fallen had it not been for Theodosia, hurrying through from her sewing room at the sound of Greene's obvious distress. He seemed, for an instant, shocked to see her, and at first mouthed something inaudible as she guided him back to his toppled chair, retrieved from the floor and the puddling wax.

After several moments of complete stillness, he seemed to reach a decision and, with a long, measured, intake of breath, reached out both hands, drawing her down to sit beside him on the cushioned sill; the rictus which had seemed to freeze his features softening its grip as he stared into the grey-green eyes he knew so well.

"My dear, I have only now come to see that there is a matter that, most reluctantly, I must discuss with you; a burden which, frankly, I must share or risk my sanity. You see, I have not been entirely frank with you of late...."

18

ITEM:

On the left Hand the CHIMNEY PIECE: a variety of Ancient
Snuffers in Brass and Steel; an ancient Iron Mace, probably
carried before the Master of the Gild of the City of Lichfield,
before its incorporation; an Head of a Mitred Bishop, in Stone
Alto Relievo, neatly carved, formerly an ornament broken from
the Cathedral of Lichfield, by the Fanatics
during the Civil Wars, 1643.

Amongst the deluge of emotions that buffeted Theodosia Greene
in the hours that followed, a desolate sense of loss was
pre-eminent. It racked the waking hours of that night and
seemed to crouch in ambush, waiting for the sour dawn. Her
husband's bleak recounting had taken her to dark places of the
soul whose existence she would later question, over and again, in
the prosaic hours of domesticity. The depths of wickedness and
cruelty to which she had been introduced left her numb with a
horror that daylight was powerless to dispel.

The added knowledge that its instigator, its *inheritor*, still
roamed – unguessed-at and unknowable – in the streets outside, brought in a lurching sense of dread with every ring of the
Apothecary doorbell. Fear, though, like pain, could be mastered,
she knew; only the Lord knew of those times beyond number that
her husband's skills had interceded in the mundane terrors and
suffering of their small city, of the innumerable souls whose health
and equilibrium bore witness to his gift. Why, then, oh Merciful
God, *why*, had he felt unable to share his *own* agony, unburden his
own dread to the wife who had shared her heart and soul with him

every hour of every day since that far-off time they had first fallen in love? Through these first years of their marriage, the struggling early days of business, the longing for a little family to inhabit the genial warren in Saddler Street, one thing had remained a constant in Theodosia's life – her utter and complete conviction that there was nothing on Earth that could come between them. But last night, her lode-star had first flickered, then dimmed almost to extinction, as she realised the enormity of her exclusion from the secret place that she, *and she alone*, should occupy.

Richard had beseeched her forgiveness for his secrecy, his almost demented self-absorption, pleading that it had been *her* peace of mind, *her* well-being, he had been at such pains to protect, though her realisation that old Michael Rawlins had shared all that she had been denied, left her shaking with anger and weak with hurt.

"How *dare* you deny me my share of your fear, your pain, Richard! Are you such a fool as to believe such things can be withheld in the name of *consideration*? Are you incapable of seeing that only by the *absolute* surrender of 'me' and 'mine' can a real marriage be made?"

Her miserable and, by now, utterly bewildered husband could only listen, while Theodosia gave vent to emotions which never before had been given expression in their lives. As she swooped between tears, shock, fury and fear, he registered – for the first time in his life – the paralysing complacency, the endless *expediency* in which he and most men pass their lives. How often do the breadwinners, puffed-up with their own busy *usefulness*, pay the slightest heed to the bread-makers and the home-builders they leave each morning? He found himself, suddenly, in a wholly alien place where the shallowness of his emotions, the sheer inadequacy of his emotional vocabulary, left him feeling unclothed and ashamed, humbled by his thoughtlessness and the paucity of his spirit.

So, when, that next day, he received a pair of requests to

attend without delay upon two of his county patients, Theodosia and Richard, both, decided that a change of scene would be no bad thing. She, by now appearing to be her usual composed and assured self, announced her immediate intention of spending several days at her sister's Cheshire home and that she would depart by the early afternoon coach to Altringham.

Pausing only long enough to wonder how such a plan had appeared fully fledged, the Apothecary wisely resisted the temptation to enquire and gave what assistance he could to a more than usually self-sufficient wife.

They parted company in the yard of The George, where a frosty smile and a very light peck on the cheek were all that he was left with as the mail coach lumbered off across the broken cobbles.

Though both his apprentice and his shop-man were busily at work on his return to Saddler Street, and their maid bustled about her usual chores, a resonant emptiness seemed to suffuse the tall old house. As he packed his own saddlebag and assembled the contents of his medicine bag, he thought again of the unseen abyss that had opened at his feet, and how those same feet, clumsy and cack-heeled, had all but stumbled into its unforgiving depths. Somehow, though, despite the crisis he had precipitated, the terrors of the night seemed less omnipotent, their triumph less assured, now that they had been shared.

The problem, though, he ruefully reminded himself, was that words once uttered can never be unsaid.

Why, then, now of all times, he asked himself, did the unbidden image of blush-red lips appear to him over and again, whispering 'I am in your debt'?

How might they look, if only they could be touched by a smile of more than gratitude?

Shaking his head as if to rid himself of vagrant fancies, he descended to the shop and left final instructions to cover his brief absence, before walking briskly down the long garden path that led to the ramshackle stable at its end. As he busied himself with the intricacies of harness buckles and straps, murmuring to the stable's ever-patient occupant, he realised that felt an emotion curiously akin to relief.

19

ITEM:

Under the large case of **SHELLS**, in a Drawer on the right
Hand: A matted tunic, or covering for the Body, neatly fringed,
from New Amsterdam. Large quantity, and a great variety of
Cloth from the Bark of a Tree in Otaheite. A Turkish Towel.

His first call was to be out by the straggling, northern reaches of
old Needwood Forest, to a gouty landowner who placed extravagant trust in the Apothecary's ability to undo the daily depredations he himself inflicted on his long-suffering liver. The second
was an invitation to call upon the very grand personage of Sir
Eldon Pagnell at his Derbyshire estate 'to discuss a matter of an
intimate nature'.

Though far from being a natural horseman, Greene opted for a
leisurely ride to them both, much preferring an aching backside to
the purgatory of coach travel across the county's lesser roads. The
offer of a good bed and more-than-adequate board being implicit
in both invitations, he had decided on a three-day outing.

For all his preoccupations, he felt his spirits rise as he breasted
the hill on the Rugeley road and the landscape of early summer
rushed to meet him. He forked off towards Yoxall, allowing his
placid mare to make the pace.

To left and right the goose-grass and stichworts had embarked
on their scrambling climb of the hawthorn hedges, the spiked
thickets already dotted, pink and white, with dog rose. It was only
as the sweetness of the afternoon air gusted lightly from the pros-
perous farmland around him, thrilling his nostrils with its scents
of corn and woodland, the air alive with birdsong, that he began to

realise just how stale and circumscribed his daily life had become.

His endless round of medicine, museum, manufacturing and prescribing, dispensing and acquisition, had exacted a price he could only now begin to perceive. He nudged the old horse into a gentle trot and began to enjoy himself.

By the time he was leaving King's Bromley he felt as if he had been released from some benign imprisonment, the self-wrought bars of an overly comfortable cell dissolving around him. An hour on, pausing to water his horse by a rutted ford, the winter cart tracks gouged and rock-hard, he sat, entranced, by the pale brilliance of a carpet of forget-me-knots glowing against the black mud. Where the water-docks spread across still water, their huge, sappy leaves were gemmed with dragonflies. A brown trout rocked in lazy suspension before darting off, scattering sticklebacks in an explosive flurry as it raced away across the dappled shallows.

The Apothecary stood, dusting grass from his coat before luxuriantly spreading his arms and taking in a few, last, savouring breaths. He smiled easily as the old horse nuzzled his neck as he prepared to mount.

"Not too far now, Rosie, then there'll be supper enough for us both," he said, quietly, and rode on into the afternoon.

Shortly before six, horse and rider turned away from the distant wreck of Tutbury Castle and entered the peeling white gates of their destination.

On that first night, Richard Greene enjoyed a most substantial dinner of beef and oysters, prefaced by Derwent salmon and followed by Mallard and Snipe – all of which, excepting the fish, he sternly forbade his suffering host.

On a perfect morning, he followed a solitary breakfast of heroic proportions with the application of fine, fat leeches, a practised scalpel, and a fruit-essence purgative to his corpulent patient. After scrutinising the diluvian response to his ministrations and having written details of a fruit and vegetable regimen of strict observance, he departed on the morning's ride across to Ashbourne.

The Buxton road, its destination many miles across the desolate high moorlands, climbed at such a rake, up out of the busy market-place at its foot, that both horse and dismounted rider were wheezing by the time its summit had been reached.

"Too much soft living," he panted to the mare as he tethered her to one of the posts outside the strategically located hilltop alehouse.

Descending towards their destination in the early afternoon, he became certain – for several perplexing minutes – that he had, somehow, mistaken his route. He was quite certain that Sir Eldon Pagnell's sumptuous house sat in the lee of the steeply climbing slopes around *this* bend, where the undulations of the softly folding hill faced out to the rougher, rockier crags of the distant White Peak, but it was approached by *a village*, surely? He could distinctly remember an unremarkable straggle of cottages and small farms that curved round to the church.

He reined in so abruptly that Rosie shied and almost unseated him. *There* was the church, but where…?

It was then he realised that – all around him – newly grassed hummocks were all that remained of close-on a score of dwellings. His mystification increased as he passed the ivy-clad tower and saw that it, alone, was all that remained of the church. The red-brick nave, the gift, he had once been told, of Sir Eldon's immediate predecessor, had joined the rest of the village in oblivion.

As if to compound the mystery, great rips and furrows scarred the park land around the plumply magnificent house, and to Greene's utter amazement a hundred men – at least – scurried about like distant ants in the further reaches of the huge domain, engaged upon some unguessable labour.

To his left, a wide serpentine mud bath glistened wetly in the soft light, its curves resembling a huge palette scooped from the grassland. At its far end, a good quarter mile from the drive where

Greene had paused in wonder, a heavily rusticated structure appeared to be either rising from – or sinking into – the quagmire, its huge stone blocks pale against the hills behind. A gaggle of carts appeared now from its lee, the distant crack of a driver's whip carrying on the freshening breeze as they meandered away up a wooded rise and disappeared into the trees.

He nudged his horse down the arcing drive towards the grey bulk of Hildershall, the house itself standing beyond palatial stables, and a sweeping curve of pillared portico that seemed to beckon the eye.

To complete his perplexity, it was as if he had entered a regimental depot preparing for imminent campaign when the courtyard of the huge stable block was revealed through its Triumphal Arch. Scores of half-dressed figures, braces dangling below coarse vests, hair slicked wetly back, others towelling down, in jostling, rowdy groups, thronged the cobbles around the horse troughs and the yard's sole pump where more muddy, work-stained men laughed and jostled.

"Bloomin' Yeomanry, Sir," replied a harried-looking Ostler to Greene's question. "Here all month for the *Landskippin*', Sir. All summer, more like, we reckon, if Mr Kent has anything to do wi' it! Pardon me for sayin', Sir."

A full and proper explanation had to wait until after Greene had been conducted to a bedroom whose outlook was limited to a view of the scrubby hillside, which rose steeply behind the house.

"*Second-best*," decided the Apothecary with a complete lack of concern, as he reviewed the opulent interior before changing for dinner, and then, descending a decidedly *first-rate* staircase to the palatial hall below.

(20)

Over the STAIR CASE; hangs a model of a thirty-two Oar'd
Galley, made by French Prisoners, confined at Liverpool,
during the last war; it is four feet and four inches long. Several
pieces of Ships bottoms, much perforated by worms.

"*Flattened*, Sir! Levelled without compunction!" bellowed Richard
Greene's host, beaming all over his florid jowls. "*What a heartless
brute I am*, you will be thinking?" – his listener's polite demurral
waved away with a lordly gesture. "And finding me quite without
remorse, wholly unrepentant, you will further enquire why I'd turf
m'own tenants out, willy nilly! Am I right, Sir? Am I right?"

Even prepared – as usual – for Sir Eldon Pagnell's rambling
bombast, Greene was unable to frame a response – let alone a
question – before the Baronet stooped gawkily from his considerable height and with alarming intimacy placed an arm, confiding-
ly, around his small guest.

"It was a sacrifice made in the name of *Beauty*, Mr Greene: the
soul's search for Perfection, nothing less! Kent is bringing *Arcadia*
to these rough old hills," his voice now scarcely more than a hoarse
whisper.

"But the cottagers? The farmers?" interjected Greene, "How...?"

"New billets, each and every last one of 'em! Kent's seeing to
it all, y'know." His eyes suddenly narrowed and he squinted at
Greene, as if seeing him for the first time.

"*Damme*, Sir, d'you take me for a *Monster*? D'you believe I'd
see m'own people without a *roof* over their heads? New village,
neat as you like, over behind the coppice. '*Nether Pagnell*', I've let

(88)

'em name it! Pretty as a picture it'll be, if you've got to look at the damn' place – which, now, I don't have to!" His guffaw rattled porcelain in the gilded cabinets flanking the room's magnificent chimneypiece.

"A Gentleman can't be doing with a rag-tag straggle of middens and outhouses on his own doorstep, d'y'see? Didn't fit into the scheme of things, simple as that! Kept the belfry, though, ivy and all – Kent's idea – damn' fine one too, don't you think?"

The frowning squint returned. "*Dammit*, man, you've precious little to say for y'self today. Best brighten up for dinner or y'll be a dull dog, and no mistake!"

Richard Greene smiled, disarmingly, realising for the first time how rapid had been Pagnell's deterioration since that first visit to Saddler Street.

"You'll not cajole me into jollity – and *well* you know it, Sir Eldon! A *dull dog* I might well be, but rather *that* than be one of those *tail waggers* you profess to despise!"

His host stepped back in theatrical amazement before stooping into another scowling squint. Then he exploded in a great spluttering of laughter, clapping the small man on the shoulder. "Capital! *Quite splendid*! Surrounded by arse lickers, day in, day out! Breath of air, Greene. Breath of air! So, what's to do, man? It's not going to be one of y'r tellings-off, is it? Y're a terror when roused, y'know, worse than any damn' nursemaid!"

Greene smiled, ruefully, before replying, watching the tics and grimaces light in the baronet's face as if being worked from within by some malign puppeteer: "I see you are engaged upon the levelling of mountains and the moving of molehills, here at Hildershall, Sir Eldon, but I'd hazard it less of a task than persuading *certain* of my patients that whilst it may, indeed, be possible to *improve* on Nature, she will not be scorned in the end. There is no fiercer, less forgiving, mistress – when all is said and done."

Any further response from Pagnell – suddenly looking fidgety and ill at ease – was precluded by the arrival of a thickset man in full uniform, his richly brocaded red coat drawn aside to reveal a hand upon the hilt of a dress sabre, the other cradling a cockaded hat beneath his arm.

"*Colonel Copeland, of His Majesty's Engineers,*" announced the liveried footman before bowing out.

"Copeland, my dear fellow! Impeccable timing! Couldn't have managed it better m'self!"

With heavy-handed geniality he propelled Greene forward with him as he strode to meet the newcomer.

"Rescued from a damn' tricky ambuscade by the Medics; fiercest buggers y'll ever face if y'cross 'em! *Forces of Nature*, nothing less, eh, Greene? *Eh?*"

With an inward sigh of resignation, the Apothecary allowed himself to be drawn into the genial banter that followed introductions – two more dinner guests arriving in rapid succession.

"*Manoeuvres!* Summer spruce-up for the Militia! That's what I put to the Duke, and *damme* if he didn't go for it, hook, line and sinker! Whitehall hardly likely to object, considering Kent has only just finished feathering *their* new billet, and wanted to make a start on Hildershall, straightway. Copeland here is keeping them all hard at it, eh Colonel?"

The soldier nodded gravely, but then spoke to the company with a humourless smile: "Though I am forced to admit that active service is more to my taste, Gentlemen, Derbyshire does have the distinct advantage of not concealing a savage behind every rock."

"I'm told that when our Soldiery are let loose on strong ale there's little to choose between 'em! Eh, Sir Eldon?" responded Pagnell's immediate neighbour, a young landowner and magistrate whose burgeoning jowls quivered at his own humour. He turned sycophantically to the Baronet who ignored him completely.

"The difference between them, perhaps, being... ," Copeland returned, without expression, "...that our lads are not known for torture, rape and cannibalism. Though perhaps you have *experience* of the Iroquois, Mr ... *Bottomley?*"

Greene hid a smile at the expert rebuff and realised that he and Colonel Copeland had more in common than might have been supposed.

"I was merely making ... I spoke in *jest*, Sir," replied Bottomley, a livid blush of annoyance rising to his podgy chins.

"A luxury that none in the Middle Colonies can afford, when it comes to those savages, which is why, perhaps, I was sharper than I intended. My apologies, Sir."

He bobbed a perfunctory bow in the Magistrate's direction.

"Thought he was goin' to call y'out, for a moment, there Copeland," boomed Pagnell, delightedly. "Y'could have set-to with *tommyhawks* out on the terrace! What a to-do! And all before soup!"

Bottomley managed a sickly smile and the moment passed.

"What little I know of the situation suggests that it is the Indians' paymasters who are the villains of the piece; they will have their forts, regardless of the infamies that such dangerous allies visit upon our people," said the Apothecary, quietly.

The soldier looked at Greene with interest, and was about to respond when Pagnell lurched off onto one of his bewildering tangents: "We've got one here, y'know, *damn'* great thing – what's left of it! Kent won't hear of ploughing it out even though it's no more than a lot of dips and hummocks. *Footprints of the Ancients*, or some such, says he. Can't see it m'self."

The guests exchanged glances that varied only in the degree of their perplexity. Pagett looked from one to another, shaking his head in exasperation.

"A *fort*! Damn' great Iron-Age bugger, Kent says. God's *teeth*, what a pack of wool-gatherers! Y'll be askin' what language I'm talkin' next!"

In spite of Pagnell's erratic weavings – in and out of commonsense one moment, the next, into some form of encrypted gibberish – Richard Greene by now understood that his host's huge wealth had purchased the not inconsiderable services of the aged William Kent, a luminary whose rise to fame remained an exemplar for the age: from a barely literate, North-country coach painter to the lauded architect of Royal Mews, Treasury and, most recently, Whitehall – to which Pagnell had alluded.

"It is all to be executed in that gentleman's *informal* manner, then, Sir Eldon? I gather it to be a stylistic model much admired in his great works for Lord Cobham at Stowe."

"*Damme*, Greene, y're well informed!" barked Pagnell with obvious gratification. "The fellow's a genius, pure and simple – can turn his hand to any damn' thing and make a silk purse of it! Give him a couple o' hundred pairs of willing hands, a trunkful of cash, and we'll see Elysium in a brace of shakes, I have his word on it!"

Dinner was announced, which brought a temporary respite to the booming monologue. As the Baronet limped ahead of them, talking now only to himself, Greene chose not to dwell upon how little time might remain for their host to enjoy the fruits of Kent's labours. His dinner companions at the all-male table were completed by the neat, soberly dressed person of Ashbourne's Rector, the Reverend Mountfield, a man of few words who shared his host's passion for Beagling.

It rapidly became obvious it was *that*, rather than his social graces, which had earned him a place at the evening's mismatched table, though, unexpectedly, it was he who prompted a return to the company's earlier conversation.

As the syllabub was being cleared away and a huge salver of hothouse peaches served to the guests, he turned to Copeland and enquired: "Did you see much evidence of the Great Awakening, Colonel? I have it on good authority that the citizens of The Connecticut Valley were much aroused by their Minister Edwards, acting in common revulsion against the disorder and emotional excess they saw all about them? It is becoming a mighty force for spiritual revival across the land, I am informed."

Before the Colonel could reply, Pagett rose unsteadily to his feet: "All due respect to y'r cloth, an' all that howd'y-do, Mountfield, but we'll not round off a damn' good dinner with talk of hymnin' and hosannahs! Got a couple o' the prettiest little bitches in whelp – show you those, quick as winkin', and be back to join you Gents at the Port. Your permission?" He belched, hugely, and, now limping more noticeably, led the uncomplaining Rector away to the Kennels.

Though conspicuously omitted from the invitation, Bottomley hurried in their wake, obviously preferring canine company to that remaining at Pagnell's table.

Copeland and the Apothecary exchanged looks of amused resignation as a blessed silence descended on the huge dining room.

"I should have been interested to hear your response to the Beagle-fancier's question, Colonel," said Greene, bringing the first wholehearted smile of the evening from the taciturn soldier. "I imagine that spiritual sustenance is no small thing to folk living in what sounds to be such daily extremity. Is it yet another full-scale Indian war? It would be the third, would it not?"

"The answer is affirmative to each of your questions, Mr Greene, though everything about that land is mercurial – it can change in an instant. Once beyond the greater towns, he who would prosper is a vigilant man with an eye to the tides and an ear to the wind."

"So the present instability...?" began Greene.

"...has been fomented by the French alone, Sir," interjected Copeland. "My regiment was briefly in Deerfield, Massachusetts, where, only a handful of years back, their Governor, Belcher, managed to negotiate a half-decent Peace with every one of the Iroquois tribes. It held, too, as much as these things ever do, until *Jacques Crapaud* stuck his ugly snout in. Day before we left, two damn' miles away, five scalped and dead, one captured – poor little bastard – and a girl tomahawked in the head, but still living, when we were ordered to *strategically withdraw*." The last words were said with a sarcastic sneer that sat oddly on the open face.

"Then possibly you will know of another vile business, probably occurring at much the same time, though at some greater remove?" Greene enquired earnestly.

Copeland shook his head in what seemed to be disbelief, and, for a long moment, simply fixed Greene in a level stare, before responding: "We sit here, at our host's gracious table, in *Arcadia-next-Ashbourne,* and yet discuss local incidents that have occurred on another continent that may just as well be another world? You have my attention, Mr Greene, of that I can assure you! To what can you *possibly* allude?"

"The murderous attack upon the Blanchmayne party, at – if I recall correctly – the meeting of the *Allegheny* and … forgive me, I cannot call the other river to mind."

Greene was abruptly aware that a cold intensity had entered Copeland's eyes.

"How you came by this information is quite beyond me, Mr Greene, but, then, the quality of your information has already been commented upon this evening. The other river is the *Monongahela.*"

"And the barbarity that took place there, Colonel?" asked the Apothecary, quietly, into the silence which grew around them.

"Yes, Mr Greene, I am all-too familiar with it. I had some acquaintance with that family, though it was a time ago. I have had no contact with any of them for a number of years."

Seeing the question in Greene's eyes, he continued: "A brother officer, Pell, led the search party out of Fort Ponchaine. He later apprised me of what they found."

"Forgive me, Colonel Copeland, but I sense your reluctance to continue with this. I have no wish to… ."

"My reluctance," interrupted the soldier, brusquely, is in having no wish to speak ill of the Dead. If I were to continue, I fear I should compound offence with indiscretion."

"I would prompt you to do neither, Sir," responded Greene, "though I feel I should explain that my interest in the matter is more than morbid curiosity. I, too, have some acquaintance with Mr Isiah Blanchmayne, his daughter and her husband. After their tragedy they returned to England, some months ago, to family in

Lichfield, where Hepzibah has been a recent patient of mine. I did not have the honour of meeting either the late Mr Blanchmayne or his unfortunate sister-in-law."

With a snort of sardonic laughter, Copeland said: "The word *honour* and the name Ned Blanchmayne make strange bedfellows, Mr Greene. I would say this of few men, but that black-hearted bastard met a richly deserved fate."

The return of their host, with Bottomley and the priest, Mountfield, from Hildershall's kennels, had brought an end to any chance of further talk between them at the dinner table. After sufficient port had been consumed to satisfy even Pagnell that he had acquitted his duties as a host, the Baronet abruptly rose from the table and announced he was off to his bed, his good humour suddenly evaporated.

Having made perfunctory farewells, he slipped and almost fell as he was leaving the company. Though he roundly cursed the footman who hurried to assist him, and at first angrily shrugged off the supporting arm, his departure was made leaning heavily on its support as he hobbled out with a broken, crab-like gait. Decency had forbidden any reference to Sir Eldon's obvious indisposition, so, within minutes of the invalid's exit, Mountfield's coach was being called. The Reverend Bottomley left with him as Copeland announced his intention to walk back to his estate lodgings across the parkland.

"I intend to be in Lichfield, shortly, Greene, and will be pleased to offer you dinner at The George, if you'll do me the honour?"

"Indeed Major, I shall be delighted, and will pay for my supper in kind – if you, in turn, will accept *my* invitation to inspect the Museum I am endeavouring to assemble. You may, in fact, be more than familiar with the few Iroquois artefacts I have managed to gather."

"*Any* form of familiarity with those particular gentlemen is a thing best avoided, Mr Greene, but yes, most certainly, to your proposal."

Treatment of the third and final stage of syphilis, was, the Apothecary found, a depressingly circumscribed affair. Virtually all the damage that the dreadful scourge could inflict had, already, been irredeemably inflicted, leaving room for little more than the alleviation of its more visible and obvious tokens. Ulcerated sores and inflamed joints had first brought Sir Eldon Pagnell to the Saddler Street Apothecary shortly after the shop had opened its doors, the Baronet being suddenly afflicted during a stay in the city for some of the Race Days. The worst of it had been that the suffering man was first astounded, and then, horrified, by Greene's prognosis. He had long believed himself cured, following protracted and excruciatingly painful treatment in early middle age which had left him scarred and half-poisoned.

That visit to the Apothecary had, however, convinced the wildly eccentric Pagnell that Greene was worth more than the sum of every other physician of his acquaintance, and, since then, a small fortune in balms, fruit purgatives, soothing lotions and dressings had flowed from Greene's prescription to Hildershall.

Sporadic house-calls – such as this – had become something of a therapeutic ritual: a brief respite in the patient's increasing deterioration. Above all else, particularly in his more lucid times, Pagnell valued Greene's utter candour quite as much as any of his treatments.

"I shall leave you with some of the fresh comfrey balm and also the *Echinacea* that I promised, Sir Eldon, but, as I have repeatedly told you, whilst the skin lesions and inflammations may be the most immediately vexing of your symptoms, it is to the longer-term defence of the heart and its functions that we must constantly look. It is a battle to be fought hourly, daily: not simply when all-too brief moments of guilt overtake you at flouting most of my advice for most of the time!"

To Greene's consternation, instead of either the genial badinage or the mock fury he knew so well, Pagnell simply stared vacantly into space before bursting into tears.

"It's all going to be so very beautiful when Kent's work is done, d'y'see?"

After a solitary lunch, served, nonetheless, in considerable state, the Apothecary left careful instructions for the increased dosage of his sedative mixture and looked in on his sleeping patient. As he had left the morose old man that morning, parting with little hope of having provided anything more than the most transient relief, Pagnell had suddenly gripped his arm and said quietly: "Due, no doubt, to the strange vagaries of my condition, I have become aware that certain, few, people are possessed of an inner light whose radiance soothes most wonderfully. You, my friend, possess this in abundance. It is a blessing and a comfort beyond compare. I thank you for it."

The day had begun with blustery showers and showed little sign of improving, so it was with some relief that Richard Greene accepted the offer of one of Hildershall's coaches rather than the lengthy ride home he had been anticipating. There was a world of difference, he assured himself, between the nicely sprung and cushioned variety and the mail coach that, within days, would be shaking and rattling his poor wife's bones on the return from Cheshire. As he settled back to enjoy the unaccustomed luxury of the brocaded upholstery and the well-sprung chassis, though, his thoughts rode ahead towards empty rooms.

It seemed that there had never been a time when Theodosia was not waiting at home to greet him – most times gladly, sometimes wordlessly – with those eloquent and appraising grey-green eyes. But then, had he not made *his* life *hers* in every way a husband could? Had they not adventured and explored, deep into the strange territory called Marriage? Why, then, was it, he found himself asking himself, that his motives – and then the perfect candour of his revelation, albeit a frankness of a reluctant kind – had caused such a fury? Especially, in a wife of such moderate temper, and one indulged in *every* way? He flinched as the memory of it capered back in sharp relief, and it was then, as if to escape that most uncomfortable place, that his thoughts slipped back and a voice seemed to enter the rhythm of the wheels … *in your debt, in your debt, in your debt …*

ITEM:

In the upper part of the window of the inner Museum: An artificial
leek of Silver with the Coronet and Motto of the P. of Wales,
embroidered and ornamented with Gold and Silver Spangles, worn
at Court by a Person of Distinction, on St David's Day. On a neat
bracket on one side of the window Admiral Hood; on the opposite
side Lord Rodney; they are twelve inches high, finely executed in
Mr Wedgwood's black hard composition, gilded and bronzed.

If the events of Theodosia Greene's recent days were supposed to
have constituted the ingredients of a restful interlude, removed
from the bustle and humdrum of her daily routine, then the lady
begged to differ.

She had arrived to a sister's house in a state of near-siege, where
that lady was, by and large, failing entirely to cope with a nursery
full of chicken-poxed young, an alarmingly scabbed housemaid
condemned as the source, and a housekeeper whose exhaustion
was becoming a threat to herself and everyone else.

As soon as the first red spots had erupted, Helena's husband,
a man of Business, had discovered a most pressing appointment,
largely involving trout and a river in Derbyshire. Admiring her
brother-in-law's discretion if not his valour, Theodosia, also, had
decamped with haste, having no intention of adding shingles to
all that a beckoning middle-age already promised.

Before determinedly announcing that she would be spending
the night at the small town's charmless coaching inn, she had sent
out for whatever of chicory, hornbeam or 'Busy Lizzie' the local
Apothecary could provide, having not the least expectation of

Cherry Plum or Crabapple from either the season or this most mundane of Druggists.

Insisting that no child was to come within hugging distance, she then briskly set about the making of a well-tried balm to damp the fire of itching, thus providing a salve for her conscience, at least, as she passed by the family pest-house on the next morning's first coach.

An indifferent supper and a leaden breakfast still sat heavily on her stomach, both setting fair to coalesce into fully fledged heartburn, when suspected footpads were scared off by the Postillion's blunderbuss, close to Harecastle.

Its thunderous discharge had probably frightened the rotund guard himself, more than anyone else, though any other lurking menace was kept at bay until the coach lurched, finally, across the cobbled wasteland leading to The George in Lichfield.

It might have been reasonable to expect that the regaining of one's home would afford the pleasure only dreamed of in the transit of execrable moorland roads and the more intimate purgatories of travelling abroad, but this particular Thursday was bidding to be remembered.

As the baggage was being manhandled down from the roof, the sight of her best travel valise with a shot-away corner failed to remind Mrs Greene of the Guard's manly defence of the coach against uncertain odds, but rather of the imbecilic nature of the male of her species.

This, generally, was the mood in which she swept home to the shop in Saddler Street, with both her baggage carrier – and anyone who had recently encountered her – lagging as far behind as could be contrived.

The sight of one of their least favoured and most self-important customers, perspiring, unwigged, and engaged in furious altercation with their shop-man, was not the homecoming she could have wished for.

"Oh, Mrs Greene! *Dear* Lady! You are the very Angel of

Deliverance and Intercession, nothing less! Convince this dolt, I beg you, that I must have every grain of Jesuit Bark on the premises if I am to save Pomlett! This wretch swears over and again that he may release not so much as a *whiff* of it without his Master's say-so! Even to a Doctor of Medicine such as myself! Does my patronage of your little shop mean *nothing* to such Monkeys?"

With a strained, conciliatory smile to her bristling steward, Theodosia hurried the unwanted visitor through to the privacy of her husband's Consulting Room before rounding on him: "Doctor Riddick, you may well be a man of parts, and are indeed a valued customer of our *little shop*, but this role of bully-boy does you no credit! The Bark is worth its weight in rubies – as you well know – and as scarce here as on any Druggists' shelves in England. What *possesses* you, Sir, to make such a spectacle in my husband's shop? What has he done to deserve such disdain? And what is this *harum scarum* about our Mr Pomlett? He looked well enough on his diet of archives and sanctimony, scarcely three days past, as did his poor mouse of a wife."

The irate man sagged visibly, holding out both hands as if to ward off Theodosia's indignation. "Oh, Mrs Greene, forgive me, I do *beg* of you! But your arrival – as timely as it is salutary – may mean the difference between that unfortunate man's survival or his certain death. I *must* have the bark – all else has failed. I have never seen infection of such virulence; its fever is consuming the last of him even as we speak. It is why I came myself, rather than sending out."

The sheer desperation and dishevelment of this, the most self-satisfied of men, dispelled all Theodosia's lingering annoyance, and she ran to the door, calling: "The contents of the small cedar box, and whatever is in the waxed paper folds of Mr Greene's small satchel. There! Quickly! No, just give them to me as you find them. I shall go with the Doctor, straight away."

"Will you be so *kind*? Oh, this is more than I could have hoped for, dear Lady. Mrs Pomlett is, herself, so reduced and distraught at the poor man's plight that I fear for her, too. Your presence will be a balm beyond compare, Mrs Greene, though let us make all haste before both pass beyond our powers."

On arriving, breathless, at the neat house in the enclosed gardens of Vicar's Court, Theodosia discovered to her utter consternation that the Doctor had scarcely exaggerated the condition of either husband or wife. The narrow, wainscoted hall stank of vomit and faeces, with stains on the stairway attesting to some desperate extremity. The Librarian's wife, her frizzy grey hair a serpentine halo about a chalk-white face and wild, darting eyes, was on her knees scrubbing at yet another stain on the little half-landing. She looked up, in a parody of comprehension, as Riddick and Theodosia Greene climbed the stairs towards her.

"Not himself at all, poor lamb. Better now though, having a lie down…."

Then, though, raising her fouled hands as if in prayer, she seemed suddenly to see their filth for the first time. Her cracked, warbling scream began just as the Doctor pushed past her into the nearest bedroom. On her knees beside the hysterical woman, Theodosia grasped the convulsing shoulders and pulled the Librarian's wife into a restraining embrace. Through the grey nimbus of hair against her cheek, she saw Riddick turn violently back towards her, a hand clasped across his mouth and nose, his shoulders heaving. He ran to the casement and wrestled it open, an instant before she heard his retching. He turned back, wild-eyed, rubbing the back of his hand across a glistening chin. "*Away!* Both of you! You must *not* see this, for the love of God!"

It was too late, though, as without warning the little woman wriggled free of Theodosia's arms and ran towards the bedroom door. Scrambling in her wake as Riddick, too, darted to intercept, they both reached her just as she gained the bedside. Theodosia reeled back as though bludgeoned by the sight of what lay in the tangle of bedding.

It was scarcely recognisable as human – a blackened, bloated monstrosity whose features seemed to have dissolved into formless putrescence.

Somehow, Theodosia managed to regain the landing before half falling, half sliding down the small stairs to the hall below. Riddick had carried Elfrida Pomlett to a settle and was gesturing urgently to where decanters stood on a dresser. With fumbling fingers the Apothecary's wife managed to splash what smelt like brandy into a fine-stemmed glass and hurry it to the figure moaning in the Doctor's grasp. He pushed it to her mouth until, spluttering and hiccoughing, she had managed several gulps through purple lips.

Outside, heard across the jumble of small houses, the bell for Evensong began its measured toll. As if its familiarity brought some blessed measure of normality, of reassurance, to the distraught woman, after a couple of moments with both Theodosia and the Doctor close by, she seemed to quieten a little and register their presence. When she spoke, then, it was in the small, wondering voice of a child: "It's a *prank*, you see? Philly says so. Just cruel silliness, Philly says. Nothing more than a scratch, you see? Silly Philly." The snigger that followed was the worst sound Theodosia had ever heard. She knew it came from far beyond the shores of sanity.

On the right hand of the Glass Case, the following Birds,
in fine plumage, and in their proper attitudes, viz: The
Ousel, Bird of Paradise, Virginian Partridge, Two Blue
headed Titmice, Barn-door Cock, Two Magpies.

"*Fishhooks*, Mr Greene, plain and simple. Maliciously secreted within a package into which poor Pomlett unthinkingly plunged his hand. Two nasty little lesions to the finger tips, though nothing that would give an Angler much pause. Damn' things looked filthy, though; source of that devilish infection beyond a doubt."

The Apothecary, his bags still propped against the Parlour door, regarded both his badly shaken wife and Riddick, both seated with a glass of his own Restorative.

"And the package?" enquired Greene, attempting to keep his enquiry one of concerned neutrality.

"Cut away, by myself, when I spied some sort of barb in it. Just a name on it – Pomlett's – in a poor hand, and not a damn' thing else, though there's not a schoolboy in the land about to own up to this, now is there?"

Mystified, Greene responded: "*Schoolboy?* You have lost me, Sir"

"Well, it's an idiot prank when all's said and done, ain't it? Even the little widow's clear on that!" He stood suddenly, bowing to Theodosia.

"Mrs Greene, may I beg the indulgence of a private word with your husband?" Seeing her frozen response he hurriedly continued: "A professional matter of some delicacy, if you'll forgive us. Scarcely the thing for a Lady's ears!"

Thinking that this bumptious booby would never know how narrowly he was escaping Nemesis, she rose with a tight smile.

"Oh, I have woman's work a-plenty to keep me busy, now that I've frittered away so much of the day," she said, and left the room.

"Indeed, indeed," intoned the Doctor to no-one in particular.

Then, oblivious to Greene's discomfiture at both Theodosia's dismissal and the conspiratorial arm now being placed about his shoulder, Riddick blundered on: "Something of an *Aesthete* was our man Pomlett, Greene, if you follow my drift?"

The Apothecary's gaze gave nothing in return.

Riddick continued, his tone confiding: "There have been, shall we say, *murmurs*, over the years, that the poor man's classical *inclinations* sometimes transgressed the bounds of scholarship. He was, shall we say, of a somewhat *Spartan* inclination, given – on rare occasions, I am assured – to a somewhat over-zealous attention to several of the youngsters that were beneath his wing."

"And you now, of course, assume that some spiteful youth was responsible for this...."

"...*accident*, Greene," interposed Rankin before the Apothecary could finish. "Nothing more, nothing less: tragic and wrong-headed, undoubtedly, but accident nonetheless."

He stood, beaming, "Lord above, what *else* could it be? I'll grant that nothing like that damned infection has ever darkened my door before, but then that's merely *one* of the crosses we in our Profession must bear."

Realising that he was not embraced in the 'we' of that statement, Greene felt a sudden wave of sheer annoyance rise within him and would have been only too happy to speed the fool on his way, had not a single question remained.

"While I think to ask, Doctor Riddick – and *apropos* another matter altogether – were you, by chance, Physician to the late Mr Neille of Dam Street?"

Comprehension slowly, almost visibly, entered the pudgy features. "Oh, you mean the sad business where you got that... ," and he raised a finger to point at the Apothecary's scarcely healed brow, before dropping it in a fluster of embarrassment.

"Or rather, I should … Yes! Yes indeed! Poor old Dick raced with us, too. Damn' good company. I'd have attended him on the day of the accident had the Thrales not been running a couple of nice little steeplechasers at Uttoxeter."

"Yes, I'd gathered he was expecting his physician, or perhaps your delivery, at least? Gout I believe?" Greene queried, in a bantering tone.

For just a moment, Riddick's pouched eyes narrowed, but then he gave his vapid smile and replied: "Clean forgot, if you must know, Greene! Not one to neglect a patient, mind; not at all, but, let's be frank, the old boy's liver pills were neither here nor there, as long as he was bled and kept the weight off his pins every now and then." Riddick paused for a moment, as if a sudden thought had occurred to his less-than-agile mind. "Strange, that, now you come to mention it, though. Left the wretched pills out with the other couple of prescriptions I'd meant…." he coughed, awkwardly, "…and there was no sign of them when I came back. Others still there, though," he ended lamely.

Forcing a laugh, Richard Greene rose decisively to his feet. "Oh well, another schoolboy prank, or perhaps – more like – one of your zealous servants!"

After an instant of uncertainty in the face of the Apothecary's response, Riddick, too, rose with a laugh of condescension.

"Indeed, indeed! If only one's patients *began* to understand the onerous weight we Physicians must bear! Can't be expected to think of every damn' thing all the damn' time!"

As he was about to descend the stairs, Riddick paused, turning back to Greene and looking upwards to the Museum on the floors above.

"My brains are scattered this evening, Greene." He fumbled open his case and extracted a folded envelope. "Why don't you add these damnable hooks to your Curiosity Shop upstairs. Just the kind of grisly memento to pull in the customers, I'd have thought. And, after all, every little counts, eh? Didn't care to leave them lying 'round at Pomlett's. Caused enough mischief, already, wouldn't you say?"

Obviously delighted by his own munificence, the Doctor turned to leave.

"Every little does *indeed* count, Doctor Riddick," responded the Apothecary, pleasantly. "So, you will forgive me if I mention the Jesuit Bark? My shop-man informs me you required our entire stock. It is, I fear, an uncommonly costly commodity – as, of course, a Physician of your standing will be all-too-well aware."

Greene returned from the welcome task of seeing a suddenly disgruntled Riddick off the premises to find his wife waiting, in obvious agitation, for him. As he came into their Parlour, she hurried towards him, taking both his hands in hers.

"Richard, Pomlett's death was an abomination. I ... I am lost for words to describe the state in which we found him. It was unspeakable what that poor man must have endured – and all in little more than hours. The way in which he had been ... *attacked* ... had more the look of some terrible corrosive acid than any contagion."

"There are poisons, though, of such caustic toxicity that they are the stuff of legends," replied her husband. "Mercifully none are to be found in these shores, though travellers amongst a number of barbaric tribes talk of monstrous harm caused by no more than a contaminated thorn or dart."

"Or *fishhook*, Richard?" Seeing the stricken look in her husband's eyes, she blurted: "It's all *connected* somehow, isn't it – all part of the same dreadful... ." She sank to her knees, suddenly, tears bursting from her eyes, the horrors of the day all rushing in on her. "Oh Richard, I'm so *frightened!* It was like seeing the Devil's own hand at work."

He sank beside her, the boards hard to his knees, his voice brisk, urgent: "There can no longer be any doubt that we face a truly satanic foe, my Dear. And yes, poor Pomlett's murder is assuredly the work of the same hellish hand. But we must be *resolute, vigilant*, if we are to stand against it! There can be no place for anything that will weaken us. You *must* understand this, Theodosia."

With her voice muffled against his shoulder, her broken sobs pulsing against his chest, she whispered: "I know, I *do* know. I'm trying to be strong, but, oh, if you had seen him, Richard. Why *him*? Why that stuffy, tedious little man? How could he have such an enemy?"

Carefully disengaging himself, Greene walked across to the Bureau, the flat sheen of its slope giving back the dimming light.

"I fear I may know the answer to that, at least," he said grimly, reaching, awkwardly, within to open a concealed drawer. He removed a small folio of papers.

"I showed you the list that Michael Rawlins came upon."

She looked up at him, puzzled, vulnerable amongst her spread skirts.

He continued: "The decayed parchment with names of all the members of that damnable Court?"

She nodded, red-eyed, in comprehension.

"What I may not have shown you was the note pinned to it, by Rawlins." He found what he sought and, squinting, held it against the twilit casement:

Promised 'forthwith' to P'lett, who insisted I sign for 'exceptional loan'.
Kindly ensure he does same on return. Mr.

"So, a *trail* was left? An indication of the *nature* of his enquiries?" Theodosia said, climbing purposefully to her feet and joining him by the window.

"Unfortunately, yes," murmured Greene, "though who could have dreamt that it would present such a threat?" As a skein of emotions seemed to collide in his wife's strained face, he hurriedly added: "Yes, I know to my bitter regret that I should have confided in you straightway – in fact, should never have kept *any* detail of this wretched business to myself, but that milk is long-spilt now – surely you can see that?"

Wordlessly, she nodded and held a hand briefly to his face. Relief swept over him, as he clasped it. Its coolness spread, delightfully but all too briefly.

(24)

A CABINET on the Right Hand the Fireplace: on the top, a grotto form'd of Ores, Spars, and other Minerals, moftly found in <u>Derbyshire</u>, covered with a large Glafs Bell. In the upper drawer: Argillaceous Earths, Gypfums, Pyrites, Selenites, Mundic &c.

It was several days before the Cathedral Library re-opened, a mark of respect for Theophilus Pomlett. His widow, sedated and restrained for her own safety, had been unable to attend the funeral, and was thus spared the somewhat perfunctory nature of the proceedings. The congregation, largely composed of his Cathedral colleagues and neighbours in the close-knit community of Vicars Close, were all-too aware of the nature of his passing, with the deceased's Physician sharing little in the way of discretion with the reluctant Mortician. As pallbearers strove manfully to ignore the fetor of their burden, the mourners seemed in no haste to follow its sad passage, and, with brief words, the coffin of the Librarian was interred down towards the South Gate.

The following morning, panting from the climb to Pomlett's erstwhile domain, Richard Greene looked, with accustomed dismay, around the once-graceful chamber, its soaring gothic curves now obscured by the makeshift shambles of what remained of the once-great collection. He was met, with nervous diffidence, by an alarmingly pallid young man, whom he remembered as the Librarian's dogsbody.

"Frederick Vale, Mr Greene, Sir. Your servant." He ducked his head as if seeking a bolt-hole.

(111)

"Sad times, Mr Vale, and, I would imagine, a difficult time to come calling? You will forgive me but I seek a small volume from, if I recall, one of Mr Pomlett's *green shelves* – or even from the Dutch Trunk."

"Well, certainly, Mr Greene, I am sure we can oblige," responded Vale, with obvious relief, "especially as you are so certain of where we must look." He spread his arms, helplessly: "It's all going to be that much trickier now, Sir, what with Mr Pomlett carrying so much of the reorganisation in his head, so to speak."

Looking at the chaos around them it seemed to the Apothecary that the hugely delayed, though much boasted of, *refurbishment* of the ravaged Library had remained firmly in Pomlett's head.

"*Diego Uffano* – his treatise on Artillery – is what we seek, Mr Vale. I need some clarification on the dimensions of cannon-shot. A bequest to the Museum, I am glad to say: three balls fired against this very Cathedral!"

Knowing perfectly well that the baize-lined shelves of the collection's best-preserved books would not contain the sought-after volume, Greene pretended to scan them rapidly before announcing: "The Dutch Chest it must be then."

Attempting to conceal his trepidation, Vale fished amongst an unwieldy tangle of keys before finding what he needed.

"It's not been opened since … what with… ."

"I quite understand your difficulty, Mr Vale. Would you like me to assist?" Greene gestured towards the locked door of Pomlett's cubbyhole, an awkwardly partitioned stud-work across what Greene secretly knew to have been a glorified privy in the wall's depth. Never once had his face betrayed a flicker when poor Pomlett had grandly referred to 'my office at the Library'.

The fact that the disarray within was as bad as that without came as no surprise to Greene, but – apparently – as a considerable shock to Vale.

"*Oh, my Lord*! This is terrible! It has been turned topsy-turvy, Mr Greene! It was not left like this!"

Greene hurried forward and, indeed, the sight that met him confirmed the young man's dismay. Bending to the strewn jumble of books, parchments and papers at his feet, he said, laconically: "Well, in spite of whatever tomfoolery has gone on in your absence, Mr Vale, here – at least – is what I sought." He held out the scuffed binding towards Vale, who continued to stare in complete dismay at the wreckage of the library's inner sanctum. "You'll doubtless discover that a cat got in, or, at worst some of those school lads who've been up to so much mischief lately – so I've been told. They have trespassed all over The Close ever since The Rebellion. Lads do so love a ruin they can improve upon!" Greene's apparent flippancy disguised consternation at the sight of the obviously burgled office and his heart beat ever faster as he added: "Does this mean we won't be able to sign out as I've always done for anything special? Is Mr Pomlett's ledger buried somewhere beneath all that? He always kept it under lock and key in there, if I recall."

He gestured through the opened door towards the spoil-heaps. Momentarily, Vale's face brightened, "Why not at all, Mr Greene! That much we can, at least, manage."

The Apothecary's heart leapt. "Oh, *capital*," he murmured.

Vale returned to a cupboard propped precariously beside the stained table that served as his desk. "Mr Pomlett entrusted the ledger to me for a repair to the spine, just before his... ."

"Quite, quite," Greene cut in, almost brusquely, "Well, I really should be on my way, so if you would be so kind?"

"Of course, Mr Greene. Let me just fill in my part. Now where is that pen?"

The Apothecary, somehow, resisted the temptation to tear the ledger from the ditherering hands and waited with all the appearance of unhurried patience as Vale laboriously entered the book's title and author onto the top of a new page in the dog-eared record. As he swivelled it towards Greene for his signature and counter-dating, Providence, panting and rain-spotted, entered the library vestibule in the form of the Reverend Mountfield, Greene's dining companion at Hildershall only days earlier.

Scarcely registering anything more than Vale's momentary distraction at the newcomer's arrival, Greene turned back the page he was signing and halfway down the preceding leaf saw Michael Rawlins' spidery signature, against '*Relic broken, on bad vellum. Consistory proceedings, for return forthwith*'.

Greene would later swear that his heart came close to stopping when he read the bold counter-signature against the entry below it, bearing the same date. It, alone, had been the point of the morning's subterfuge. A *Geographia* – the supposed loan entered against the damning signature had obviously been an irrelevancy, Greene knew, no more than an excuse for the supposed borrower to determine Rawlins' purpose. The half-dozen subsequent entries, ending on the day that Pomlett's sentence of death had been delivered, were scanned in little more than a blink; names as familiar to Greene as the hairs on the back of his hand; aged scholars, bumblers about libraries, and as dependent upon their regular dosage of book-dust as most were of their port. He could dismiss them without second thought, now that he had found what he sought. He realised, then, that he had only known what he expected to find in the split instant of its discovery. Then, and only then, did *anything* begin to fit into place.

"Why Mr Greene, I had not expected the pleasure of your company again, so soon, and certainly not in this sorry place," said Mountfield, weaving between book-heaps to reach him. With an audible sniff, Vale excused himself, disappearing off into one of his labyrinthine burrows.

Wishing only that that he could free of the dreary dog fancier, the Apothecary made to escape with the barest pleasantries, but Ashbourne's vicar had obviously decided that any company was preferable to the cheerless shambles all around them.

"To think, Mr Greene, that a dozen or more of England's great collections, *knowingly* in possession of so many of the looted treasures from our Cathedral library, refuse *absolutely* to consider their restitution! It is a sad comment upon the paucity of Christian virtue to be found in public life, these days, is it not?"

Normally, Greene could have happily engaged in a topic close to his heart. At that moment, though, he had little time for anything but the signature that remained, imprinted, behind his eyes.

"For some time I have been planning a letter on that very issue to my cousin Johnson, at the *Gentleman's Magazine* – but, speaking of time, Sir, I must ask you to... ."

He got no further, realising his mistake even before Mountfield's delighted response: "Why, Mr Greene, I had no *idea* you were related to the admirable Johnson – I myself have made one or two humble forays into print in that excellent publication: a short epistle on Coursing, you may recall? A brief *vignette* on the improved Gin-Trap?"

"Alas, Sir. I seem to have as little time for reading as I do for most things outside a welter of daily demands that seem to be ever-multiplying!"

"Ah, but what *would* become of us, Mr Greene, denied recourse to the pearls of experience and learning? A descent back into Barbarism! Nothing less, Sir; nothing less!"

Desperately, Greene tried another tack: "Well, I must certainly not be responsible for denying you *your* recourse, Mr Mountfield, so if... ."

"Actually, Greene, you could do me a service, if you'd be so kind," responded the oblivious vicar, *sotto voce*: "My eyes are willing, but weak, I fear. In the absence of Pomlett's fellow, perhaps you could assist me in the search of this *Haystack* he inhabits?"

"It will be my pleasure," said Greene, resignedly. "Which pearl do you seek today?"

The search took half an hour, with defeat only finally averted by the summoning of Vale, who located the prize in several smug minutes.

"*Webb* on *Canon Law*, Sir. I *could* have saved you gentleman the wasted time," adding: "If only I'd known what you sought," and failing to keep the petulance from his voice: "It's what a Librarian's *for*, after all."

"Then we shall just have to hope that Pomlett's replacement is appointed without delay, shall we not?" responded the Reverend Mountfield, icily, raising an eyebrow to the Apothecary. Vale retreated without another word, as soon as the damp-stained book was duly processed.

"You'll forgive me for observing that your choice is a trifle dry for a sporting gentleman," observed Greene smilingly, as, finally, they made progress towards the door.

"Oh, no more than a spot of procedural swotting to do, before the Bishop's visit next week – a tiresome disciplinary matter: Parish politics. Wheels within wheels – you know the kind of thing! Won't bother you with the details. Old Webb's still the best there is, though. As acute now as the day it was written, which is no mean feat when you think of when *that* was. Mind you, if truth be told, not that much *has* changed since King James' day, when all's said and done. I doubt that his Bible will ever be improved upon."

With murmured assent, and farewells as brief as decency permitted, Greene seized the opportunity presented by the sight of the approaching stairs. With a levity he didn't feel, he called back over his shoulder: "I wish you joy in your Canon Law, Sir, though I shall stick to the mysteries of my own calling, I believe!"

With benefit of hindsight he would come to wonder whether it had been *then*, or later, that a suspicion had begun to enter his mind: a niggling unease that somehow, *somewhere*, he had missed something of importance.

(25)

ITEM:

Beneath the Cabinet in a Drawer with 4 cedar sides: a coll.
Of Roman Coins in number 184 among which in large Brafs
are Nero, Anton. Pius, Empresses Faustina and Lucilla. In
middle Brafs, Tribonionous, Dioclesianus and Miffius Decius.
Small Brafs, Posthumus, Tacitus, Heliogabulus and &c.

Theodosia Greene was busy with one of her regular ladies as her husband came through the shop door. With a brief smile she indicated that she would join him upstairs as soon as she could, and he waited, chafing with impatience until he heard her on the stairs.

She spoke before he had a chance to pour out his discovery: "Well, this is a day of surprises, Richard. You'll never guess what has occurred while you've been out. A mixed parcel if ever there was one!"

He knew the only course was patience, as she continued: "The first piece of news is that, just after you'd gone, word came that the wretch responsible for burgling poor old Michael Rawlins has been nabbed, red-handed. He was taken at Alrewas last night, at another house-breaking. He'd fallen, apparently, and broken his leg. The parish Constable searched wherever it was he lived and found a pocket watch engraved with the old gentleman's name. They've got him locked up here, in the Guildhall cells, Richard. Apparently, he's singing like a bird, so that he'll get some attention for his leg."

A return to barbarism. The words, heard less than an hour earlier, echoed uncomfortably.

"Perhaps they'll break out the cat'o'nine tails into the bargain," he said, so angrily that Theodosia was taken aback. "Dear Lord, what are we come to when torture reappears on the agenda, Theodosia?" Before she could reply, he had gone for his bag. "The rest of your news must wait, I fear, Theodosia. I shall attend to him if no-one else will."

As he hurried out of the shop, his pensive wife could have been forgiven uncharitable observations concerning the occupying of moral high ground, and the possession of hidden agenda.

The City Gaol was no worse than many others, and though Greene had not penetrated beyond the more sociable façade of The Guildhall until now, the gaoler-cum-janitor was known to him. He was a slow, decent-enough man, in Greene's nodding acquaintance of him, who was mightily taken aback by the Apothecary's greeting.

"Who's responsible for this shameful business, Utting!? Why has your prisoner received no medical attention? This is a disgrace!"

In a tone of injury and resentment, the Gaoler bristled in response: "Now that won't do, Mr Greene, Sir. That's not it at all." He raised stubby hands in mollification and continued: "It was *you* we was waiting for, honest as I'm standing 'ere! That's why word was sent, wasn't it?"

"*Me*? Why *me*? Why not one of the City's physicians?" retorted Greene, suddenly feeling far less certain in his indignation.

"Well, let's be honest, Mr Greene, Sir. The Doctor gentlemen ain't never over-keen on my cells and who's in 'em – takes some folk that way – but *you* know we've all got our jobs to do, like. Everybody knows you do."

Then, as if to cover his awkwardness, Utting added – almost as an afterthought: "Any'ow, 'e asked for you by name, didn't 'e? Didn't want anyone else, did 'e?"

A mystified Greene was escorted past the heavy iron gate and down the cobbled tunnel to the cells.

It was several moments before the Apothecary's eyes became accustomed to the grey half-light whose pallor seemed to leach the colour from the cramped prison and its single sprawled occupant. In the sour, stale air, dust motes flared as Greene disturbed the new straw of the floor. He stared down at the dishevelled figure on the palliasse for several moments before it came back to him. This man had once stood, unkempt and ill at ease beside his small daughter on a far-off day when the Apothecary had gravely examined a handful of rusty tokens the child had come across at play. He had explained that, whilst it was not the treasure both had obviously hoped for, here was a sixpence for her kind consideration of his museum.

"You came, then, Mister. Thanks." With evident pain he propped himself up on his elbows. "Broke the bugger bad. Reckon you could fix it for me walk to the 'angman, do you, Mister?"

Not yet trusting himself to speak, Greene simply gestured for the man to lie back and went about his business. He paid Utting for hot water, towels and sent across to The Three Crowns, for a flask of gin. The fractures – there were three, Greene thought, at first sight – were as bad as any he had seen, with splinters of bone gashed through the blackened, inflamed flesh, above and below what little remained of the kneecap. "Tried a bit of a turny-key on 'im, but left it on a bit long, did we? Bleedin' like a stuck pig, we was, though."

In complete silence, apart from admonitions to drink more gin, the Apothecary cleaned, cut, sewed, probed, re-set and splinted what he could: the occasional shuddering groan the only sound to issue from the suffering prisoner.

"If you're as brave a man, sober, then the Lord only knows what brought you to this pass," the Apothecary said, unheeded, to the unconscious figure on the stained mattress, as he made to leave the cell.

It struck him, suddenly, that he didn't even know the thief's name, far less who had despatched him to the empty Friary on that terrible day. That, like so much else, would have to wait, sighed Greene inwardly, as he turned at Michael Jackson's sparsely filled window, and hurried home down Saddler Street.

(26)

On the left hand the Fireplace, A medal, four inches in diameter, turned in an engine lathe, on a piece of Canal Coal, finely polished, of the Chevalier de St. George. A Stag in Wood, turned in like manner.

"An invitation to *Dine?* In The Close? This afternoon?" repeated Richard Greene, stupidly, staring at the invitation: *the second surprise* that Theodosia had handed to him on his return.

"I thought it might improve your humour, frankly, Richard," she replied stiffly. "Though you seem more taken aback than gratified!" Then, in a softer tone, continued: "I grant you it is uncommonly short notice, though that, surely, is explained in Mr Clarke's note. I think it is a most gracious acknowledgement of your services. We get little enough of that, Lord knows," she added, a tart note creeping back into her voice. Greene once again scanned the perfect penmanship of the note:

In the hope that you will forgive the most unmannerly lack of notice for this long-overdue expression of our admiration and gratitude, we felt, Blanchmayne and I, that this suggestion – made, today, and most spontaneously by our dear Hepzibah – was the most perfect expression of the full health to which she has been so providentially restored.
As such, we overcame the natural inclination towards hesitation, the better to seize the moment. I trust you will forgive my impropriety and wish to share our joy.
Your most humble &c. Willm. Clarke. Prebendary House, No.15. The Close. Lichfield.

"I think it is most charming, Husband – and I have always wanted to see the inside of one of those houses." The matter, as far as Theodosia was concerned, was settled. "I sent word back, straightway, that we shall be *delighted*. Now, what news from you, my Dear? Did your visit to the Library – and, of course, to that wretched man in the cells – reveal any of what we hoped for? I have had no opportunity to enquire until now."

Greene, offering a silent prayer for forgiveness replied: "Early days, on both counts, Theodosia. Perhaps tomorrow will tell, though I'm encouraged by what little progress I have managed. I'll not bore you with it now, though." He looked at his watch: "There's little enough time if we're to be in full fig and on parade at four."

William Clarke had been born to the role of Genial Host, a talent that had served him well. In all the little *accommodations* and *easements* that had oiled the wheels of his various business ventures, a nicely turned profit could usually be relied upon between gentlemen who appreciated matters *comfortably* transacted.

So, arriving as the clock in the Jesus Tower rang out four, Apothecary and Mrs Greene were greeted effusively by the temporary master of the Prebendary House, having been helped from their cloaks by staff a sight more attentive than Greene remembered from any previous visit.

"Your acceptance was more a measure of your graciousness than of my *punctilio*, I regret," Clarke puffed, standing back in theatrical admiration to take in the full length of Theodosia's gown, "though one might have expected *days* rather than mere *hours* to be required for the furbishment of such elegance, Mrs Greene, if you will *also* forgive such presumption."

Theodosia blushed with pleasure, replying: "One just gets on with the job in hand, Mr Clarke, though, admittedly, some are far greater pleasure than others."

"Oh, delightful, *delightful*, Mrs Greene. *The job in hand*, indeed!

Now, come through and I shall introduce you! Your hostess will be joining us momentarily, I believe," he added, offering an archly confiding smile to Greene.

Timothy Sharratt and Isiah Blanchmayne were standing against the graceful Oriel that overlooked the gardens, in conversation with a sharp-featured man and an equally angular woman, her shoulders protruding like ploughshares from a dress of palest yellow silk. Both came forward as Theodosia was led in by the beaming Clarke, followed by the Apothecary.

As introductions were made, and Theodosia treated to the full intensity of Blanchmayne's piercing, blue-eyed approbation, the Greenes learned that the other couple were a Mr Aloysius Hoare, Clarke's Banker, and his wife; residents of Clifton, Bristol.

The latter fact was revealed in less than two minutes by Mrs Hoare, as she peered down her blade of a nose and said sweetly: "Oh, Mr Greene, I was saying, just before you arrived, how blessed you all are to live in this little Sea of Tranquility! It is as if one had stepped back into the pages of a Romance, these little narrow streets and quaint yards – and more ancient timbering than one could shake a stick at! Whilst we, my poor, dear, husband and I, are *engulfed* in the beautification of Bristol. Do you know Clifton? No, of course not. How tedious of me – but simply imagine *all* you remember of Bath and transport it a cliff-top eyrie above the Severn! And such *landscaping*, such terraces and squares a-building! It is firmly expected that, for all the monstrous inconvenience to us poor residents, our Hustle and Bustle will be finished to perfection *long* before Mr Wood's adventure in Bath!"

As Greene finished a brief silent prayer concerning the seating plan for dinner, and before he could frame a response, the door opened to the arrival of their hostess.

He felt a seismic lurch inside him, and it was all he could do not to gasp aloud. Dressed in an unadorned bodice of white satin and moving in a cloud of black-feathered skirts, she wore her ebon ringlets down to sculpted shoulders, gathered in bunches and entwined with tiny white flowers. The Apothecary simply hoped he was not gaping like a gaffed codfish as he tried to connect this Vision with the dessicated creature he had coaxed back to fragile health.

And then she smiled.

Suddenly there was a curve – a quirk – to her mouth that lifted the cheeks into perfect oval moons beneath eyes that seemed to dance and sparkle with some inner radiance. Small, perfect white teeth, framed in a blush-rose pink. Greene suddenly realised that not only was he being spoken to but that he had completely forgotten where he was.

"…than the last time you saw my daughter, Mr Greene? It was Hepzibah's wish to thank you, here amongst her family, was it not my dear?"

Blanchmayne turned, smilingly, to her. Avoiding her father's gaze and seeming to have eyes only for him, Hepzibah Sharratt advanced on the Apothecary, the room seeming, to Greene's wide eyes, to dissolve around her. With the smallest bob of a curtsy she offered a satin-gloved hand, her eyes demurely downcast.

"Mr Greene, and you have brought your charming wife. I fear, Mrs Greene, that I have been the cause of many hours lost to your husband's company. Neither of us would have had it so, I am certain. Please forgive a weakly woman's need. We can be such a tribulation to our menfolk, can we not?"

Before Theodosia had even begun to dissect the multiple ambiguities of what she thought she had just heard, a salver of champagne was brought, with a flourish, into the salon, and small, inconsequential conversations sprang up between the guests. The Apothecary had not noticed the dark, thick-set servant on any of his previous visits, and noted, with interest, the distinctively American twang to his apology as he inadvertently nudged Greene's shoulder in passing. A brief glare, directed at him by Timothy Sharratt, seemed to confirm it.

"Far more at home with *Pemmican* than with Parlours, is our

Sam Blain, I'm afraid, Greene," the young man laughed.

"He was my late uncle's help, can turn his hand to anything – especially hard liquor, if he gets half a chance!"

Dinner was announced, and in answer to his prayer, Richard Greene was seated beyond the immediate range of the Banker's wife. The plan set him, undeniably, in the place of honour: to the right of his hostess who, tonight, took pride of place at the head of the superbly set table.

Beside him, Blanchmayne resumed his easy conversation across the table to Hoare – both obviously well at ease in the other's company – before turning to the Apothecary. "Your business interests take you as far-afield as Liverpool, brother Clarke tells us, Greene," he nodded towards Hoare, continuing: "There are some mighty interesting schemes afoot – both there and at Bristol – though perhaps you already have wind of them?" Before Greene could reply, Clarke's avuncular boom sounded from his most temporary place at the foot of the table.

"Gentlemen, for shame! Let's not drive the ladies into a Vapour with business at the table. I'm sure our Mr Greene must endure more than enough shop-talk as it is! Tonight, let us discuss the very *latest* modes, and plays and whatever else takes our Fancy, and let the Devil take the bank – 'til the morning!"

To polite laughter the meal was set on a well-trodden path of frothy inconsequence, diverted only by a succession of toasts and the comings and goings of course upon course. Apothecary Greene, meanwhile, was fighting a losing battle in his desperate attempt to ignore the proximity of Hepzibah Sharratt's *décolletage*, revealed tonight in such a manner as to make the Apothecary doubt that this could be the same bosom he had sponged so clinically scarcely weeks before.

As it seemed that both men – to Hepzibah's left and right – were equally aware that the entire topic of America was best avoided, conversation tended towards the quirks and customs of the little Staffordshire city in which they all found themselves.

As the wines were served or replenished, the volume rose around the table with conversations engaged in tangents across it, until Clarke, perhaps a little more boisterously than he intended, called down: "Do tell everyone about your *Gable*, Greene!

He added, turning to the Banker's wife at his elbow: "It's priceless, quite *priceless*!"

Misreading the Apothecary's bewilderment as reluctance, he repeated: "Oh tell us, *do*, Sir! – This in no place for hiding lights beneath bushels! You are among friends!"

All attention turned to Greene, comprehension now dawning across his somewhat flushed features. "I think you must be referring to my *Porch*, Mr Clarke?"

"The same, Sir, the very same," puffed Clarke, "we pray you!"

Warming to this relief, Greene said, smilingly: "Strictly speaking it is *part* of a porch, only, the rest having, sadly, decayed beyond repair."

The smile now widened to a grin as he saw the mystification around the table.

"Your intelligence is of the highest order, Mr Clarke, as I was only able to have the relic dismantled some days ago. It lies in my stable, as we speak, though I have hopes to install it in my new Museum room." He broke off to say, disingenuously, to Theodosia: "Did I not mention that, my dear? How remiss of me."

In the still-puzzled laughter, he continued: "It is all that tangibly remains of one of the City's most stirring – some might say *uncanny* – events: the death of Lord Brooke, General of Parliament, as he directed the fire of siege guns against where we now sit at Dinner!"

He smiled around the table. He had them now.

"There's a fine marble memorial in our Cathedral's south aisle to the Royalist Commander here, at that time, which describes the Cathedral and Close as 'this great fortress', and that is precisely what My Lord Brooke was up against: a stronghold unlike any other in the Midlands."

"And the *porch*, of which I was unaware, Mr Greene?" cut in Theodosia, to general laughter.

"All in good time," chuckled Greene, and continued: "The General was well-known for his fiercely anti-clerical sentiments, and so one can only imagine his *particular* vexation at confronting not only a monument that he abhorred, but also one so heavily fortified and resolutely held for The King, that neither storm nor bombardment had, thus far, even *dented* its resolve. So, in the year 1643, on the 22nd of March – and I ask that you note that date – His Lordship was taking shelter from the Garrison's fire, beneath a certain porch in Dam Street. Unknown to him, one of the defenders, a deaf-mute named Dyott, son of an old, old City family, had climbed to the battlements of the Great Steeple with his duck gun. Our General, taking the shelter afforded by his refuge rather too much for granted, lifted the visor of his heavy siege helmet, the better to spot his next target – little knowing that he was about to become one, himself! Dyott's sharp-shot, from many hundred yards, struck the porch and ricocheted into Brooke's unprotected brow, wounding him to death. The mark of that very shot is, I maintain, still visible on the relic that lies, *temporarily*, in my stable!"

"And *the date*, Mr Greene? You asked particularly that we note it," prompted Blanchmayne with good humour, obviously aware that he was feeding the storyteller his cue.

"Oh, did I not mention it?" responded the Apothecary archly. "It was the feast-day of Chad, the Cathedral's patron Saint." Greene's *coup de grace* was delivered into the murmurs of his audience. "Yes, and even stranger to tell: the bullet which sent the General to his Maker was cast from the roof lead of that same great church."

"Bravo, Mr Greene, on all counts!" exclaimed Hoare, drily, "I see there is far more to Lichfield – and its citizens – than might at first be apparent."

He turned to his hostess, who, Theodosia had noticed, had

responded to Greene's monologue with little more than polite attention, failing to share the general amusement.

"You are fortunate indeed to be living in the shadow of such history, Mrs Sharratt. It must be a daily inspiration to see that great Spire above one's windows."

"The Cathedral and all it represents has long had its day, Mr Hoare. As for the shadow of history, it is one I would gladly shed." Hepzibah Sharratt rose, abruptly, "Ladies, shall we leave these gentlemen to their *business*?"

The sheer gracelessness of her departure, with Theodosia and the Banker's wife in awkward train, left a palpable silence in the Dining room until Blanchmayne said, heavily: "Please forgive my daughter's manner, she has...."

"Dammit, Sir!" interjected Sharratt, furiously, "Hepzibah is my *Wife!* Her name is *Sharratt,* in case you or anyone else has failed to notice! If there are apologies to be made, then *I* shall make them. We are not *adjuncts* to your life, your misadventures! We have our own star to follow, my *Wife* and I, you shall see if we don't, Sir!"

With that, he rose from the astonished company.

"You will forgive me Mr Greene, Mr Hoare?" he said, woodenly, turning on his heel and leaving the room.

Hoare pursed his lips and, with raised eyebrows, looked from Blanchmayne to Clarke, then back again.

The American sat, pale beneath his walnut tan, hands clenched on the table, wordless.

Clarke, in a babble of embarrassment, mouthed a succession of inanities before walking to the dresser and helping himself to a brimming glass of brandy.

"Oh, the impetuosity of Youth, gentlemen. All that fire and mustard, eh!? D'you know it reminds me of when *I* was a lad and...."

Unaware of her husband's outburst, Hepzibah had acted with complete unconcern as the Ladies settled in the opulent parlour, just as if she had not spoken minutes earlier. Cordials were served, with little ratafia biscuits of exceptional lightness, and within minutes they had fallen to discussing baking recipes.

In the chit-chat that followed, it rapidly emerged – along with the accent to accompany it – that Lizzie Hoare came from Devon farming stock, far less grand than might be supposed; whilst Hepzibah Sharratt, herself, chose to bring up the pro's and con's of cookery in the Middle Colonies, along with an animated description of the game, fish, herbs and flowers that flourished there in such natural abundance.

"Do you miss it most awfully, my dear?" asked Theodosia, following the only lead that the evening had presented.

"It is a land beyond imagining, Mrs Greene. To be deprived of it and all else in my life, is to endure a windowless, airless, confinement. I loathe this place, as any prisoner would his cell. I wish to offer no offence: that is the simple truth."

There was a look so alien, so detached from every emotion either of her listeners knew, that the Banker's wife excused herself in a flurry of awkwardness, quite unaccustomed to any display of raw emotion.

Alone, and expecting nothing more than an instant rebuff, Theodosia reached out and took the younger woman's unresisting hand in her own: "I cannot offer any of the endless vistas or the excitements you have lost, Mrs Sharratt, but I *can* offer a little company and gossip beyond the walls of this dreary old place, if that might provide even a brief respite in the long hours of your day. You spoke with such enthusiasm for the flora and fauna of your home, that perhaps you might even care to join me in my flower painting?"

Seeing what she read as amused refusal hovering on Hepzibah's lips, she hurriedly added: "It is neither so old-maidish nor prim as you may suppose. I find it a wondrous way to clear one's head of all the nonsense and bustle of the day. It is a *refreshment*, more than aught else. And, the Lord knows we all need one of those at times!"

To Theodosia's surprise, the young woman gave an outright grin.

"That would suit me very well *indeed*, Mrs Greene. The menfolk of this family seem to be convinced that society is circumscribed by the walls of this wretched Close – as it's so aptly called! To escape it will be my pleasure. When shall I come?"

ITEM:

A small glass case with folding doors; a variety of Sea-fhells
of the larger sort. In front of which stands a glass jar in which
are enclofed 3 Crucifixes carved in Wood and Painted. The
middle Crucifix represents our Saviour, the outer thofe of the
thieves; on top of the middle cross is seen a Dove defcending.
The work of fome French Prifoners confined at <u>Bristol</u>.

"Oh, Richard, did you ever see such a shade of yellow in your life?
It made poor Mrs Hoare resemble a wan daffodil," said Theodosia
happily, "and as for poor Mrs Sharratt's little *event*, I feared we
might all be struck by lightning, to hear such sentiments voiced
in The Close! She really does *hate* it, poor child. I have offered her
refreshments tomorrow afternoon. A change of scene may serve
to raise her spirits."

"Hepzibah Sharratt is neither poor nor a child," said her husband with a gruff sternness that took his contented wife by surprise. "The enterprises in which the Brothers Blanchmayne were
involved must have made them a fortune, for all their eventual
*mis*fortune. And, presumably, it will all pass to the Sharratts, one
day. There is no other succession involved."

"Granted," replied Theodosia, "but why so dour about our sweet
hostess?"

A flush of guilt seemed to pass through Greene's whole being
before he replied: "As a physician I sense a detachment, a *disaffec-
tion* in her that troubles me deeply, for all her undoubted bloom
this evening. There is a steely resolve, an edge, there, that does not
sit happily with her femininity."

"Oh, indeed? And we women are all such *soft* biddable creatures, are we Husband?" said Theodosia, annoyance beginning to spoil her mood. "I think it nothing less than remarkable that she bears her losses with such … *character.*"

Had his wife but known the nature of the *character* displayed – unobserved – by their hostess, as cloaks were being fetched, and farewells made, Greene dreaded to even consider the outcome.

Hepzibah Sharratt had passed close by him, moving to bid farewell to the Hoares, when the back of her hand had brushed, for an instant, across his crotch.

It was as if he had received a galvanic shock, but as frantic desire and stupefied embarrassment collided within him, the bustle of departure had managed, somehow, to conceal it.

"Oh, perhaps you are right my Dear, though I must confess to being thrown into the strangest of moods by the whole affair."

"There is something you have not told me, Richard," said Theodosia, stopping abruptly. "What is the matter, to cast such a pall over the evening? You know you must tell me." If he entertained any doubts on that score, the note of warning in his wife's tone was unmistakable.

"This will take some explaining, my Dear, and I do not think Breadmarket Street the best place to do it. Let us at least get home."

"The name in the library ledger was *Blanchmayne*? Then, surely Richard, that confirms your strange sighting after poor Mr Rawlins' death. Isiah Blanchmayne is somehow the link you sought. He could be the … Oh, Richard, why didn't you *tell* me what you'd found? Your silence meant that we have been sitting at the same table as the man who… ." She couldn't bear to finish.

"On the contrary, my Dear. It was at that very table that my precious *construct* crumbled into worthless pieces – all my suspicions are proved groundless, brought to nothing by what Hoare said."

"And what in the name of Goodness was that?" asked his wife, bleakly.

"It cannot have been Blanchmayne that I saw on Greenhill. He was, indisputably, with the Banker in Bristol on the day itself and, subsequently, in London. They travelled back to Birmingham together, I gathered, though Blanchmayne was collected by the same idiot coachman to whom I spoke later that same day."

"And how was this information volunteered so conveniently?" she asked coldly.

"It arose in the most innocent and roundabout manner, as it transpired, my Dear."

Talk had turned to the perils and inconveniences that face the traveller, and it was Clarke who brought up the shooting on Bower Day. "You've scant need to travel abroad for tragedy – or plain mischance – to befall, gentlemen," he'd said.

"Look at the death of the old boy from The Friary! Hit by another of your famous ricochets, Greene! Scarcely out of sight of his own home and at a carnival, dammit! You missed all that to-do, Isiah. It must have been the day you signed us up for the Sugar?"

"Would that have been the twelfth, Hoare?" Blanchmayne had enquired, with complete composure, Greene following his every move.

"Indeed it was!" the Banker replied, "A day for a double celebration, you'll recall – it was Lizzie's birthday, too'" he turned to Greene, "We all dined most extravagantly in Bath, though with two good excuses!"

He had gone on to say, though, that both his and Blanchmayne's satisfaction at a most profitable transaction had been tarnished by the awfulness of their subsequent journeys to London and back to the Midlands.

Blanchmayne, with heavy humour, recounted a tale of incompetence and appalling horsemanship at Oxford, and how the sole comfort in hundreds of miles travelled in coaches had been provided by William Clarke's vehicle – for the last twenty of them. The conversation had moved on to the huge advantages to be gained from the creation of a country-wide canal network, and it was then that Blanchmayne demolished the last plank of the Apothecary's carefully constructed suspicions.

Excusing himself, momentarily, he'd fetched that same *Geographia* Greene had seen entered into the Library ledger and opened it on the dining table to reveal several pages of notes. The fact that here was a book borrowed for the most innocent of reasons had been infuriatingly reinforced when he'd gone on to illustrate several well-informed observations about such a commercial network – and, unknowingly, to leave the Apothecary faced with a slate wiped clean.

"So, all in all, I am back exactly where I started," finished Greene, morosely.

At that same moment, in one of those unlooked-for conjunctions that seem sent in mockery, their housemaid bobbed at the door to say that an urgent message had arrived: *Would Mr Greene attend on Mr Utting at The Guildhall with all haste?*

White-faced, the Apothecary sprang to his feet, knowing with sick certainty that a bad day was about to get far worse.

(28)

ITEM:

Under the large case of Shells, in a DRAWER on
the left hand: a piece of Cloth from <u>Ehoe</u> and from
the Gold Coast in <u>Africa</u>. Charles Ashwell Efq, St
Vincent's Ifland. A Quiver from <u>Sandwich</u> Island.

A cresset, smoky in the freshening breeze, lent a hellish dance of
shadows as Richard Greene hurried down the gaol tunnel to the
cells, footsteps echoing dully in the brick vault. The heavy iron
gate at the top of the passage had been open – itself a surprise –
and Utting's cubbyhole stood empty.

The distraught Gaoler met him as he reached the cells.

"'E's *dead* Mr Greene! Done away wiv 'isself, the bastid! In my
custody, in my bleedin' cells! 'Anged 'isself!"

"But you had his belt and laces as a matter of course, man!,"
shouted Greene, unable to contain himself. "How could he…?"

"Wiv *your* bleedin' bandages, is 'ow, Mr Greene," Utting cut in,
"Beggin yer pardon, Sir, but *that's* 'ow! I'll not be blamed fer this!
See 'im yerself!"

To the Apothecary's horror, the nameless thief hung, scarcely
a foot above the straw, a crude twisted noose knotted to the bars
of a small blind grille, the cell's sole ventilation. A crude wooden
stool – the cell's sole furnishing apart from the palliasse and a
reeking bucket – lay, upended, close to the dirty, calloused feet.
In the straw, the stick splints, bound on with such care only that
morning, were cast aside, close by an upturned slipware bowl, its
contents glistening in the straw. Greene bent close to it, identifying large lumps of mutton and carrots.

(135)

"You fed him well," said Greene, staring intently at the mess, avoiding Utting's gaze as he tried to marshal his whirling thoughts.

"Nuffin' to do wiv me, Sir," sniffed the Gaoler. "'S'all gone to bleedin' waste, any'ow."

"*Nothing to do with you?* How so, Utting? You're alone here, surely?"

"Bought an' paid for by some poor sod as did'nt know 'e'd kick it," said the Gaoler. "Brought in, from the *Crowns*. Lot's of 'em do it, if'n they've got the ready. Pays me 'emselves, or some poor bleedin' wife or sweet'eart does. Better'n porridge, I'd 'ave to agree, though."

The Apothecary's pulse quickened. "Someone brought this in, then? At what time?"

Utting's pouched eyes narrowed. "Why d'you ask, Sir?" He saw the look in the Apothecary's eye and hurriedly continued: "Around five, but this bugger must've bin all right then, cos' the bloke from the *Crowns* got tired of waitin' for it and said 'e'd come back for the bowl. Saw this one meself, like, lyin' there like 'e was supposed to be." He nodded at the empty palliasse. "It was 'im from the *Crowns* raised the alarm, like, when 'e come back for it."

"Let me get this straight in my head, Mr Utting," said Greene, as nonchalantly as he could manage. "I need to be in full possession of the facts so that I can attest to your blameless role in this sorry business." He watched slow comprehension enter the Gaoler's face, and a look of complicity cross the flat features.

"Look, Mr Greene, chummy was goin' nowhere, not wiv 'is leg like that – we both know that...."

"So, you let the servant from The Three Crowns into the cell and left him to wait. Was that normal?"

With a gross leer, the Gaoler replied: "Well, that's often the 'ole *point* of things, ain't it, Mr Greene? 'Specially wiv' one or two of them girls as comes across, if there's a bob or two in it."

"But you said *he*, a minute ago, the *bloke* from The Three Crowns?"

Now Utting looked flustered. "I didn't mean they was a couple of bum-boys! Nuffin' like that Mr Greene! Just that, like I said, this poor bugger weren't going nowhere, and there din't seem any 'arm in it. Can't say I'd seen 'im before, but 'er at the Crowns never could keep staff. Piss-poor wages and a sharp tongue."

At that, the Gaoler obviously decided that not only was there nothing more to tell, but that he'd vindicated his own actions to everyone's satisfaction.

"Would you give us 'and getting' 'im down, if you don't mind me askin', Mr Greene, I'm not much on climbin'."

The fact that a crippled man had, supposedly, managed the feat, did apparently not strike the Gaoler, but, wordlessly, the Apothecary re-set the stool and, stretching uncomfortably, tugged at the knotted bandage as Utting took the dead weight.

Straining, close by the twisted, engorged neck, Greene had the opportunity of noting heavy bruising around the windpipe, well above the viciously taut noose almost buried in the swollen flesh. It was only as they laid the pathetic husk on the palliasse that Greene noticed another object half-buried in the straw beside it. A crude, half-begun doll, its legs and arms no more than knots of grass, its torso a loose-balled nest.

Again, a memory of a far-off afternoon. A little echo, that just for one moment seemed to hang in the foul air: *'E's got two 'eads, Sir.*

(29)

A great variety of Gun Locks, which ſhew the gradual progression
of fire Arms, from the first invention of Gunpowder to the
present time; Four brass heads of the Roman Spear; seven
bolt heads of the Roman Balista, in Braſs; the head of a
Roman Celt, or sacrificing Axe, found in a Tumulus.

"*Murdered?* Oh, Sweet Lord, not *another*," whispered Theodosia, "Could it have been to stop him testifying – talking, at all?"

"Without a shadow of doubt, my dear, though it suits that dullard Utting to suppose otherwise. I honestly don't think any other possible cause of death even entered that thick skull."

"But Richard," Theodosia said with sudden urgency, "whoever killed that helpless man – whoever knew where to *find* him, how to *get* to him – must also know that you ministered to the thief only hours before. *We* know that you learned nothing from him, but his killer could not be sure of that!"

The implications of her words lay between them like a stain upon the day.

"How was it done, Richard? How could there have been time to do away with the poor soul, fashion that noose and hoist him…?"

Words failed her.

"It was done with a cool deliberation that freezes the blood to even consider it, my dear. He must have throttled his victim as soon as Utting retreated to his comforts; unbound the splints that providence had provided and made the halter from the bindings. Utting, if he bothered to note *anything*, would have seen only what little he expected to: a prisoner laid out on the floor. The fact that this was a dead one would not have entered that leaden brain."

"But if he *had* noticed something untoward, Richard...?"

"Oh, I have not the slightest doubt that he would have suffered the same fate, my dear. What would one more death mean to this monster? No, once again, circumstances alone provided him with all he could have hoped for. He gambled brazenly with the simple fact of a Gaoler's inertia – and won! It was no more than the work of a moment to hoist that poor dead soul up to the bars and kick away the stool. He will never admit to it, but I know – and Utting is *aware*, I know – that the cell had not even been re-locked. His prisoner was a helpless cripple – and that was all the idle incompetent needed to know, to save himself a walk! We shall now await the astounding discovery that no such servant is in the employ of old Mrs Meade at The Three Crowns, and that no such meal was ever ordered for the Gaol. Let Utting sort *that* one out – I shall not lift a finger to save his lazy, negligent hide!"

"If there is one crumb of comfort to be found in this, it is that Isiah Blanchmayne is again proven blameless, Husband. He could not have been at The Guildhall *and* at Mr Clarke's table – that much is certain."

"You will forgive me if I derive no comfort from the fact," Greene retorted, bleakly.

"There have now been four deaths – murders – that I – *we* – alone know of."

He reached out for her then, lost in a wilderness of doubt and fear.

"Has it been my own wretched silence – my craven self-absorption – that has permitted this foulness?" He bowed his head as misery engulfed him. "Who, though, would have believed a *word* of this nightmare in which we are enmeshed? What could they – *anyone* – have done to protect against a crazed, *unseen* assassin? Fire, bullet, poison, and now choking with bare hands. Oh, dear God, Theodosia, what is out there? How can we prevail against such satanic wickedness?"

Now it was her turn to be strong. "I believe that the will of the Good Lord will prevail, Husband, and if, as it seems, we have been chosen – God help us – as His agents, then we will prevail in righteousness."

She saw the look on her husband's face and managed a small smile: "And if I sound like one of the Bible-thumping fraternity, it is not that I've undergone some glorious enlightenment, but because I have seen evil incarnate revealed in this, Richard. I am neither vain nor foolish enough to believe that we can stand alone. And stand we must – there is simply no choice. That is all."

Then, to the Apothecary's amazement, she sprang to her feet. "And soon Mrs Sharratt will be arriving to take tea. I must make myself presentable."

Rising, Greene took her in his arms. "*Presentable* will be the least of it, my dear. I am a weak, dithering ninny of a husband and do not deserve you."

It was as she smilingly disengaged herself that he seemed to hear the voice again: *In your debt, in your debt…*

He hurried away, downstairs, to the reassurance of pestle and mortar, hoping that his coat skirts would conceal what he could no longer hide from himself. She would be here, in his house, with his wife. As he busied himself behind his counter, he seemed to feel the brush of a satin-gloved hand, over and again.

(30)

On the wall of the left hand of the ORGAN: a large pair of Rams
Horns, ditto of the Bald-Faced Antelope. A Cocoa Nut divested
of its external covering; a Highlander's Mull or Snuff Box.

A late autumn was giving ground to the first frosts before the
long-overdue invitation arrived from the Apothecary's dining
partner at Hildershall.

*I plan to put up at the George for the week commencing October
24. Shall you join me on that Wednesday at 4? If I hear nothing
to the contrary I look forward to the pleasure both of your company and your Museum.*
Your servant Henry Copeland.

The days had become weeks, the weeks, months, since the death
of Jack Davey. When Greene had put a name to the Guildhall
corpse, supplied by a fawningly attentive Utting, it had seemed
that it would lead him no further than a ramshackle hovel on the
edge of Barton-under-Needwood. As he had stood, disconsolate-
ly, outside the closed-up squalor – its garden a ruin of tares and
bramble – an old man hobbled out from a neat cottage across the
lane, stopping when he saw the Apothecary.

"Gone away, Master. No sense in waitin'. Nothin' to come back
for, see?"

"And who might that be?" Greene had enquired, disingenuously, raising his hat to the Methuselah.

"'Er you'm looking for, I was s'posin'. Aggie, Aggie Davey.

Lost her kiddies to the mumps, then 'er old man killed 'isself. Terrible business, Master. On the Parish at Croxall, so I've 'eard."

The nearby village of Croxall, had, by coincidence, been Theodosia's birthplace, and it was at its small manse, once her family home, that he next presented himself.

Admitted by an aging housekeeper, he was taken through the well-scrubbed hall to a study redolent of its equally aged occupant. Despite a sour squint bestowed on him as he entered – *It's a Mr Apothecary Greene, from Lichfield, he says. Hasn't got an appointment* – by way of introduction, his reception was polite, if not fulsome.

"Down the road from Michael Johnson's, if I'm not mistaken? No call for your services, glad to say, but I've seen your pretty glass," said the Rector of Croxall after a limp, dry handshake. "Can one be of some assistance?"

Saying as little as possible of the circumstances, Greene explained that he was pursuing something of a *professional obligation* in seeking out Davey's widow.

"Then that duty ends here, sadly," intoned the Vicar. "The poor woman did away with herself shortly after coming back here. Drowned, out by Catton Hall, apparently. The Trent is an unforgiving river. It seems she had nothing to live for, poor creature."

"You said *came back*, Sir. Did she hail from here?"

"I believe so, Mr Greene, though long before my time. *Bellis* was the family, I believe, though they're all gone too. Nothing to hold our young people, with Burton's *attractions*." He'd grimaced at the word and peered accusingly at the Apothecary: "Not to mention Lichfield, so close-by."

The Apothecary knew now that this was another blind alley, though before excusing himself, he'd said conversationally: "A name you may be more familiar with is *Webb*. My wife Theodosia was, in fact, born in this very house; the only child of the Reverend *Abraham* Webb?"

"I know the name, of course – painted it onto our list of Rectors myself," replied the elderly incumbent, pausing, eyes screwed tight in concentration. "1711 to 1722, if my memory serves."

"That would be it, no doubt," said Greene, "though I was denied the privilege of knowing either my wife's father, or her mother. He died when Theodosia was a girl," said the Apothecary rising to leave, "and her mother not many years later, I gather. As the only surviving child, she moved to family friends in Uttoxeter until her majority."

"That's about the sum of what I could tell her Cousin," the Rector replied, also rising, to indicate that time was up, "though if genealogy were his passion I suggested he might find greater reward with grandfather Webb of many removes." The Rector shrugged, a trifle petulantly. "It seemed, though, there was little I could add in *that* direction, either. He seemed to know all about it. Hardly surprising, I suppose – a life as well-documented as it was fertile. Few men could ask for a worthier immortality."

The Apothecary was scarcely following. *Grandfather? Immortality?* For Greene, one word, alone, hung in the air: *'Cousin'.*

Theodosia had no living relative, even describing herself light-heartedly as 'an orphan from the storm'. Showing not the least regret when her husband-to-be had pointed out that marriage meant the extinction of her family name, she had whispered that they would just have to populate the County 'with little Greene shoots'.

It was only as he realised the old Priest was holding something out to him for his inspection, that he seized the lifeline to haul himself clear of the maelstrom that was filling his head. It was that book once more; he could scarcely believe his eyes. *Old Webb's still the best there is, though. As acute now as the day it was written.* He had been so busy searching for the needle that the haystack had eluded him.

"Ah, yes. Great, Great Grandfather Webb. *On Canon Law...,*" croaked the Apothecary, silently cursing himself. He had failed totally, utterly, to make the connection, *any connection*, with the long-dead author and his own wife's maiden name, though it had already been dangled before his purblind eyes, shouted at his cloth ears. "*Immortality* indeed," he managed, "It must be, oh, how many years old now?"

As if amazed that Greene could fail to have such information at his fingertips, the Rector peered, peevishly, at the old book's *frontis*:

Printed 1611, by Swainson at Eagle and Child Yard, Stafford. Dedicated to His Most Catholic Majesty King James the First of England and Sixth of Scotland, Protector of the Faith.

"Well, the old boy certainly knew where *his* bread would be buttered, did he not?" said Greene, failing entirely to achieve the bantering note he sought.

The elderly clergyman bridled, visibly, replying: "Few monarchs could expect a more punctilious servant than King James found in Webb of Croxall. The Law was his life, though he saw little enough recompense for it. King Charles had little regard for such scholarship."

Greene seized his chance: "And talking of which – though I must detain you no longer – would it have been Cousin *Peter* or Cousin *Paul* who sought you out, I wonder? Both short, one fair-haired, the other bald? There are that many In-Laws I lose track altogether, I must confess."

"I recall no name. It was several months ago. He was a big man, with a brogue – a drawl – that was not immediately comprehensible. Well-travelled I would say: heavily scarred above the eye, though he kept his hat on, for some reason."

A disparaging sniff indicated both the vicar's opinion of the visitor's civility and an end to the conversation.

Forcing a smile, Greene replied: "Ah, yes, Cousin *George*. Something of an aenigma to us all, I fear."

ITEM:

An ancient Drinking Cup in the form of a sharp toed Shoe,
mounted with Silver wherein is engraved the inscription
"Adjum ex Inferis Ubi bibitur in Ocreis" Two Glass Cases
which contain 126 different specimens of Wood; each
specimen three inches long and one and a half wide.

The Apothecary's ride, back from Croxall, had seen his hat, wig,
and all pretence of dignity, lost along the road to Lichfield. Aban-
doning his exhausted, sweat-rimed mare to fend for herself in the
garden stable, Greene ran headlong into the scullery door, past
a gaping housemaid and on to the stairs. He scarcely heard the
maid's forlorn call behind him.

"Mistress is out, but she asked particular would you..." – the
words lost in his clattering ascent.

Pausing only to drag a heavily carved box from beneath the
window seat in the Parlour bay, he carried it through to their dining room and hoisted it onto the table's open leaf. Next, he ran
back to the bureau.

After a moment's fiddling he lifted the small folio from its
place of concealment, bringing it, too, to the table. He lifted the
enormous book – Theodosia's family Bible – out of its box and
flung open its front cover. There, on the flyleaf, in a dozen different
hands, was the story of the Webb family: its births, marriages and
deaths. There also, in a firm, scholarly hand and, just as he had
expected, the *Pater Familias*, the book's first owner, had inscribed
his name and issue.

With shaking hands, the Apothecary opened the folio and

found the vellum rag that, finally, had confounded both his and Michael Rawlins' attempts to decipher.

Now though, with sickening certainty, his finger traced out the gaps in the illegible final line: ... *olome ... bb ... f ... roxa.*

Bartholomew Webb of Croxall: it seemed so damnably obvious now.

Who more suited to burnish the dignity of Bishop Neille's court than this, the coming man of Church law?

Though the Apothecary knew, with nauseous conviction, that it was a futile exercise, his trembling finger traced down through the generations as they were excised by the strokes of a pen. Only one descendant of Webb of Croxall remained.

Only one name on that ragged index of death sentences was unaccounted for. Half a thousand people might know her as Theodosia Greene; one, though, knew her by another name. Born as Webb, she must be made to perish, hideously, as Webb – for the demented circle to be closed.

32

ITEM:

Within the Bureau: a naked Chinese female Figure, neatly carved
in Ivory; a cumbent Figure in Ivory of a pregnant Woman,
wherein is shown the contents of the Thorax, Abdomen &c.

Dinner was not going well. For all Greene's evident pleasure at
meeting the soldier, again, the conversation seemed to lack any
of the shared enthusiasms that had drawn the two men to one
another, that night at Hildershall. Greene, with his ever-present
headache and bilious stomach knew he was solely to blame.

Copeland had been frankly alarmed at the first sight of the little Apothecary, as he entered the panelled bustle of The George's
taproom. Glancing nervously from left to right, peering myopi-
cally into the amber gloom around the fireside settles, Richard
Greene was not the best of advertisements for his profession. The
sweaty, unhealthy sheen of his face gave back the firelight, though
that did little to relieve its gaunt pallor, his cheekbones sharp-
slashed shadows across the waxy skin.

Greene had downed two strong ales to the soldier's one, before
they had gone in to the busy dining room.

"How did you leave *Arcadia*?" the Apothecary enquired, after
an embarrassingly obvious scrutiny of their fellow diners.

"I am expelled from Eden, you might say, Greene," the soldier
replied. To the Apothecary's raised eyebrows, he continued: "You,
of all people, will not be surprised to hear that Sir Eldon's decline
has accelerated to such a degree that it has become insupportable.
He rages at delays, though causes ever more by his vacillation and
flights of fancy. When his wretched Bridge was all-but complete

he ordered it dismantled and moved *one hundred yards to the right, in order that it should harmonise more prettily with the lie of the land.* It stands, presently, half demolished, and the subject of yet another altercation with William Kent. That saintly man has endured tantrums, declarations of undying admiration, unpaid wages and the legion day-to-day eccentricities of which his client is capable."

"And your own exigency?" enquired Greene, with a tired smile.

"Was brought about when I refused to embark upon the defensive earthworks around the House."

The Apothecary's eyes widened. "*Defences?*" He shook his head sadly. "Oh, my Lord … Against *whom*, pray?"

"Against the Poor? The Mutinous? The Disaffected? Who can tell how such aberration is fuelled?" Copeland shrugged with weary resignation: "All I knew was that he expected my men to spend weeks, *months*, throwing up breastworks, counterscarps and moats as if we were defending what little remains of the wretched man's sanity. I could endure it no longer."

Copeland stretched, luxuriantly, eying the comfort and decorum of their surroundings. "I am thus a free agent, and mighty glad of it – until my masters decree my next billet, and I decide whether to accept it or hand in my papers. I intend to lodge here, in the meantime – it appears one could do far worse."

"Then, if the former, let us most earnestly hope it may not be the Indies, or any other of the fever-grounds to which our troops are routinely consigned," said Greene morosely.

"Amen to *that*," murmured Copeland, "though, if you will forgive my impertinence, Sir, you look as if you, yourself, have recently been victim of such a posting. You are much altered since our last meeting, if I may speak with a soldier's candour? Have you been unwell?"

Copeland's sharp eye saw annoyance, discomfiture – and something akin to a plea of desperation – jostle in the small man's face before he answered, falteringly: "I have had … there has been … Oh, *damn and blast it*, Copeland, I've become such a sore-headed bore that I cannot even dine in the company of a friend without imposing my black humour on the occasion. I really must beg your pardon, I am simply not fit company, tonight."

He made to rise from the table, drawing curious glances from other diners, when the soldier reached across and grabbed his arm, all-but forcing him back to his seat.

"No, *damn and blast it*, Sir. I shall *not* excuse you!" and, to the Apothecary's amazement, he continued – *sotto voce* – having discouraged attention with a brief but ferocious glare at their neighbours: "I am all-too-familiar with the face of Extremity when I see it, my friend, and I see nothing less at this table. As a soldier these twenty years I am a stranger neither to fear itself, nor to its power of attrition. I have seen it destroy better men than me; an unseen enemy that gnaws at heart and soul. It *must* be withstood, *mastered*, or it destroys everything within its ambit. But then, I suspect such thoughts come as nothing new to you?"

With a miserable shake of his head, the Apothecary replied: "I employed almost exactly those same words to *another* ... only weeks ago. Though what has occurred since then...."

His eyes darted to left and right, once again, before he continued, bleakly: "...what I have learned since then is that words are but words; they offer scant protection in the face of ... that which I am attempting to confront."

"Then, if your invitation stands," Copeland gave a wintry smile, "and if I have not already trespassed irredeemably upon your private affairs, I can provide, at least, a pair of well-seasoned ears? I fear there is little left to shock me in our mongrel world, so if to unburden yourself will offer some relief...?"

Greene nodded mutely in assent and attempted to address the food congealing on his plate.

"Please enjoy your meal, Colonel Copeland," he said, ruefully, "it may be the only pleasure on offer this evening. We can take our port, though, at Saddler Street, if you are agreeable?"

In a heroic attempt, then, to rescue something of an evening he had awaited with such anticipation, he said, lamely: "Have you read Farquhar? George Farquhar? Or perhaps seen one of his plays? His *Beau Stratagem* is a lampoon about this very Inn."

"I regret not," replied the soldier, addressing a cold steak.

33

ITEM:

On the left hand the FIREPLACE: a neat impression, from
a Bras Seal of <u>Henry</u>, Prince of Wales, Son to Henry
4th in red Wax in a circular Frame. A neat profile of the
Duke of Cumberland. An Indian Ax of stone, used by the
Charibee Indian before the discovery of <u>America</u> and the use
of iron among them. They are found in all the Islands.

"This is extraordinary, Mr Greene. I have never seen anything
quite like it," breathed Copeland, staring around the first of the
Museum rooms.

"It is as if you are in possession of some specie of lode-stone
that draws the world to it. How in the name of Goodness have
you accumulated this astonishing array?"

In frank wonder, the soldier went from case to cabinet, from
pedestal to drawer, with the Apothecary – in spite of himself –
warming to his accustomed curatorial role.

They had returned far earlier than either would have foreseen,
to a note from Theodosia Greene, saying that a severe headache
had driven her to bed, and to *be certain that the Parlour fire is not
over-banked. The girl is not to be trusted.* After first collecting the
decanter of Port and a couple of glasses, the Apothecary had led
the way upstairs.

Even before they had entered the Museum proper, Copeland
had spent many minutes admiring the blades and firelocks in what
Greene would liked to have called 'The Armoury Corridor' had
not its length been little more than his own abbreviated height.

He knew, though, that what followed spoke for itself – experiencing a frisson of curatorial pride as his visitor gazed in wonder around him. Out in the corridor Greene had been fascinated to watch the soldier's minute inspection of a pair of Buffalo-hide gloves and a Rifleman's coarse linen jacket, both gifts from the American colonies.

"*The stem or woodwork of a Cross-bow,*" read Copeland aloud, peering at the neat plate beneath the blackened relic, "*found many years since, in digging up the ground in the Field of Battle, near Bosworth in the county of Leicester: it is made of Yew-Tree, perfectly found and very neatly carved.*"

"Why Mr Greene, it surely does not take a soldier to recognise that even an article so apparently humble is nothing less than a national treasure?"

The Apothecary glowed with gratification. "I believe so, with a passion, Colonel," he said quietly, "it is what drives me."

An hour, and more, slipped past, as one label led to another, one story melded into the next, until Copeland, catching sight of a display on the closet door of the second room was brought up short.

"I regret that I need no explanation of these fellows," he said, flatly, gazing at the fan of arrows displayed above their tasselled quiver, "nor of those," he added, nodding towards the tomahawk and scalping knife labelled below.

"Made in bloody Birmingham, traded at huge profit by bloody merchants and put to bloody use by their bloodstained owners," said the soldier, with the merest slur to his words. "There is a dreadful poetry to it, don't you think?"

The Apothecary poured them both another glass, before replying: "I would not wish to lead you into indiscretion, Sir, but you may recall that we were interrupted, at Hildershall, when you were describing just such an event – as *bloody* a one as ever was, I believe."

"Ah, yes of course," replied Copeland, with a sardonic smile. "The long-overdue passing of that unlamented bastard, Blanchmayne."

"You hated him with a passion, it seems, Colonel."

"I had every reason to, Mr Greene."

Staring up at the arrows, he began: "I was a Lieutenant, seconded to the 42nd Foot on bridge-building duties, garrisoned at Hartford, Connecticut. Old Ed Blanchmayne had long been a force to be reckoned with in those parts, and the army contracted with him for timber supplies and the like. Mind you, he would have dealt in smoke and moonbeams if there was a profit to be turned – he and his sons had a finger in every pie across the frontier. I met their womenfolk at some social junket during my first Christmas in the Middle Colonies, having done business with father and sons in the preceding Fall. There was old Ed and his wife – who'd die within a month of each other that Spring – Ned, the eldest; Isiah, a year or so younger and Isiah's wife, and, of course, their daughter, the lovely Hepzibah. Ed was a rogue but a likeable one, it must be said. Ned, though, that was another matter. He may well have inherited all his father's cunning, but when the old man passed over, found to his fury that he'd inherited only *half* the business. He'd be senior partner, but partner, nonetheless."

"He and his brother had never been close. Ned had little time for anything or anybody that didn't serve his interests, which is probably why the old man made certain that Isiah would get his spoon in the pudding." Copeland gave a small smile. "You are being most patient, Mr Greene. I shall come to my point without excessive delay."

"I am all ears, Colonel. Have no fear on that score," demurred the Apothecary.

"It may come as no surprise to you," continued Copeland, "that I formed a romantic attachment with Hepzibah Blanchmayne, which in my callow way I thought reciprocated. At first, both brothers were frequently away on their business and I was a welcome guest at Isiah's home. Before long, though, it became apparent that Ned's tastes ran more to the comforts of home than to the business of earning the wherewithal to pay for those comforts."

A note of sardonic bitterness had entered the soldier's voice, and Greene sat forward intently as Copeland continued.

"It would have taken a blind man not to see that Ned was treating his brother like hired help, but, for some reason not then apparent, it was *equally* obvious that Isiah was only too happy to be from home whenever the opportunity presented itself. It was his energy, his acumen that kept the cash flowing in, with his *senior partner* content to enjoy the fruits of a brother's labour. It was the merest accident that brought me to Hepzibah's home during one of her father's absences. There was an Easter fair being held close by – no more than a village féte, but I'd thought it would provide an opportunity for us to be together. I had no way of knowing that her mother had already granted leave for the household servants to attend – diversions of any kind being all-too-few, God knows. She had allowed them to drive with her, it transpired, though Hepzibah had found some pretext to remain." Copeland stopped, then, fixing the Apothecary in an unblinking stare: "What I shall tell you now must never be repeated, Sir. It is a confidence shared with a physician, Hepzibah *Sharratt's* physician," he said, through a mirthless smile. "Do not mistake it for some blabbed indiscretion let slip after a glass too many."

The Apothecary nodded, solemnly, in agreement, wondering if somehow the race of his pulse might be apparent to his visitor.

"I found her, *them*, engaged in an act too foul to describe, Greene. Ned Blanchmayne was debauching *his own niece*, beneath his brother's roof."

Greene tried to keep his feelings from his face as the soldier continued.

"To this day I don't know whether he saw me – he had his back to the door and was … in rapture. She though, my *lovely* Hepzibah, did." Copeland's voice trembled with emotion: "Scarcely pausing in her … *labours*, she smiled at me, Greene, a smile of such mockery, such *knowingness*, that it sickens my soul even to remember it. It was the last time I ever saw her."

Greene, caught in a welter of emotions, laid a hand briefly on the Colonel's arm. "This will go no further – you have my word on it. It is unspeakable. What though of young Sharratt? Where does he enter the picture?"

"I can only put two and two together concerning that, but I do know that there was a lost child, a miscarriage, not so many months after they wed. *A whirlwind romance* was what local society termed it. We shall never know what the term of that pregnancy might have been, though I believe young Sharratt would have been given pause for thought."

"You mean…?" began Greene.

"Oh yes, Hepzibah would have borne her uncle's child with delight, Greene. I am in no doubts on that score. She was in thrall, and the bastard revelled in it."

"But her mother? Isiah?"

"If Isiah had any inkling then he chose to ignore it. Ned was a dominating, ruthless man, his brother was no match for him – much as the old man had known. As for his wife, Hepzibah's poor mother, she took solace in religion as only a desperate woman can. There was little love lost between mother and daughter, Greene. Hepzibah had always been too much the hoyden – the tomboy – for the poor woman to cope with. By the time she was ten, the girl could shoot the eye from a pheasant, or so Isiah used to boast."

"It would appear she grew into more *womanly* ways," murmured Greene, continuing: "So, was it the Iroquois that put an end to this…," he searched vainly for the word.

"Finally, it could have been little else," said Copeland, flatly. "Theirs was not a taste to be outgrown. One could only have wished that the savages had not botched their first attempt."

"*First?*" echoed Greene, puzzled.

"Two years earlier some Brave came close to sending Ned to perdition. He was almost blinded in the right eye, from what I heard. A tomahawk wound, I believe."

"And finally? By Fort Dummer?"

"Oh, they did the job properly that time, and no mistake, though I wonder if the bastard was alive at the end?"

"How do you mean?" asked Greene.

"They heaped live coals on his feet first, then on his genitals – finally on his head. Nothing recognisable was left, so I was informed. For all my sentiments, it is a sight I am grateful to have been spared."

He stood and walked across to the casement high above Saddler Street. A silence fell on the lamplit room as the soldier gazed, wordlessly, out across the roofs to the Cathedral, its bulk a huge, half-seen, presence in the mist. Without turning he said: "And now what a pretty trick fate has dealt, Greene, for here they are again: father, daughter and her devoted swain. For he *is* devoted is he not? Hepzibah would settle for nothing less."

The bleak bitterness in his voice hung in the silence, Richard Greene finding no words to fill the void, until, finally, Copeland seemed to shake of his melancholy.

"I must be the most thankless oaf to ever stand here, in the midst of all your wonders, Greene, when it was *I* who offered a ready ear to *you*, my friend. Forgive me, but there are some wounds that will not heal. Though, clod that I am, I've denied you any salve for yours, tonight."

The Apothecary joined him at the window and peered out into the dank night. His gaze carried across to where the house near the South Gate stood, concealed by trees and shadow.

"I don't begin to understand how, or why, Colonel Copeland, but there is some awful *congruence* between your miserable tale and my own. I am mocked by utter impossibilities that offer the sole solution I can discern. It is driving me to the edge of reason. In the face of appalling danger I find I can do no more than await its approach, with no vestige of control over the time, the place, or the means, of its coming. I am unable, even, to confide in my wife, such is the nature of the burden I carry. If that sounds no more than self pity, then so be it, but no man should have to face what

I must, bereft of any skills or armour – uncertain, even, of who or what I must stand against. There has been no one to whom I could turn."

"Then we must look to your defences, Mr Greene, though at present I have even less idea of the nature of the enemy than do you! I think you had best start at the beginning."

She'd been woken by some sound from the street outside, her headache now only a ghost of the raging attack that had driven her to bed. Sensing immediately that she was alone in the curtained tester, she drew the heavy fabric aside and peered, blearily, across to the mantle clock. She felt a flutter of concern: two o'clock? He should have been well home by now. Or, had he returned, having drink taken, and nodded off in a chair? Though the 'morning after' was no less than any sozzled husband deserved, she had spent more than enough time massaging out those self-inflicted cricks and twinges. She rose with a shiver and pulled on her winter shawl, gathering it tight as she was met by the draught on the landing.

She heard the low murmur of conversation coming from the Museum rooms on the floor above. Though it was never her way to interfere in her husband's avid collecting or the business and trafficking that went along with it, she found herself – for some reason – climbing the stairs to the weapon-hung landing above. The Turkey rugs from her old home in Croxall, absorbed any sound made by her stockinged feet, as she approached the half-glassed door. She stopped as if she had walked into an unseen wall, as the words – Richard's words – carried through to her, where she stood, unseen, in the darkened passage:

… I am unable, even, to confide in my wife, such is the nature of the burden I carry. If that sounds no more than self-pity, then so be it, but no man should have to face what I must, bereft of any skills or armour; uncertain, even, of who or what I must stand against. There has been no one to whom I could turn, Copeland."

Fury – utter speechless *fury* – was the emotion that triumphed.

She stood, frozen, for just a moment more, her ears filled with the roar, the outrage, of what she had just heard from her own husband's mouth. The husband who'd wept as he admitted his earlier deceit? Who'd sworn, in tears, that no such secrecy, such poor faith, would ever again come between them? *The husband who'd just driven a blade of ice into their marriage.*

She turned, and walked with complete composure, back down to the bedchamber they had shared. Shared since the first day they had embarked upon the adventure of Saddler Street. With quiet, unhurried deliberation, Theodosia collected her husband's nightshirt and dressing gown from the closet door, walked out onto the landing, and folded them, neatly, over the rail at the stairhead. Then she carefully locked their bedroom door before regaining the tented enclosure of their marriage-bed. Then the tears came. Scalding.

(34)

Between the Eastern and middle WINDOW: a piece of wood, rudely carved, taken from the roof of the Parish Church of Stone, Staffordshire, with the letters IHS MCDIV.

Throughout the following day, Richard Greene – perplexed, though too preoccupied to feel annoyed – was vaguely aware of his wife's cold civility and her increasingly obvious preference for her own company. He'd slept badly, despite his aching tiredness, in an un-aired bed. He'd registered that, for whatever reason, his own was being denied to him, but was beyond caring. Had he given the matter any great thought he would have put it down to 'a woman's mood' and trodden with a somewhat lighter tread. As it was, his announcement that they were having company for supper, in the form of Colonel Copeland, was met with a mask-like lack of reaction and immediate instructions issued to the housekeeper. That lady, since first light, had been engaged in treading as lightly as she was able, around her stone-faced mistress.

In the smaller hours, whilst a pall of silence still hung across the sleeping, mist-shrouded city, Copeland had walked back to The George. Until shortly before dawn he had sat, listening, with growing astonishment, as the little Apothecary's eldritch tale unfolded. The soldier was not a stranger to violent death, but this was of a different order. As the horrors were revealed, one upon another, he came to understand the paralysing fear that now gripped Richard Greene, a terror rendered doubly baneful in its invisibility, its facelessness. He understood, too, that this was an enemy that would seek to destroy anyone who became privy to its existence –

and, whether he liked it or not, he was now among that number.

As he listened to the account of Pomlett's death, and Greene's telling of Theodosia's eye-witness to its unmitigated horror, he'd stood and walked over to the display of feathered shafts above their quiver. "These, I believe, are arrows of the *Tuscarora*, one of the six nations that make up the Iroquois League. I have seen too many good men die from what seemed little more than flesh wounds, for all that savage band of brothers favour poison on their blades and arrowheads alike. There is one, though, whose effects most resemble what you describe: these foul things have no names that I know of, but this is made from putrid deer liver. Even a scratch," he smiled humourlessly, "from a barb much like this will mortify within the hour."

He'd carefully lifted one of the hooks that the Apothecary had laid on the table and peered at its cruel tip. There was a dark smear just visible on its underside, which he raised to his nose. With a wrinkle of disgust he replaced it beside the others.

"Even now it stinks. One would have more than sufficient."

Copeland looked across at Greene, bone-weariness etched across the small man's face. "You've given me more than enough to sleep on, my friend. For myself, I need time to order all that I've heard tonight."

He stood and looked down at the Apothecary. "If I am unable to promise you sweet dreams, Sir, then I can at least assure you that you're no longer alone on this dark path. If you'll accept what assistance I can offer, we should meet tonight."

During those small, dark hours, when the souls of sleepless men are at their most beleaguered, the Apothecary had risen inestimably in the soldier's esteem, as his steely determination in the face of such odds was revealed in his halting account.

Greene had struggled to his feet. "Somehow, we must keep this from my wife, Colonel, though I doubt that will be easy. Please, dine with us, tonight. Theodosia will be delighted to meet you." The only delight the Apothecary's wife appeared to be deriving from dinner was in causing indigestion to the two men at her table. When her replies were any more than monosyllables, they sailed so close to *ennui* or – worse – downright mockery, that Richard Greene could scarcely credit it. Copeland had struggled to conceal his embarrassment as gambit after gambit had failed to raise conversation above the leaden, and only admitted defeat with Theodosia Greene's parting salvo.

She'd risen from the table with the words: "It would appear, Colonel, that what with bridge building, landscape gardening *and* service in the Americas, you and my husband have simply *everything* in common! I shall not keep you from such delights a moment longer. There are a hundred and one little tasks to occupy the little woman."

As the door closed behind his wife, Greene's gesture of hopeless discomfiture was forestalled by the soldier.

"I fear your good lady is all-too aware that something is amiss. Forgive my presumption, but might it not be the wisest course to enlighten her?"

"And inform her that she is under sentence of death, Sir? What words should a husband employ to that end?"

"I regret I have little experience in that area, Mr Greene," replied Copeland with enough stiffness for Greene to quickly respond: "Forgive my sharpness. It was not intended. It seems to be in the air tonight."

Copeland smiled and waved his hand in dismissal. "Well, I doubt that my contribution can do much to clear the air, my friend, but I have made an *aide memoire* of my thoughts on last night." He unfolded several sheets of paper from a pocket. "There are some observations and some questions. Shall we discuss them here or…?"

Once more the Apothecary led the way upstairs to the Museum, ensuring that the door was firmly closed behind them.

"The fact that all of this business stems from Wightman's burning is beyond dispute," began Copeland, "so we must ask who has the strongest reason for seeking vengeance. The answer to that, surely, must be his family or his associates. Anabaptists, you said?"

The Apothecary nodded, only too relieved to listen.

"The killings cease abruptly in 1634, at five perfectly spaced intervals over twenty years. They begin again, for no apparent reason, one hundred and twelve years later. I discern no pattern or significance there. Why, then, did they cease at all? We must, I think, look to Burton on Trent, to see what – if anything – survives of the Wightman family, or of that sect. I fear that could prove to be a cold trail, to say the least, but it will be a beginning, will it not? I intend to ride there tomorrow."

Copeland stared intently at his notes, before continuing: "You, Sir, are the sole witness to the murder of old Mr Neille. There remains no trace of the killer's hand there, no spoor to lead us anywhere. You missed Michael Rawlins' death by a moment, identifying, as you thought, Isiah Blanchmayne, in the vicinity – no more than that – of where you believed the shot was fired. That must now be ruled out?"

"His whereabouts that day are fixed without doubt," replied the Apothecary. "Then, again, there is no scent there, apart from that unknown man's resemblance to *Cousin George*, from which one might suppose that they are one and the same, and that he is actively seeking out *Theodosia Webb*."

"From your perspective, Greene, the Court document provided the link between Rawlins' and Pomlett's deaths. It was the librarian's knowledge of the document that sealed his fate. The name *Blanchmayne* in the library ledger provided you, as you thought, with damning confirmation of his involvement: his guilt. Apart from the fact that his borrowing from the library now seems blameless, no Court in the land would accept the simple *presence* of the name as proof of any damn thing, my friend."

Seeing the stricken grimace on his rapt listener's face, Copeland raised a hand in mollification before continuing: "I however, would have shared both your instinct and your conclusion in this.

Who is to say that the ledger did not provide the killer with what he sought? We should enquire who else might have had access to it."

"You are right, of course: I looked no further than what I hoped to find. How easily we delude ourselves, Colonel."

"Just as a Gaoler saw only what he expected, Mr Greene: a serving man not an assassin, a prisoner rather than a corpse. Do not blame yourself. What little the dullard *did* notice was that, once again, our man was big and dark complexioned – with a hat of some description worn low on his brow. *That* one will believe, by now, that yet another of his crimes has gone undetected – unless…."

"Unless he has discovered that it was *I* who attended on the wretched Davey," interjected the Apothecary. "He would judge me by his own debased values and assume that I had seized the opportunity to wring whatever information I might from the helpless thief."

"Which places you in ever greater jeopardy, my friend."

Seeing the expression on the Apothecary's face, the Colonel added: "Though you are, of course, only too aware of that. Forgive me."

The soldier walked briskly up and down the length of the Museum room as if to focus his thoughts. He stopped and turned decisively to Greene.

"As I see it, we are faced with two distinct threats, my friend: one – to yourself – is the most immediate and will require the utmost vigilance to guard against a crime of opportunity. This bastard has demonstrated his resourcefulness. The second, I believe, will seek to maintain its air of *ritual* – a foully perverted one – but ritual nonetheless. The perfect synchronicity of the killing dates says it all. I believe that your wife will be safe until Holy Week of next year. Easter Saturday to be precise, four months or so distant. It may not presently seem so but that knowledge gives us a measure of advantage."

"A precious small one, Colonel, though I am forced to agree with your assessments. Both terrify me."

"Only a fool would deny it, and you are no fool, Mr Greene. So, *whoever* the foe may be, Sir, it is at least possible that you have made the only sighting of him – another measure of advantage. For if – as I believe – you're right, then he dares not show himself in your vicinity." He smiled broadly, before gesturing around him at the brimming displays. "So, unless these walls have ears – and The Lord knows they have most other things! Our alliance is, as yet, confidential. The advantage here is that I can be seen where you should be not, and ask what you cannot without exposing yourself to greater peril. So, you see, my friend, we are not without assets, though we must employ what we have to the full. I shall be away for some little time as I have some family business of my own to attend in Newark. I may need to stay over, a day or so, at Burton, too – for that is where *our* business must begin, I am certain of it."

"Then I heartily welcome your certainty and your resolution, Sir. They are qualities in short supply here, I regret."

"We shall speak on my return. To my mind, Mr Greene, you have in no way overstated the menace that exists out there. Be certain, though, that you don't underestimate you own ability to withstand – and defeat – it."

The two men walked to the door.

"Perhaps you'd be good enough to make my farewells to your wife, Greene, it's later than I thought."

(35)

ITEM:

On the left hand of the eastern **WINDOW**: two glasses,
which contain fluids of different specific gravities, which
being inverted, pass through each other without mixing.

They had been meeting over several months, never for more than a couple of hours, during which Theodosia Greene had watched the young woman's progress with growing fascination.

"You have a remarkable eye, Mrs Sharratt," she said, towards the conclusion of one such occasion – neither of them knowing at that moment it was to be their last. She stared intently at the tiny watercolour sketch. "The way in which you've captured the tone of that Cloth of Gold recaptures the depth of colour I love best in my garden. It's a blessing that it dries so well, though you've managed to banish its dustiness altogether."

The younger woman gave a small smile. "I'll settle for the fresh variety any time, Mrs Greene, and the fresh air it grows in. I thought that winter in Connecticut was dull enough, imprisoned by the weather for weeks at a time, but there we were at least free of these fogs and mists and endless drizzle."

Realising that she sounded defensive, the Apothecary's wife replied: "Well, yes, it has been drab of late, I must confess. Lichfield scarcely looks its best when the Trent Valley murk descends, but soon you'll see us in a different light, I'm certain. With Christmas scarcely more than a week away, we may well expect a white holiday! There have been times in recent memory when oxen have been roasted whole out on the ice of the moat and the Pools. It really is a picture then."

For just an instant, and gone before it had even formed, a look of such patronising derision seemed to flick across the young woman's unlined features, that, for that same split second, an old, hard face seemed to smirk behind them. A radiant smile dispelled the illusion before it could do more than cast a melting shadow.

"Snow and ice hold few charms for The New World, Mrs Greene. We are all still too close to the edge of extremity."

Taken aback at the tenor of the young woman's response to light-hearted conversation, Theodosia replied: "How so, Mrs Sharratt? Surely the Middle Colonies can now boast fine towns – cities, even, such as Boston? We are constantly assured that polite society in the Americas lacks nothing in the way of culture and refinement."

Hepzibah Sharratt gave a most un-ladylike snort. "*Polite* society, perhaps, Mrs Greene, though its politeness is eggshell thin and its boundaries extend no further than the end of the last boardwalk. No, I'm talking about what the British would call the 'Generality'." Again, momentarily, the flash of a sardonic edge. "The ordinary folk live a life bounded by what can be harvested or bought before winter, what can be defended against filthy Savages and what can be planted in spring. They talk less about the threat of hunger, than about the *certainty* of starvation. That is what I mean by extremity. No-one here can possibly understand."

"I regret to say that you are mistaken in that, Mrs Sharratt. The cause of the rural poor is something close to many decent hearts," said Theodosia, evenly. "The poor, who, no doubt, are sitting by their *decent* firesides, in the midst of *decent* lives with a *decent* chance of seeing out their allotted span," said the young woman, vehemently, rising to her feet.

Suppressing the flash of anger, the Apothecary's wife managed to say, quietly: "Perhaps presumption is one of my many failings, Mrs Sharratt, but I count myself as one of the *decent* people you seem to hold in such disdain. I fail to understand why my sentiment should merit such contempt."

Ragged emotions chased across Hepzibah Sharratt's delicate face, and it was several seconds before she replied: "We inhabit different universes, Mrs Greene. I should not have come. Perhaps close confinement is all I'm fit for."

Before Theodosia could stop her, she crumpled the watercolour between her hands and tossed it onto the small fire burning in the Parlour grate.

In spite of her shock and annoyance, the Apothecary's wife began: "My dear Mrs Sharratt, I know what a terrible... ." She got no further.

"You know *nothing*, Mrs Greene! Do not suppose otherwise, or I shall disappoint you more!"

With that, Hepzibah Sharratt hurried from the room, leaving Theodosia lost for words.

As the Autumn weeks passed into Winter, the young woman had seemed to lose something of the guarded tension she wore like a shawl, relaxing into the shared stillness of their painting. She had shown no impatience with her first clumsy attempts and even laughed at their crudity, apparently happy to accept the light touch of the older woman's guidance. There had never been much in the way of conversation, but Theodosia's instinct had been to give her visitor the rare space provided by companionable silence, sensing that small-talk was the last thing that the young woman sought – or needed.

Gazing, as the flame licked about the ruined sheet, Theodosia felt an aching sense of loss, of wasted, misdirected love, of caring frozen by indifference. The rumpled ball now disintegrating in a gout of flame, wasn't the half of it, though.

36

ITEM:

A CABINET on the right hand side the Fireplace: Silicous Stones, Semi Metals, Inflammables, Fossil petrified Bodies, Stone with Worm Tubes, petrified Mufles, a curious reticulated slate found over a Bed of Coal at <u>Brown Hills</u> Works.

"Burton's as drab a town as the inhabitants are dour, Greene, and I am well-pleased to see the back of it," said Copeland with feeling. "The Lord knows I enjoy my ale as much as any man, but to live with the stench of its brewing, day in, day out, would drive me to temperance. However, to business: you do not wish to hear any more about my delicate constitution, I'm certain." Suddenly, the soldier was all seriousness. "If I had only thought to enquire of you what were Wightman's views on Baptism, I would have saved myself several days' fruitless search for notaries and registers."

"Oh, indeed," said the small man, "he and his brethren loathed it with a passion. It was one of the accusations made at his trial."

Before the soldier could demur, Greene opened the folio and lifted out Rawlins' copy of the death sentence.

"Yes, here we are...."

...concerning the wicked heresies of the Ebionites, Corinthi-ans, Valentinians, Arrians, Macedemians, of Simon Magus, of Manes, Manichees, of Photians and Anabaptists, and of other heretical, execrable and unheard of opinions, by the instinct of Satan, by him excogitated and holden. Viz...

Oblivious to Copeland's strained silence, he scanned the lines.

…That Jesus Christ is not the true natural son of God… that he is only man and a meer creature… that Christ our Saviour took not human Flesh…

"It's here somewhere. Ah!"

*That the baptising of Infants is an abominable custom…
That the use of Baptism is to be administered in Water only to converts of sufficient Age of Understanding, converted from Infidelity to Faith… That God hath ordained and sent him, the said Edward Wightman, to perform his part in the work of Salvation of the World.*

Finishing, he looked guilelessly at the soldier. "So, no: registers and such-like won't have been a promising start, but forgive me, I interrupted you – pray continue."

"What little I have managed to discover was achieved only by one of those coincidences that never lose their power to amaze me," said Copeland, who now had Greene's undivided attention.

"The Bear Inn, where I had intended to lodge, was full, and I was directed to a smaller, new, establishment out on the Rolleston Road. Who should its proud new Landlord be, but a Sergeant of Sappers who had served with me in '39! He'd been attached to Lord Gower's regiment only last year but had sickened of the treatment handed out to the Pretender's men after Culloden – though not, I suspect – before he'd provided for his retirement! Trimmest little billet you could hope for. Made me damn' welcome too."

Now it was the Apothecary's turn to be patient.

"After two days of drawing blanks, I'd achieved no more than a conviction that the trail was as cold as we'd feared. That night, I was sharing my frustration – and drowning my sorrows – with Sergeant Quigley – though no confidences were betrayed, I can assure you. I'd concocted a vague fabrication concerning the dying wish of one of my men to be reconciled with his long-lost family, hence my search. I was just hoping that the Good Lord would agree that the ends justified the means, when he says, out of the blue, that his old grandma might recall a thing or two. You really should have seen her, Greene, like something out of The Ark! She claimed to be one hundred and one years old – and looked twice that! She may have had no teeth and less hair, but, by Heaven, Greene, the old biddy had lost none of her marbles! Fortunately, Quigley was on hand to translate, as the tongue she spoke bore little resemblance to our own – though her grandson was obviously used to it! When he asked if the name Wightman meant anything to her, she seemed to pause for thought – and then the laughter began. I thought, Mr Greene, that I had provoked some kind of seizure she took on so, spluttering and chuckling like a madwoman!"

"You mean she *recognised* it, the name?"

"It had been a family joke, Greene, shared year in, year out. *She'd grown up with it!*"

Bewilderment and impatience threatened to make the Apothecary explode.

"Her father had been a Cooper – and a sporting man, too, Quigley conveyed to me. The old lady told how he'd once had a lucky day at the Races and blown all his winnings – to her mother's fury, apparently – on the finest tool chest that money could buy, swearing that its contents, and his skills, would make their fortune. He'd bought it at the best ironmongers this side of Derby, *Wightman's* it was called. Wightman's of Lichfield Street. He'd proudly show off the shop label to anyone who'd look."

"But why in the name of goodness might a child remember such a thing?" blurted the Apothecary in scorn.

"Simply because her poor father was never allowed to forget it, Sir," said Copeland, with obvious satisfaction.

"From that day on, whenever anything needed mending about the house, or the family needed extra cash, 'Wightman's will see to it' was all that was needed to put her old man on the spot. It became a byword across generations, the way these things do in families. By the time his Grandma had finished, even Quigley swore he could remember it from his own youth. Though the shop itself was already gone when she was a child, its premises were, by then, occupied by a mercers and haberdashery – just the kind of thing a girl remembers. The shop-girls there had a standing joke, too, apparently."

"Which was..?" the Apothecary asked, shaking his head as if in disbelief.

"If they were having a particularly bad day they'd declare that they were 'off to Mericky, too'. "

Greene gazed at the soldier in complete incomprehension until Copeland concluded: 'It's where the previous owners, the Wight-mans, had *gone*; d'you see, Greene? They'd moved lock, stock and barrel, around the 1640's – as far as I can work out ... to America."

37

ITEM:

In the lower Drawer the **CABINET** next the Fireplace: Fluor
called Blue John, from near <u>Matlock</u>, a Chalk Nodule
changing into Flint, Hypocephaloides or Wedge Cock-
le, Crab Stones, <u>Sheppey</u>, Pectunculi, <u>Bath</u>, Canal Coal,
polished, <u>Lancashire</u>, Inflameable Earth, <u>Devonshire</u>, A
sprig of Virgin Silver from <u>Christiansburg</u>, <u>Norway</u>.

Theodosia's prediction of the holiday season's weather had come
true with a vengeance. By the morning of Christmas Eve, only the
hardiest souls – or the tardiest shoppers – were in evidence along
the city's snow-banked streets, as a vicious north wind scythed
down from the distant Peaks. The length of Saddler Street shop-
boys with shovels and besoms were losing the impossible fight to
keep access open for last-minute trade. By two o'clock, in an already darkening afternoon, the streets had emptied and the shops
were closing their shutters, one by one.

Inside the Apothecary Shop, its air redolent of nutmeg, cloves,
cinnamon and muscovado, the Greenes and their small staff made
the accustomed celebration of well-fortified mulled wine and hot
fruit buns. By four, the last had been waved off, bearing a gift and a
modest cash bonus to their wages. The business, at least, was pros-
pering at Saddler Street, even if its owners were presently deriving
scant gratification from the fact.

To a casual observer nothing amiss would have been apparent
in the couple's mutual civility and cooperation. They had a flourishing, multi-faceted trade that required all their energies, leaving
little – by way of leisure – to share. Neither would the same

observer find any cause to remark upon the divergence of their few pastimes, and the paucity of mealtime conversation.

Is Mr Greene the Apothecary, not master of his own Shop, his own Museum and his own Table, to converse, or not, as the fancy takes him? one might enquire.

Where is the Marriage contract that promises chit chat and pleasure without cease, for pity's sake? one might ask.

It is a Sacrament concerned with duty, obligation and obedience, nothing more, nothing less, one might firmly aver, *and is the daily life of Mr and Mrs Greene not a paradigm of those Virtues?* One would expect no reply to that, the question being largely rhetorical.

The Apothecary had never felt more miserable in his life, and the prospect of Christmas – with none of the blessed distractions of work – was doing nothing to improve matters. For days that became weeks, Richard Greene had tried everything, *anything*, to break through the carapace that his wife had drawn about herself. She responded either by avoiding his company whenever possible or, even worse, with a pretence of bewilderment at his concern. So, it came as no surprise when his wife announced that – in spite of the weather – she was joining other ladies of The Box Club for a festive soiree.

"I've told Maisie that I don't want the York ham touched until Boxing Day, but she'll leave soup and pie for your supper."

Greene looked puzzled.

"I *did* tell you that I've given both her and Jane leave to go to the carol service at the Cathedral this evening, so you're to be left to your own devices. I shall take a Chair. It's ordered for six, so you'll be spared escort duty." With that she departed, closing the door quietly behind her.

Left to the eloquent emptiness of the room, the small man was torn between the desire to smash something or the compulsion to bellow at the top of his lungs. He stood trembling in a barely suppressed fury of frustration and resentment, both underpinned with the sense of dread he carried like a stone in his gut. If he had caught sight of the sallow, pouch-eyed figure he'd been reduced to over the past months, he might have had taken more care to avoid what came next.

When an appeal to attend upon Hepzibah Sharratt 'without delay' was delivered by a blue-lipped boy, the Apothecary had just finished a most perfunctory meal, eaten alone in the silent house. He felt a physical thrill of panic mixed with a frisson of sheer excitement. He had studiously avoided contact with her during her regular visits, managing to nod politely if their paths crossed and busy himself with some distraction. Even now, months on, it took no more than the memory of that brushing hand, that *caressing* hand, to arouse him and alarm him in equal measure.

He had given little thought to it until this moment, but now realised that the young woman had not visited these several weeks past, though Theodosia had not commented upon the fact. Perhaps Mrs Sharratt had been subjected to his wife's glacial humour, he thought sourly: that would have sufficed to keep a regiment of Tartars at bay. He realised he was standing already cloaked and with his bag in hand.

Of course he must go to Hepzibah Sharratt's side. It was his professional duty, nothing less.

38

ITEM:

Beneath Handel's bust: a model of a gothic Tomb in Card
Paper; the work of the ingenious Mr <u>Jones</u>, Comedian.

The Apothecary's carefully schooled expression of professional insouciance lasted only as long as it took to register who had opened
the door to him. He had trudged, waded and stumbled his way up
through the South Gate, the snow knee-deep as soon as he had
left the shovelled alleys of Dam Street. He was perspiring beneath
his heavy layers by the time he reached the well-lit porch. Flambeaux snapped and crackled in the gusting wind throwing dancing
lights from the holly wreath decorating the imposing door, red
berries like blood-pricks against the black wood.

"Why, Mrs Sharratt, I…!"

"You'll freeze us both, Mr Greene. Come in quickly."

The moment he entered the house its silence seemed to enfold
him, and even as he allowed the young woman to help him from
his topcoat and cloak he knew he was standing on a foreign shore.

"Your message asked that I…."

"Attend on me *without delay* Mr Greene. I have been counting
the minutes since I despatched it. I thought perhaps the boy had
become frozen in a drift!"

"You seem quite … *well*, Mrs Sharratt, if I may say so. How
may I be of service?" he asked, as the piercing eyes held his.

"Firstly, you will take something to dispel the chill, Mr Greene."
Without waiting for a reply she led the way into the softly lit parlour. "And then I am certain you will have the remedy I require."

Completely abashed, the Apothecary looked helplessly around

him as a brimming glass was placed in his hands. "Mrs Sharratt, I am sure you are most kind," he said, faltering for words, "but are we *alone*? Is there no-one at home? Surely we … this is hardly…?"

"Oh, Mr Greene, I do believe you are concerned for my reputation!" she let out a peal of laughter that seemed to light up the room even as the scarlet blush rose to his hair. "And now I have embarrassed you into the bargain! What a thoughtless creature I am."

She reached out and, before he could withdraw an arm gone suddenly numb, led him to one of the room's richly brocaded sofas.

"Everyone is out, down to the last boot-boy, Mr Greene, I cannot deny it: though neither could I deny my aversion to the seasonal nonsense to which they have all flocked. My indisposition was real enough though even these few *moments* of your company have been enough to dispel it, where I never could."

"I am suffering, Sir, from the combined effects of this pestilent climate, this insufferable boredom and this damned town!" she laughed at the Apothecary's reaction. "Do I shock you, Mr Greene, with my un-ladylike sentiments and expressions? I can assure you there's far worse where that came from! I grew up among wagon masters and muleskinners, Sir, not the prissy dried-up old maids who are considered suitable company in this gaol."

Desperately attempting to maintain some professional gravitas, the Apothecary began woodenly: "Are there *particular* symptoms Mrs Sharratt … rather than just this general feeling of…."

"Feel *this*… ," she said, suddenly hoarse. Before he could believe what was happening she had seized his hand and plunged it into her décolletage.

"…then there'll be no need to explain."

Suddenly he was rolling a hardening nipple as it swelled from its aureole between his fingers, feeling the firmness of the breast cupped in his squeezing hand. As his mouth sought her lips they parted wetly, a darting tongue flicking, serpent-like, between them. As it wormed into him he felt her hand rubbing, pinching, scratching at his crotch whilst a gasp of pleasure hissed in his ear and she strained towards him. Now both breasts were free of her loose gown, no stays or corset to impede his urgency. He pushed his head into her bosom, licking, nibbling at their swollen tips, both glistening with spittle, as she moaned and swayed. With one hand rubbing ceaselessly against his throbbing crotch, she had lifted her skirts with another which was now lost deep between her splayed thighs. She was gasping and whinnying with pleasure as he staggered to his feet, preparing, with no other thought in the world, to rip open his buttons and take her there on the parlour floor. As his hands fumbled to free himself she raised both hands to her breasts tugging, tweaking, then hissing: "Quickly, *quickly*, whilst there's still...."

The jangling doorbell, down the corridor and out in the hall, shattered the moment as surely as a bucket of ice water, Greene spinning round in frantic disarray, attempting to cram himself back into his pants as he hauled them up over his thighs. To his amazement Hepzibah Sharratt, one moment splayed in utter abandon, was – the next – quickly rearranging her bodice, smoothing her ruffled skirts and hurrying past him to the hall. The Apothecary hobbled behind the protection of the open door, attempting to catch his breath and slow his pounding pulse as the sound of an urgent voice carried down the corridor.

Moments later Hepzibah Sharratt reappeared, looking flushed, but otherwise composed. "There's been an accident, it appears. Over towards Johnson's Parchment Mill: A chair has gone into the Pool. They're trying to revive the passenger. They said at Saddler Street you were here, so the lad came back as fast as he could."

The word *chair* seemed to blare in the small man's head. *'You're excused escort duty'.*

With speed born of desperation the Apothecary struggled into his coats, shrugging off Hepzibah Sharratt's half-hearted attempts to help him. Throwing open the front door Greene ducked out into the snow.

How long had the lad wasted, getting all the way to the shop and then back along the Dam?

The cold sliced between his gritted teeth setting nerves jangling through his gums and cheeks. In his headlong struggle towards the South Gate he was heedless of the lanterns swaying behind him, the torches pushing through the violently gusting snowflakes, as the Cathedral congregation emerged from the South Transept into the ferocious night.

With his breath coming in gasping sobs, Greene skidded round into Mill lane, the dull black expanse of the huge pool ahead piercing the wheeling flurries like an immense hole in the face of the earth. Ahead he could just make out a dying torch guttering through the white pall. As he stumbled towards it, the dwindling flame revealed two figures bent over a bundle on the bank, reeds a white curtain behind them. He shouted as he approached, snow spitting into his open mouth and stinging eyes.

He threw himself to his knees by the shrouded form just as a tall black figure and then another loomed above him. Richard Greene caught just a glimpse of a wide-brimmed hat pulled low over piercing eyes, a heavy scarf over nose and mouth. Then an immense, blinding detonation crashed in on his senses and an eternity of blackness rose to take him: *There could have been no-one at Saddler Street to know his whereabouts.*

A frosted boot hacked cruelly into his prone body. With grunted satisfaction the big man stooped and dragged the senseless Apothecary up by the lapels. The other bent and took the feet. Together they edged towards the reeds and, with a nod from one they swung the slight figure, once, twice, hurling it out onto the new-formed ice. With a splintering crack it shattered on impact and the Apothecary slipped below its jagged rim. Then, though, as the big man stooped, peering, towards the water, another crack rang out. Sharp. Staccato. The smaller of the pair yelped in pain and clutched at his cheek. With a muffled curse the other grabbed him by the arm and yanked him away from the waterside.

A shouting figure fought through the storm towards them. Wordlessly, both turned and lumbered away into the howling darkness.

Attending the Carol service had not been a good idea. The soldier had stood for what seemed an eternity, amongst the standing congregation in the shadows of the South Aisle. Rocking to and fro on increasingly cold feet as the profound chill of the ancient flagstones penetrated his boots, a smell of mildew and dust combined to catch the throat and sour the nose.

The packed pews in the body of the Cathedral had effectively muffled even the bombastic organ as it fought, and lost, against the cutting shrillness of the Guild band's brassy anthems, though they – and most of the proceedings – went largely unnoticed by the uncomfortable man. In spite of himself, his gaze kept returning to the distantly observed heads of two men amidst a larger group, both well muffled against the dank cold.

Copeland had recognised Blanchmayne and his son in law, Sharratt, as soon as they'd entered – though the sole reason for the soldier's presence was conspicuous by her absence.

It had been more than curiosity and less than indifference that had prompted him to venture out this night. For many weeks he'd known where Hepzibah Sharratt resided, though, whether by accident or design – he could not have distinguished – had managed to avoid so much as a glimpse of her.

Normally the least sentimental of men, the Officer of Engineers, earlier that afternoon, had been comfortably ensconced in the back parlour of The George, preparing to enjoy a solitary Christmas and planning an early supper. Hunger, though, had little to do with the odd sense of emptiness that gradually possessed him, as he found himself remembering other Christmases, other times spent among a distant family or among his peers, of friends unseen for years. And, of course, a black-haired girl who'd maimed his heart.

He'd known suddenly that he had to see her.

Her presence at the Christmas Eve service – along with what seemed likely to be most other citizens of the small city – was more than likely, it being one of those annual events, he'd been reliably informed, that were *de rigueur* for local society. The prospect, however, of encountering Mrs Apothecary Greene, in the forlorn presence of her husband, was not something he would relish. On his visits to Saddler Street over the past months, her civility had never been less than perfect, her manner never less than glacial. He had watched, powerless to intervene, as his friend's spirits flagged in the glare of her relentless pique. Now, though, his thoughts turned back once more to another face, to an etched memory of eyes that could blaze like ice-diamonds from the snow of skin.

With a mixture of apprehension and excitement, he'd joined the throng braving the foul conditions, jostling and wobbling good humouredly on their way towards the Cathedral.

From Greene's description of the Prebendary House, Copeland guessed that its occupants would enter through the South Transept, rather than endure the icy walk around to the main door at the West Front. He felt his pulse rise as, first, the unmistakable figure of Isiah Blanchmayne, followed by Sharratt and then a portly form he assumed to be Clarke, came in from the porch, shaking snow from heavy topcoats. No-one followed them.

He ducked back into the shadow of an immense crossing pier, his spirits plummeting – even though it was a disappointment strangely spiced with the relief of being spared sight of her. He was about to leave when a hand took him by the elbow and he turned to the smiling faces of a couple of his recent acquaintances among city society, both confirmed bachelors whose company he'd enjoyed. One pressed a silver flask conspiratorially into his hand before insisting that he join them on the standing fringes of the large congregation. "Easier for a quick getaway," had been the other's laughing remark, as Copeland had accepted their invitation to cards, later, at a nearby house. *Why not?* he'd decided, *this is not a night for one's own company.*

They'd been amongst the first to leave, already pushing their way out, through the sheltering Chairmen and Linkboys in the great porch, as the strains of the last anthem hung beneath the Nave vault.

Copeland could not have failed to recognise the bent, ungainly figure that cannoned out of the house ahead, the sudden spill of light from its open door, golden against the eerie blue of the snow-fall. He saw the small man fall almost immediately, but struggle – in what seemed like desperation – to his feet and go lurching off into the night. With hasty, garbled apologies to his surprised companions, the soldier took off in pursuit of the disappearing shape of Richard Greene.

Once through the South Gate, Copeland had struggled across the Mill-race bridge and into Dam Street where the way was passable from earlier clearance. Even through the wheeling vortex of flakes he could just make out the empty road ahead, and knew he'd gone wrong. With a curse he turned back for the Mill lane. He was in time to catch a single glimpse of a blurred figure fight-ing its way towards the Pool. There was something terribly wrong about the obvious panic that drove it, and the soldier felt instinc-tively for the pocket pistols he always carried in his topcoat. He stopped for a moment and, turning his back to the tearing wind, quickly – expertly – saw to the priming of first one and then the other, before ploughing on in the direction of the faint flicker of light that had seemed to be Greene's direction.

(39)

ITEM:

Over the CLOSET DOOR: two Woodcocks, a Pigeon,
two Wagtails, a pair of Barbary Doves, a Jackdaw and a pair
of Bullfinches, a Pigeon beautifully displayed, a Cock Jay.

Whether *persona non grata,* or not, Colonel Henry Copeland was certainly not leaving Saddler Street that night.

The astonished and furious lady of the house had rushed to the passage door in response to hammering, kicks and bellows from the street. She had assumed, first, that her husband was – as usual – oblivious somewhere above, either in his Museum or already in bed, and second, that the tumult was the work of drunken roisterers who would – she promised herself – never make this mistake again. The sight that met her was not what she'd expected.

With the aid of several passers-by, themselves returning from The Close, Copeland had bundled the scarcely conscious Apothecary through the freezing streets. Both men were drenched to the bone; Greene's face a blood-slicked waxen mask, blue-white beneath matted hair; Copeland shaking uncontrollably from exhaustion and exposure.

Tottering, with the last reserves of his strength gone, the soldier delivered his burden onto the kitchen settle, scarcely feeling the blessed warmth of the house enfold him. "Look to your husband, for the love of God!" he gasped, as the mistress of the house, immobile with incredulity and shock, could only stare, aghast.

The spell broke and she rushed to the slumped form of the Apothecary, tearing off the sodden, ruined clothes, and shouting for towels, brandy and blankets.

She looked wildly back at the swaying, grey-faced soldier. "Off with your things, *everything*, for God's sake, man! You're perishing!"

White-faced with panic or red with embarrassment, housekeeper and maid scurried to do their mistress' bidding, as the sight of two naked men – one of them the Master – filled their domain.

Within moments the Apothecary's swaddled form had been hoisted onto a hastily manhandled table in front of the glowing range. As his wife spooned brandy between his blue, unresponsive lips, Richard Greene was suddenly wracked with coughing, water spewing from his nose and slack mouth. Copeland gulped down a glass in one, gasping as its fire coaxed agonising sensation back into numb limbs and red-raw knuckles.

With the combination of spirits and warmth, the ragged gash behind the Apothecary's ear reopened and Theodosia urgently cleaned it with more alcohol, steeling herself to ignore her husband's agonised cries as she dabbed away the mud and weed around the edges of the vicious wound.

As the last swathe of bandage was tied off, Maisie arrived with the earthenware pot she'd been sent for and, handing it to her Mistress, watched open-mouthed as she urgently spread its contents across her husband's heaving chest, ribs and back.

A smell of camphor, garlic and goose grease overwhelmed the already-stifling atmosphere and set Copeland coughing violently at its bite. By now draped decently in blankets, he paced, unsteadily, up and down the kitchen flags, knowing he must restore his circulation rather than surrender to the numbing exhaustion that threatened to overwhelm him.

He came to the table and peered bleakly down at the small man, whose cheeks were now painted with a faint flush of colour, a sheen of sweat across the brow throwing its patchwork of old scars into glistening relief.

Across her husband's prone body, the Apothecary's wife gazed with quiet ferocity at the trembling soldier.

"When I've seen my husband to his bed, Colonel Copeland, I would ask you to join me in the parlour, if you feel able. Otherwise, your own bed will be prepared immediately. You'll be our guest tonight." It was not a question.

He inclined his head by way of agreement, his gaze not flinching from her cold intensity.

"You and I, Sir, must have words."

"Indeed, Madam, we must."

He was asleep in her husband's chair when she finally came down, thick woollen socks encasing his large feet and an old patchwork quilt shawling his broad shoulders. Assuring herself that his voluminous wrappings covered all that needed covering, Theodosia Greene sat quietly across from him, watching as the light of the small fire played across his weathered features. Suddenly the soldier jolted awake as if a charge had passed through his body. In an instant he focused and absorbed his surroundings – making as if to rise when he registered the seated woman.

"I scarcely think we need stand on ceremony, Colonel. I assume from your presence that you feel able to tell me what's occurred? *All* of what's occurred?"

He nodded, meeting her stare.

"Then allow me to say one thing before you speak. It is quite evident that you have done my husband – and me – a great service tonight. He is most unwell, and may get worse, but, by the grace of God, has been delivered from extremity. Whatever else is said here tonight you have my heartfelt thanks for that."

She stopped, then, and sat back in her chair, waiting.

Eventually the soldier spoke.

"Mrs Greene, to come between husband and wife is not a course I ever thought to embark upon. I am no stranger to hostile territory, but this is terrain I enter with the gravest trepidation, for to share confidence with one is to betray the other. There is, however, no other course open to me now. If you chose to believe me, I have neither strategy nor plan of campaign in this, only the skills the Lord saw fit to bestow – and I fear they'll be woefully inadequate in explaining what I now must. I'm mindful of your gratitude, Mrs Greene, and thank you for it, but I would rather crave your *understanding* – and your forgiveness. I have been a party – albeit a reluctant one – to what's been kept from you, though I was convinced into so being only by knowing the evasion to be based on the selfless courage of your husband and his desire to protect you."

"To *protect* me Colonel? What price my sensibilities in the face of the incessant nightmare in which Richard is embroiled? He already *knows* my feelings are far from delicate in this vile business, Sir. You – and he – will have to do better than that!"

"Forgive me. You misunderstand, Mrs Greene. It is not your *sensibilities* that Richard is so desperate to protect. It is your life."

Somehow, he found the words.

40

ITEM:

On fome Shelves next the ORGAN: a Roman Urn, found in a
field near Yoxall in the County of Staff. Containing Afhes and
fragments of burnt Bones, a small urn found near <u>Colchester</u>,
a Head in Stone, neatly carved found in <u>Raunton</u>, an Earthen
Veffel, which contains nearly two quarts, found with several
others of a smaller size in the walls of the Conventual Church of
<u>Fairwell</u>, at the time it was taken down in order to be rebuilt.

She sat in such profound stillness that the silence seemed to take
form around them, as if the panelled, fire-lit room had become
some hermetic cell detached from the world, its clocks and its
passions.

An occasional blink, flickering across the grey-green eyes, and
the almost imperceptible rise and fall of her shoulders were the
only signs of life in Theodosia Greene's rapt introspection. It was
only as she moved, finally, her face to the dying embers, that he
saw the glistening trail across each cheek, though her features
were still fixed in mask-like serenity.

"The best of it, Colonel Copeland, is that he loves me too dear-
ly to load me with such a burden. The worst of it, that he does
not love me sufficiently to do just that. Is it possible that men
understand so little?" she smiled, ruefully, "or impossible, the ex-
pectations we have of you?"

"It would take a wiser – and less cautious – man than me to
answer that conundrum, Mrs Greene. I can only answer for your
husband's courage in taking the solitary, thankless route he chose
– whether rightly or wrongly."

"Thankless, certainly," said the Apothecary's wife, quietly, "and I have guaranteed its solitude, have I not, Colonel?"

He shook his head with infinite weariness, holding both palms open towards her.

"Do not ask me to presume further upon your private concerns, Madam. I have done so, thus far, only with the gravest reluctance. I do not *withhold* judgement of your husband's handling of this terrible affair, Mrs Greene. I simply have *no* judgement to pass. Extremity writes its own rules."

After another long pause she spoke again: "My eavesdropping, however unintentional, provided me with a half-truth that has blighted my life – our lives – since that night, Colonel. As I raged against what I believed to be Richard's lack of faith, it was my own that provided me with all the fuel I required to turn supposition into fact, and fact into the lash I've wielded since that moment."

Suddenly, her appearance of equanimity was pierced by a look of naked anguish, as she whispered: "Do you think he will ever forgive me?"

"*With all my heart*," came the spectral voice from the doorway, as both turned in astonishment.

In another context the wraith-like figure of the Apothecary would have been comical: turbaned in dressings, draped in a blanket, his bony knees protruding beneath a red flannel nightshirt. He stood swaying in the doorway, one hand propping himself against the frame.

"I could not rest, Theodosia, before I told you. The time for passivity is past. I know now that we must take the fight *to* the bastard before he can…."

They caught him as he fell.

"*Bath?*" chorused the soldier and the Apothecary's wife.

"Bath!" repeated Greene, with as much conviction as he could manage. "We shall announce our imminent departure as soon as I'm on my feet."

Propped against a hillock of bolsters he seemed almost child-like in the huge marriage bed. His cheeks had regained their customary bucolic flush and the extravagant bandaging had given way to a dressing pad. The room still regularly shook to the alternate sneezes of Copeland and the patient, though both had escaped the worst that Theodosia had grimly expected. The two men were suffering nothing more grievous than clogging head colds and hacking coughs that she was treating with unswerving sternness, as Christmas gave way to the passing of the old Year.

"But I don't *want* to go to Bath, Richard! The cost is prohibitive, the waters are noisome and the company will be little better – especially out of season. Besides, have you forgotten we have a shop to run and a living to be earned?"

"I have no wish to go to Bath, *either*, Theodosia, and have no intention of approaching within fifty miles of the wretched place," smiled the Apothecary, wanly. "I said we shall *announce* our imminent departure, and the world and all our customers shall see us *prepare* for that departure! There'll be no shortage of well-wishers, I'm sure. Word will travel, you'll see."

His wife exchanged a look with Copeland that managed to combine mystification and concern, as he continued: "We shall be going for a good three months and will not be returning until after Easter. It falls particularly early this year," he added, helpfully.

Seeing a smile of dawning comprehension on the Colonel's face, Theodosia Greene glared at her husband, saying: "Don't laugh at me you *infuriating* man! Simply talk sense or you'll find your soup in your lap."

Copeland cut in, evenly: "I believe it is a *feint* your husband proposes, Mrs Greene, though I agree he is trying both our patience. His health must be rapidly improving."

"I think, in all seriousness, my dear, that for you to express your lack of enthusiasm for such a protracted absence – to all and sundry – will add a tasty pinch of veracity to our subterfuge," said the Apothecary.

"*Our* subterfuge, Richard? It seems to exist only in *your* bruised head. Explain yourself, for pity's sake, before I lose all patience with you."

"To permit our enemy – or enemies, I should say – the choice of time and place for their next move," he reached out and took her hand, "is to waste a valuable weapon. Left to their own filthy devices I have absolutely no doubt that they would be reserving that move until Holy Week. The choice of Easter Saturday – the day of Wightman's burning – has held a blasphemous potency these hundred and fifty years, and they will not be diverted from that ghoulish adherence unless they think their entire enterprise to be threatened. Wherever there has been the opportunity, their foulness has been accomplished within the bounds of the City."

He looked from one to the other, before concluding: "This way, and this alone for all I can see, we force their hand. Be mindful of the fact that on every other occasion they have acted against unsuspecting and wholly unprepared victims. This will be different."

"But Richard, I still cannot credit that I am condemned by no more than my bloodline." In spite of herself she trembled as she continued: "What, in the name of all that's blessed, could be accomplished by the murder of an Apothecary's wife, a century and a half on from that poor wretch's death? It is lunacy, sheer demented lunacy."

"And to recognise it as such is nothing less than paramount, Theodosia. We are dealing with deranged adversaries who have stepped beyond any bounds of restraint or decency. They are driven by an obsession which makes them dangerous beyond belief."

Looking at his wife's distraught expression, the small man added, gently: "Now I think you understand the dilemma in which I've been mired, my dear. This terrible knowledge exacts an equally terrible price. It was my dearest wish to somehow spare you that."

"Practicalities, then," interposed Copeland briskly.

"From the moment that the news of your departure is broadcast, we must assume that some form of attack will be formulated.

Too much ingenuity has gone into the other crimes for this to be any different. This, in turn, suggests that attempts will be made to ascertain your movements, or the layout of this house. You might instruct the staff that they should keep eyes and ears open for any undue curiosity from customers – particularly ones not known to them – on the pretext, perhaps, that a sneak-thief is believed to be active in the city. In a place this size that could be true at most anytime, I would imagine?"

"Indeed, and what could be more natural than such concern on the eve of prolonged absence," agreed the Apothecary, "though we must give serious thought as to how our very real business can be managed for the duration of our fictional absence. We must be seen to make viable provision for more contingencies than I care to contemplate." He looked tiredly at his bedside companions. "I fear my little plan could turn into a very large stick for our own backs. Do, for Heaven's sake, speak up if you can see a better alternative."

"I think none of us will need any urging in that direction," said the Colonel with a wintry smile, "though, in the meantime, I want you both to have these."

From a canvas bag at his feet, the soldier took a wrapped bundle that he now spread open on the quilt. Revealed was a boxed pair of small pocket pistols. In a tone that brooked no argument he said: "You must each carry one at all times, and, Mrs Greene, be familiar with its loading and priming."

The silent woman made no attempt to interrupt.

"And when I say 'at all times', I mean nothing less. Delicacy forbids me to expand on that, but do I make myself clear?" He handed one to the Apothecary, saying: "I had only to see a fraction of your Collection to know you are well versed in firearms, Richard" – the new familiarity went tacitly acknowledged – "but are you as familiar with *discharging* them?" Seeing Greene's expression, he smiled and said: "No, I thought perhaps not."

Handing the other to Theodosia, he withdrew one of his own

pistols from voluminous pockets. "Had it not been for these, your husband might still be beneath the ice of Stowe Pool, Mrs Greene. In fact, the wound I think to have inflicted on one of your attackers, Richard, might still lead us to them. That is how important these grim things can be, Mrs Greene, so we shall commence with the naming of the parts."

41

ITEM:

Beneath the Birds in a Glafs Case: a calculus extracted from
the Bladder of a Woman in <u>Lichfield</u>, with her own hands;
weight two ounces. A double Placenta, injected, the red
colour'd Wax represents the arteries, the yellow, the veins.

Her tongue wormed, slithered, into his ear as his head buried itself in the white flesh of her exposed breasts, her breath coming
ragged and urgent as her fingers raked his neck and back. Nipples,
stiff with her need, pushed against his lips and teeth, her body
arching and bucking beneath him, his…

"Mr Greene! Mr Greene, Sir!"

He jolted from the dream as if plucked bodily from another Universe; sound, sight, smell, rushing in to occupy the fevered
void of his imaginings.

The Apothecary stared wildly up at Tillett, the shop-man,
standing awkwardly in the parlour door.

"Mrs Greene said I could disturb your nap, Sir – on account of
it seems quite urgent. What with it being Mr Clarke, Sir, from The
Close? She thought you'd want to see to it, Mr Greene, on account
of she was on her way out? Sorry to startle you, Sir."

Regaining his composure, and thanking Providence for the
all-concealing rug over his lap, Richard Greene responded:
"What about Mr Clarke? Is he below? In the shop? Why can't
my wife…?"

"No Sir, begging your pardon, that's just it. Mistress is out, left
us to it for an hour, she said. The gentleman's had a seizure – it's
the young gentleman, Mr Sharratt, who's come for you. Says can

you come straight away? No-one would've disturbed your nap otherwise, Sir. Sorry, Sir."

Tillet had misread the colliding emotions in his employer's face as annoyance, when, in fact, guilt had met dwindling lust with both heightened into sharp relief by the shock of waking. For a split instant he had pictured the entry of a betrayed and outraged husband. Now, though, as he properly absorbed the import of the summons, he managed to nod in what he hoped was a confident and business-like manner and clamber to his feet. He had been taking these extended naps, on his wife's insistence, ever since he had resumed work, earlier that week. This, though would be the first call he had made since ... *no*! He banished that thought resolutely as he hurried downstairs to meet Hepzibah Sharratt's husband.

"Mr Greene, I must apologise for intruding on what I'm told is your convalescence. I'd not realised you'd been unwell, Sir, but it's Uncle Billy: he received – *we* received – some very bad news that has completely felled him. I fear the worst, Mr Greene, and being alone at the house could think of no-one else to turn to – especially with all you've done for my... ."

"*Alone?*" interjected the Apothecary, far more sharply than he intended.

"My father-in-law is away – as ever – though this damn' business is all to do with him; and my wife... ," a bitter, humourless smile twisted his open features, "is out – as ever, at her dressmakers, or perhaps her milliner today. I lose track of all the demands which keep her days so full. If it is not tea and floristry twice or three times a week with Mrs Greene, it's busy here, busy there."

"Then we should waste no more time, Mr Sharratt, especially if your uncle is unattended," said the Apothecary briskly, the questions already forming in his mind.

The drooling, slack-featured figure of William Clarke bore scant resemblance to the avuncular host who had welcomed the Apothecary and his wife to the Prebendary House scarcely months earlier. He was half-propped, half-sprawled, on a sofa all-too familiar to Richard Greene.

"How long ago did this happen?" he panted, the exertion of their hurried passage through the icy streets still rasping sore lungs and pumping blood noisily into his cold ears. "It will be close on an hour, now, Mr Greene. At first I tried to get the women to help me with Uncle Billy, but they were of little use."

"Well, I suggest you put them to use now Mr Sharratt. Warming pans for your uncle's bed, and as quick as they like! You and I must get him there, even though I'm loath to move him. Where is that fellow of Blanchmayne's when he's needed?"

"Sam Blain? Oh, he's *needed* all right, if my wife has her way. Treats him like her personal footman, he's off holding horses and opening doors wherever it may be that Hepzi's decided to favour today. Not that there'll be much more of that, though. Not any more."

Saving his energies for the lifting of Clarke's deadweight up stairs achingly familiar to him, the Apothecary knew that questions must wait, as he and Sharratt managed the stairs and corridor to the master bedroom, where they deposited the unconscious man into his hastily prepared bed.

"Leave him to me, now, if you please, Mr Sharratt. I'll do what can be done."

For the next hour, Richard Greene's mind emptied of everything but the need to rouse the palsied Clarke. After bleeding, he applied vigorous massage to the limp arm and a gentle application of warm oils to the flaccid cheek and lips, employing a dropper to trickle a stimulant into the lolling mouth. Finally, and with a scarcely audible groan, the right eye opened as the other twitched and flickered. In the minutes that followed, blank incomprehension slowly gave way to a look of uncertain, fearful, awareness.

"Don't attempt to speak, Mr Clarke. The worst is past and help is at hand. You need do nothing but rest. There will be someone constantly at your side. There is nothing to fear." Clarke seemed to sink into a stertorous calm, with Greene remaining at his side until he felt there was nothing more he could accomplish. Then, though, just as the Apothecary made to leave, the single eye opened in wild, unfocused panic and the twisted mouth tried to form a word, words, before the suffering man slumped into unconsciousness. With a heavy heart, Greene left the bedchamber, the sound of the mangled word still in his ears. He was sure it had been 'ruin' groaned over and again.

"Embezzlement, Mr Greene – and I betray no confidence in saying so – soon it will be common knowledge. Not only is Isiah Blanchmayne a ruined man, but it is all-too likely that he will pull poor old Uncle Billy down with him. What a curse this family has brought home with it."

Looking strangely at young Sharratt, the Apothecary enquired: "How so?"

"As if the deaths in America were not enough to ruin our lives, it's the crooked legacy of the late, unlamented, Ned Blanchmayne that has returned to haunt us all, Mr Greene. It was common knowledge that he was a black-hearted bastard in trade, but I would never have dreamt that his malevolence could spill over into the wilful destruction of his own family's fortunes. It appears that he was systematically stripping the assets of the company, leaving always just sufficient balance for him to manipulate affairs, though – suddenly – he was no longer there to camouflage his sleight of hand."

"But what has occurred to reveal his trickery, Mr Sharratt? I was under the impression that Isiah's business was flourishing?"

"So, unfortunately, was everyone else – including my father-in-law! Not long after our arrival, he persuaded my uncle to invest heavily in Sugar – far more heavily than was ever advisable, in all honesty – though poor Uncle Billy was quite besotted with what he supposed to be Isiah's business acumen. The Blanchmayne reputation as traders and entrepreneurs goes back generations, Mr Greene, and with what Billy and the world saw as the family's assets, how could this new venture fail?"

"But fail it did? And it's this that has revealed the true situation?" asked Greene, in rapt attention.

"Just so, Sir. No-one had counted on a slave revolt in the Indies and the fire-starting that went with it. So, no crop this year, no return to the investors, no servicing of their investment loan with the bank, Hoare's Bank. The loan was called in against the Blanchmayne guarantees, only to find that the Vault was empty! The company's capital reserve had disappeared into the pockets of Brother Ned, who was then despatched to a place of no redress. Wherever that fortune went, the knowledge died with him. The bubble burst, apparently, some weeks after we'd left for England, with creditors cutting up rough at the company offices, and seizing anything they could lay hands on. Now it's all finally caught up with Isiah here, with Hoare instituting bankruptcy proceedings against him. He'll be locked up, quick as winking, as soon as he shows his face. Whether or not Uncle Billy can survive it, is another matter. I don't know how his finances stand as there has never been cause to fear such a thing."

"There is, I regret, more to fear than simply Mr Clarke's *financial* health, Sir. Your uncle may never recover the use of his faculties – either that or he may be grievously incapacitated. The prognosis is not good."

At that moment, before Sharratt could react to the Apothecary's concern, the noise of hooves sounded from the road outside.

"It appears my wife is about to honour us with her presence, Mr Greene," he said turning back from the window. Unwittingly, the small man found himself drawn to the window beside Sharratt, even as he was saying: "I must take my leave, there remains much still to be done before our departure."

Sharratt seemed oblivious to the remark, staring without expression at the sight of his wife being handed down from the small carriage by the heavily wrapped figure of Blain.

As the erstwhile driver turned towards the house, Richard Greene's gaze was suddenly torn away from the caped figure of his passenger to the sight of a dressing pad covering one ear, startlingly white against Blain's black hair and swarthy features.

"Your man has been in the wars, by the look of it, Mr Sharratt," observed Greene with an equilibrium he did not feel.

"Not *my* man, Greene. I'd have left him in his precious wilderness had it been up to me, but then I have little say in such matters. He's a veteran of Tavern Wars, though, I'll not deny that. The brute had half an ear ripped off in his most recent brawl."

"Ears can be a nasty business if they're not well-attended to. When did he risk his?" the Apothecary asked lightly.

"Christmas Eve, Mr Greene. The perfect start to the Season of Peace on Earth, Goodwill to Men, was it not? I'd have shown him the extent of *my* goodwill – there and then – given the chance. My dear wife prevailed, however."

Any further remark, in the same sour vein, was forestalled by the entry of that lady.

"Why Mr Greene, this is an unexpected pleasure," said Hepzibah Sharratt with a brittle smile. "I'm quite restored to rude health – as you can see – I trust you've not felt the need to call on my account?"

Before Greene could reply, Sharratt stepped forward, an arm extended towards his wife's shoulder: "Hepzibah, we have received very bad news, of a family nature. When Uncle Billy received it the shock brought on…."

With the slightest sway of her shoulders, she evaded the reaching hand.

"Oh, families! Families! Are they not the bane of your life, too, Mr Greene?" cut in the young woman. "Scarcely a day seems to pass when one fails to annoy another. Its pettiness is…."

"*Hepzibah!*" Sharratt's voice cut like a lash into her asperity.

Just for a part of one second, Greene caught the molten flash of fury in her eyes as her husband's voice stopped her dead.

"I know Mr Greene will excuse us, but what I have to tell you will not wait."

Already Greene was making a quiet departure.

"I must accede to my husband's sense of urgency, Mr Greene, but there will be another time, assuredly," she said modestly, eyes downcast, unreadable now.

Not trusting himself to reply, the Apothecary hurried from the Prebendary House. Somehow, in a manner he would never fully comprehend, the sight of the bandaged Blain had ripped a veil from his eyes. *I am mocked by utter impossibilities that offer the sole solution I can discern,* his own words to Copeland, months before. With devastating certainty, he knew the identity of his enemy.

42

ITEM:

On the left hand side the FIREPLACE: an Indian Ax of stone, used by the Charibee Indian before the discovery of <u>America</u> and the use of iron among them. They are found in all the Islands.

If ever there were times, in later years, when Richard Greene had cause to doubt the hand of Providence in men's affairs, he had only to think back to this midwinter day to reaffirm his faith.

He'd arrived back to a slack afternoon in the shop, where a much-needed reordering of seasonally depleted shelves and dwindling stocks was already well-advanced, the prospect of the Apothecary's forthcoming absence appearing to have a salutary effect on staff hoping for preferment during his absence.

"Mrs Greene asked that you be told she's gone to Edial, Sir. To see about the wool," said Tillett from his step-ladder. "With Colonel Copeland, she said to say, about the wool."

Greene realised, with a humourless smile, that his immediate reaction to Tillet's message had been to feel for the pistol in its accustomed pocket. He relaxed, reassured, in the knowledge she was not alone.

"A box of stuff from The Friary arrived while you were out, Mr Greene. I took the liberty of leaving it in the Museum for you," said his Apprentice, with a prickly look at the occupant of the ladder. "This is the end of the clearing out, they said. New owner takes up residence next week."

There was little love lost between them, the Apothecary knew, though he refused to become involved in squabbles over pecking order. If only his problems were of similar magnitude, he thought wistfully, climbing to the floor above. At least here's an end to the dismal business of settling the Rawlins estate, he told himself, regarding the oak box without enthusiasm. A cousin in Devon, simply a name in a lawyer's diary, was to be the recipient of the bulk of Michael Rawlins' fortune. The elderly man had never mentioned kin of any kind, and the weary, pre-occupied Greene could do no more than assume that the fortunate recipient knew as little about her benefactor as he, apparently, had cared for her.

The Museum had benefited handsomely from Michael Rawlins' particular bequests: a suit of chainmail on a woebegone dummy, a gun rack of ancient firelocks, several exotic presentations of tropical birds under glass, and several dozen fine quality bindings of antique texts, maps and engravings – all of which awaited attention from their distracted custodian.

As Greene grasped the lock hasp and lifted the box lid, a scent of woodsmoke and beeswax filled his nostrils and transported him, just for a moment, back to the old man's well-loved library. He winced, as a physical stab of loss seemed to pierce his diaphragm. As a sense of solitude and dread rose in him, he stood abruptly, blew his nose and stared sternly at his reflection in the over-mantel. "*Won't do at all*," he said, aloud, to himself, and turned back with a new briskness to the contents of the box. Heavy wax seals were attached to the larger documents, whilst loose leaves from broken volumes, some particularly fine botanical illustrations and a variety of ephemera would normally have enthralled the Apothecary. Now, though, he simply leafed absently through the contents, a large part of his mind elsewhere.

It was towards the bottom of the piled contents that his eye caught a pinned note attached to an unremarkable loose leaf, looking as if it might have come from a work on heraldry or genealogy. In Rawlins' unmistakable hand, it read: 'show to RG'.

This time, the sensation was as of a blow to the solar plexus, a winding assault that was gradually replaced by the chill of sheer incredulity, as Greene read – and reread – the small page:

…of some substance, being not only well-set in Trade but claiming Noble lineage of significant pedigree. Within the family was preserved a chart illustrating descent from that Robt. de Beaumont, 3ʳᵈ Earl of Leicester, Crusader and companion to Richard Lionheart. The aforesaid Robt. was named also Blanchmains, in French, on account of his exceeding white hands – token of the leprosy contracted in the Holy Land. The name became anglicised to Wightmains, then to Wightman, though, in the hour of that family's extremity, all claim to the protection afforded by such ancient kinship, was roundly rebuffed by the Noble House.

With his heart beating a wild tattoo, Richard Greene began, distractedly, to pace the Museum rooms, his eyes registering nothing but the etched sequence of those names upon the page – *Blanchmains, Whitemains, Wightmains, Wightman* it had the meter and resonance of some nightmarish children's rhyme and now whirled and spun in the Apothecary's head.

Since that sight of Blain, bandaged, he'd known to the roots of his being that only the impossible could be believed. *Blanchmayne*, the name mocked his myopia, scorned his stupidity. The answer had been dangled in front of his purblind eyes, the name spoken, over and again, into his cloth ears.

Sounds from below began to intrude into his pacing reverie, signalling the return of Theodosia and Copeland. He ran to the stair-head, calling urgently for them to come up.

"Ned Blanchmayne, 'mutilated beyond recognition – the wagon master never seen again', your own words, Harry!" said the small man with absolute conviction, continuing: "How was the body identified at all? Do we know?"

"Simply by virtue of a decorated weskit, Pell said," replied the soldier. "A vile, mustard-coloured thing – even I remember it. Ned had worn it for years – like a second skin. It was almost like his trademark."

"So what better way to lay a false trail?" enquired Greene urgently, "than to conveniently disappear with pockets well-lined at his brother's expense. Could it be the Iroquois *colluded* in this?"

Copeland gave a bark of mirthless laughter. "How little you know of the Six Tribes, Richard! Even had they not been seduced by the French, any man jack of them would have killed Blanchmayne inch by inch, rather than deal with him."

The soldier turned to Theodosia, who'd been listening in rapt attention since her husband's astonishing revelation. "It was the strangest thing, that whilst he was able to rob his own people blind – with apparent impunity, he was shunned by the tribes. They'd trade with *anyone* fool enough to risk his scalp, but it was only ever Isiah that did any fur trade with the Mohawks, or the Tuskarooras. They said his brother had the Evil Eye or some-such nonsense. I remember Ned used to laugh about it."

"So, we must assume that Ned Blanchmayne simply took advantage of a situation that presented itself." The small man paused. "The implications that accompany that are unspeakable."

"Then *I* shall say the words, Richard," said Theodosia in scarcely more than a whisper. "If you are right, then he must have been nearby – in concealment – when the Iroquois did ... all that they did ... to Hepzibah's mother, and their wagonmaster – and done nothing to stop it. What kind of monster could witness that and then seek to turn it to his advantage?"

"The same kind of monster who has been responsible for the cowardly, cold-blooded slaughter of four souls in our city, Theodosia. Now, though, he has a face *and* a name. Are we all agreed on that?"

"I can offer no better explanation, Richard," said Copeland, "though it is beyond my comprehension how your conviction of the identity of Blain's master could have coincided, in such an eerie fashion, with Michael Rawlins' revelation of the true lineage of the Wightman family. To him, of course, it held nothing more than historical interest: not being acquainted in any way with the new occupants of the Prebendary House, or even the name of Blanchmayne. He had simply chanced upon family roots whose significance – for him – ended with Wightman's burning." He looked to Greene for confirmation, before continuing: "They must have readopted the old family name to start anew in the Americas. The mystery is, what could compel such a self-serving swine as Ned to revive, *fulfil* – whatever you will – an age-old vengeance?"

"When – *if* – we discover that, I think there will be no more questions left to answer," said the Apothecary, "but until then, we must assume that his own devious reasons brought him to blacken these shores, and that Blain remained the conduit to ... the family."

Only Copeland noticed his hesitation, but Theodosia, as if by some sixth sense, suddenly asked: "Are we saying that Isiah, the Sharratts, poor Mr Clarke – *all* are complicit in the brother's filthy deceit?"

The look that passed between Copeland and the Apothecary rang a sudden alarm bell in her head, as she saw an inexplicable flush rising in her husband's face.

With what now read as sudden haste he exclaimed: "No, surely not, as Isiah has had proven alibis earlier and was sitting – along with Sharratt and Clarke – in front of Harry, in the Cathedral, as my attackers were already in place by the Pool."

"And young *Mrs* Sharratt?" asked Theodosia quietly, looking intently at her husband. He stared in what looked like desperation at the soldier, whose attention was resolutely fixed elsewhere. She continued: "I've never been sure, in my own mind, how the false message actually reached you that night, Richard. You've never mentioned the identity of the messenger, now that I think about it, and yet there was no-one else but you here to receive one? Surely it would have been a first line of enquiry for either of you," she looked piercingly, with growing suspicion, at the two men, "to determine its source?"

"I – I had already been called out, my dear," said the Apothecary in a forlorn attempt at insouciance.

"*On Christmas Eve?* Pray, where exactly, Richard? How can it be that I know nothing of this?"

"It simply didn't seem important, Theodosia, but if you must know, it was an urgent summons to the Prebendary House. The message for me arrived whilst I was there."

Appearing suddenly thoughtful as she gazed into some middle distance, she said quietly, patiently: "So Hepzibah Sharratt had been seized with such a *grave* condition that medical assistance must be urgently summoned on a Christmas Eve? Summoned with all her menfolk at Carols?"

A stricken silence seemed to become almost tangible, as she added: "So, was she undergoing some sudden *relapse* – after all the attention you have lavished upon her already?"

The Apothecary's hopeless discomfiture was so eloquent that Copeland wished himself anywhere but within the ambit of Theodosia Greene's mounting annoyance. Then, though, she turned to him.

"Colonel, do you see two heads? *Claws? Serpents for hair?* Am I so ferocious that my own husband cannot explain himself?"

He knew better than to reply, so she then turned back to the hapless man.

"What, I must ask myself, could there have been about this particular *house call* that it should have been kept from me?"

"It is not that it was *kept* from anyone, Theodosia…," began the Apothecary, helplessly.

"But I am not *anyone*, Richard. I am your wife! So, *what*, I repeat, was the emergency?"

"It turned out to be nothing more than a *maladie imaginaire*, my dear, when all's said and done. Mrs Sharratt is prone to depressive humours, and a certain … *instability* … which prompted her call – and which I saw no reason to mention," he added, lamely.

"*No reason to mention?*"

The frigid echo hung between them, as Theodosia Greene

paused, closing her eyes as if deep in thought. Without opening them she said, in ominously measured terms: "Am I alone in wondering how a messenger knew where to find you, when this house was empty and you were busily attending upon your *patient*? Any word summoning you to the Prebendary House would have been delivered by one of Mr Clarke's servants, would it not? So, who else could have known, Richard? Colonel?"

"Obviously, that has been on my mind, my dear," said the Apothecary hurriedly, "although I must concede that I've been prepared to entertain any possibility other than what now seems to be emerging."

As if he had not spoken, Theodosia continued – another thought only now seeming to occur to her: "Or perhaps, just like *our* staff, *their* staff were elsewhere, leaving an empty house. Did you both have to shift for yourselves, Richard?" She stood and walked across to the fireplace. Her next words were addressed to the mirror above it, her back, rigid with anger, turned to the seated men. "Was there ever a man in history, immune to wide eyes and secret smiles?"

For the first time, Copeland spoke, into the aching pause. "Mrs Greene, *Theodosia* – if I may be so bold – you and I have managed to arrive at something far better than the armed truce I feared, have we not?"

She returned his gaze impassively, waiting for him to continue.

"As you've not denied it, I'll presume that the somewhat *singular* bond of our friendship will entitle me to speak freely. Not without cause, you are supposing that, once again, certain information is being withheld from you – and you are correct."

As she stiffened, the soldier held up his hand, and continued: "Your husband has not spoken of certain confidences I shared with him as a physician and, more particularly, as Hepzibah Sharratt's physician. Until then, no living soul had been party to them, and, you'll be the first to understand, the information I shared was not his to divulge."

Theodosia Greene sat, immobile, listening intently now.

"Hepzibah *Blanchmayne* was, quite simply, the love of my life...," he began.

"*Tea and floristry twice a week? ... With me?*" the Apothecary's wife repeated, angrily. "That wanton chit has not only been abusing the friendship I tried to show her but must have been laughing at me from the start. Think on it now, Colonel, Richard." She looked from one to the other, anger replaced by a fierce animation. "It was at Hepzibah's insistence that the dinner party at the Prebendary House was held at such short notice, allowing her ... *paramour* ... uninterrupted access to the cell of that poor wretch Davy. It must have been *Ned* Blanchmayne you saw that day on Greenhill – no wonder you mistook him for his brother. You say the resemblance was striking, for all their difference in age, Colonel?"

"It was, certainly. They were both peas from the same pod," replied Copeland.

"Ned's marksmanship would have been more than enough to nail a sitting target such as Michael Rawlins: he'd grown up as an Indian fighter and that's the hardest school I know. In the same way, he'd be only too familiar with the type of poison used on Pomlett. Even to my knowledge, Blanchmayne and Co. must have lost half a dozen men, over the years, to just such wounds."

"Ned had the luck of the Devil to have cheated death from his own injuries, which, incidentally, will explain the hat, pulled low to cover that tomahawk scar, no doubt. It was most disfiguring."

"So, you know now, Richard," interposed Theodosia, "worse, *far worse*, than the fact that she was prepared to abuse my trust, the Colonel's trust, and that of her own husband, Hepzibah Sharratt was prepared to lure you to a certain death."

Her husband, looking intently at his feet, responded quietly: "Then I shall just have to make sure that she and Blain are employed to lure that murdering bastard Blanchmayne to *his*, shall I not, Theodosia?"

Then, suddenly, as if possessed of a whole new resolve,

Richard Greene stood, saying, with a bleak smile: "There are seven days prior to our *departure* for Bath;. This is how I propose we fill them...."

43

ITEM:

On the Front of the Organ: in a neat oval frame carved and
gilded is a beautiful nofegay of flowers worked in Silk on a
ground of white Satin, by Mrs Short of
Newport in the county of Salop.

The tent appeared on the edge of the trees below the Bishop's
Palace, shortly after a blustery dawn had broken over The Close,
its erection managed with notable efficiency by two soldiers of
his Majesty's 37th regiment of Foot. Their comrades, at the edge
of the roadway, were unloading a wagon with cheerful profanity.
Stacked with all the ropes and paraphernalia commandeered by
a senior Officer of Engineers, it was drawn up now in the lee of
the windswept church, its horses fidgeting in the traces, its driver
commandeered into the chore.

The previous evening, in the boisterous dining parlour of The
Swan Inn, Colonel Henry Copeland had announced to a less than
enthusiastic group of junior officers that as soon as dinner permitted they were to make the necessary dispositions for an Exercise
in Surveying, to commence in the Cathedral Close at first light
next day.

He would arrive at eight o'clock, he informed the flushed faces,
to inspect the preparations he then ordered. "…As an exercise for
the enlivening of both brain and body, Gentlemen! We all shall
find it most stimulating after a winter of cosy Billets, I'm sure
you'll agree."

With a clear view of the Prebendary House and its stable yard across the sloping green, Copeland sat at ease in the shadowed interior of the tent as the squally wind banged around its bleached walls. He watched as his young officers hurried away to their allotted tasks after a briefing remarkable for its brevity. He looked at the workmanlike timepiece pulled from a fob and nodded to himself. *About an hour before it begins* he thought.

As the shutters were being taken down in Saddler Street, Theodosia Greene looked up from her day-ledger when a young man hurried into the shop.

"Good morning, Mr Sharratt. I believe you have received my message?"

"I did, and thank you, Mrs Greene – though I was about to come of my own accord."

"A happy coincidence, then," replied the Apothecary's wife. "Please come through."

Once in the privacy of the small room behind the shop, the Apothecary's wife said: "Mr Greene is most apologetic for his sudden departure, but one of his county patients is gravely ill. I know my husband will want to stay with him till the end."

"Has this taken him far afield, Mrs Greene? For, if so, I regret that we shall miss our own farewells unless he returns by the day after tomorrow."

"To answer your question, Mr Sharratt, he was called to Hildershall, Sir Eldon Pagnell's house, by Ashbourne," said Theodosia evenly, "but I am quite taken aback! You are leaving us at such short notice?"

"Not by choice, in any sense, Mrs Greene, though this – apart from your note – was why I had to see Mr Greene. I've been forced into the decision to take my uncle to his sister's house at Stratford. I got word to her as soon as Uncle Billy was struck down. She, my Aunt May, is his closest kin, and I thought... ."

His voice tailed off, strain and tiredness glowing in his eyes.

"You acted most commendably, Mr Sharratt," said Theodosia, "I'm certain your uncle would have wished it."

He shrugged. "I don't seem very good at pleasing anyone at the moment, Mrs Greene – least of all my wife. She seems most unhappy at the prospect of leaving Lichfield so shortly, though," he managed a small bitter smile, "we both know she has had few good words to say about it during these past months."

Almost apologetically, he added: "As she will doubtlessly have been confiding to you over many long weeks."

She felt a sudden welling of pity for this hopelessly betrayed man.

"So, you are both accompanying your uncle to Stratford?" she said quickly, ignoring the tacit question.

"Lord, no, Mrs Greene. Hepzibah has only days to prepare herself as it is. I go alone and then must return with all haste."

"Then where...?" began Theodosia.

He seemed suddenly furtive, glancing around before he continued: "We have received word of how we are to join her father, Mrs Greene. It came this morning, within minutes of the delivery of Aunt May's reply to me. In the circumstances you'll forgive me if I disclose no more about it, but we're all he's got, Mrs Greene. Regardless of what his daughter may feel, we'll not abandon him when he needs us most."

"But surely Hepzibah can understand that? It seems, if you will forgive me for saying so, that your father-in-law is more sinned against, than sinning."

"Mrs Greene, ever since the loss of our first, unborn, child, Hepzibah seemed to take against us all, but her father particularly. Then, with the horrors he brought down upon his own kin and the loss of our second child...," he broke off and shrugged, miserably. "But I should not be burdening you with this, Mrs Greene."

"The burden would seem to be all yours, Mr Sharratt." She reached a hand to his arm. "I had no idea that your wife had lost two children. As I know to my own cost, such loss can seem like the end of the world, but she is still a young woman."

The tired eyes filled with anguish as he replied: "No, Mrs

Greene, she knows that she can never bear another child. I think it has been that, more than anything else, that has turned her so … into such… ." He seemed unable to continue.

Not knowing how to respond, the Apothecary's wife suddenly became all business and bustle. "Well, the last thing you can afford is for me to detain you with my chatter, so here are the several prescriptions left by Mr Greene and a note on the dosage and application. We ourselves leave for Bath at the end of the week, so this is – most likely – farewell, Mr Sharratt."

"Shall you not come to make your farewells at Uncle Billy's, Mrs Greene? Your friendship has been much appreciated, though Hepzi's mind will doubtless be elsewhere with all there is to do."

"I regret not, Mr Sharratt, though do please tell your wife that, had I not been left alone and single-handed, I should have liked to see all we have accomplished together, just one last time."

As she took payment for the neatly wrapped packets, Sharratt said, wistfully: "I can share your disappointment, Mrs Greene, though my wife has yet to share a single one of her paintings with me. But then," he added, shaking her hand, "I suppose we must all have our little secrets."

(44)

In the Lobby by the Stairhead: beneath the pipe-clay
Model of the Cathedral Church, an ancient Patriarchal
Chair which formerly belonged to that Church.

Within minutes of each other, the soldier had watched a succession of visitors arrive at the door across The Green. The first, a boy, had run up through the South Gate, pausing only to thrust a message at the maidservant, before jumping the low railings beside the house and disappearing back down through the battered arch. The next two, both with a look of *Postillion* about them, came and went, having made their respective deliveries. Around nine, the hurrying figure of young Sharratt left the house and followed in the errand boy's footsteps, the soldier's discreet observations being then interrupted by the arrival of a heavily muffled figure emerging from the trees behind the tent and ducking in to join him. Some thirty minutes later, both men watched Sharratt's return, packages in his gloved hands as he disappeared through the grand door.

"It could be quite a wait now," Greene said. "The pattern, if pattern there is, seems to be that it's mostly in the afternoons when our Mrs Sharratt contrives to make all her *visits*."

Copeland grunted and sunk deeper into his canvas-slung chair, his eyes not leaving the house beyond. It was, in fact, more than an hour before both were galvanised by a sudden flurry of action across in the stable yard.

"That's Clarke's coach being harnessed," said Greene, urgently, "not what we expected at all!"

(212)

Copeland said something about *imponderables* and continued his surveillance through the part-drawn flap – now with a short telescope that had appeared in his hands.

Greene himself could make out the swaddled form of William Clarke being borne to the waiting coach, his nephew frowning with concern beside him, and, within minutes, both men, attended by two of the household servants, were driven away at a steady pace.

"The Lord only knows what's going on now," said Greene, in concern. "It's little short of folly to risk poor Clarke with a journey. What's to do, Harry? This is beyond me."

"Well, whatever it is, it's certainly producing results. Look *there!*"

Scarcely moments after the departure of the coach bearing the invalid, the watchers were rewarded by the sight of Hepzibah Sharratt hurrying across to the Mews at the far side of the stable yard. Apparently oblivious to her agitation, they watched as Blain hauled the small Barouche out of the Coach House with little appearance of urgency. Seeming to ignore the young woman's angry gestures, apparent even to the watchers, the heavy-set man ponderously enacted the rituals of trace and harness to his own satisfaction. They saw Hepzibah Sharratt angrily disdain his hand as she hauled herself under the folding canopy, gesturing for their immediate departure.

As the light vehicle rolled away, the soldier stood, stretched, nodded to Greene and stepped out to call for his own mount. Before the small man could speak, Copeland turned back to him: "Yes, I shall do exactly as we agreed, Richard. I let her lead me – we hope – to Uncle Ned and return forthwith. No heroics. As prescribed!"

With that, he mounted gracelessly. "It can be no more than five miles, I'm sure of that," he said, looking down on the small, earnest face turned up to him. "Not if she's been flitting there and back so often. Expect me within two hours at the most." As he pulled his horse's head round, he added almost as an afterthought: "You're sure the City constables can be relied upon in this, Richard?"

"Oh yes," replied the Apothecary wryly, "my good friend Utting will be only too keen to do me a service. He'll guarantee they jump to it when prodded."

With a final nod, the Officer of Engineers nudged his mount in the direction of the West Gate and trotted after the dwindling coach.

Richard Greene settled back in his chair to wait, confident that little of interest would occur across at the Prebendary House. In spite of the blustery morning the tent was snug enough for him to take out a fold of papers – from the pocket shared with his pistol – and to soon begin to lose himself in its contents, elbows propped on the trestle table that was the tent's only other furnishing. Copeland's officers, all by now taken up with a weighty schedule of tasks to be completed, set down and reported, paid no attention to the civilian observer they had been told to expect. Had they known, though, that the same small man had been the architect of their travails they may have paid him greater heed – though not necessarily of an appreciative nature.

By the ancient Common Law, Burning was the punishment for heresy, but the Party accused was first to be tried and convicted thereof by the Bishop and the reſt of the Clergy of his Province assembled in Convocation. After Conviction the Offender was delivered into Lay-Hands, and the Sherriff of the County, by virtue of the Writ, de Haeretico comburendo, was to cause him to be burnt.

The accustomed sadness touched the Apothecary as he followed Michael Rawlins' spidery script in its meander across the page. He paused to glance sourly in the direction of the ramshackle housing of the Library beyond The Green before returning, as he'd done so many times before, to the leaden litany of accusation that had delivered Edward Wightman to the flames.

… and he did maintain his most perilous and dangerous Opinions that Jesus Christ is not the true natural son of God, but is only Man and a meer Creature, and not both God and Man in the same Person.
That the Soul of our Saviour did sleep in that sleep of Death as well as His Body. That Christ our Saviour took not humane flesh of the substance of the Virgin Mary His Mother, and that the promise 'the Seed of the Woman shall break the Serpent's Head' was not fulfilled in Christ.
That God hath ordained and sent him, the said Edward Wightman to perform his part in the Work of Salvation of the World, to deliver it by his teaching, or Admonition, that the promise may be fulfilled.

As a particularly violent gust strained the guy ropes to their limit, the Apothecary glanced up from his reading, some flicker of movement off to the edge of his vision carrying his eye to the approaching rider who now emerged from the lee of the great church. The Apothecary felt a stab of panic deep in his gut as the rider came clearly into view: a big, heavy-set man with an ankle-length riding coat and a wide-brimmed hat pulled low over his eyes. As both horseman and mount flinched at the renewed onset of the wind, the rider paused to clamp the hat more firmly onto his head whilst seeming to carefully scrutinise his surroundings before nudging the stallion towards the house across The Green.

The Apothecary was transported back to that momentary glimpse on Greenhill – the same heavy topcoat, the low-pulled hat of Rawlins' assassin – this had to be Ned Blanchmayne, he told himself with dread certainty. Where, though, had Hepzibah led Harry Copeland, and where was the soldier when he most needed him?

The two hours were well past with no sign of his return. Look-ing down, Greene was amazed to see his pistol in his hand, its loading and priming now almost second nature to him. As the rider dismounted in the stable yard, Greene watched as he led his horse to the nearest loosebox, neither ostler nor house servant attending the arrival. The tall figure emerged from the stable and, after once again seeming to scan his surroundings, moved out of sight as he went towards the side door of the Prebendary House. Some moments later, the Apothecary saw the pale orb of a face, momentarily, at the bay window of the dining room, though it was gone within the blink of an eye. He knew what he must do, though the thought of that confrontation brought a spasm of nau-sea to the small man now struggling into his topcoat. He stood for a still, inward moment with eyes tight shut, before clasping a large pocket-handkerchief to his nose and face and with ap-parent unconcern ducking out of the canvas shelter towards the trees once more. Once at the top of The Close, he descended the rampart walk above the weed-choked moat, down towards the South Gate.

The side gate by which he entered the Prebendary garden was scarcely used at this time of year, and, glancing to see he was un-observed, Greene had to put his shoulder to it to force its ledge past the bank of windblown leaves lodged behind it.

Once through, he passed along the bare, raised beds of the kitchen garden, pushing past bushes of rosemary that left a clean pungency on his coatskirts as he came to the scullery door. To his right stood the washhouse, a gleam of copper just visible against the limewash within. Checking his pistol once more, then easing it back into his pocket, he lifted the latch, his right hand still grip-ping the butt, and stepped over the scrubbed threshold.

Silence. No sound of kitchen or pantry, no clatter of pans or murmurs of conversation. Had he not seen the face at the window he would have thought the whole place empty.

Closing the door with elaborate care, he worked out the unseen geography of the house whose public face he had cause to know so well. When he was satisfied with his intended route, he moved cautiously forward, pistol at his side, his heart in his mouth. Once through the empty kitchen and past the unoccupied housekeeper's Snug, the green baize door that marked the domestic frontier of the Prebendary House gave noiselessly to his hand, and the Apothecary entered the familiar landscape of hall and dining room passage.

He froze as a series of creaks sounded from somewhere above his head, beyond the balconied landing, towards the rear of the house. Keeping well to the wall of the cantilevered stairs so no sound would betray him, Richard Greene gained the landing and, fighting to control his breathing and his pounding heart, realised he had been holding his breath for the whole stealthy ascent. After pausing to take several deep breaths, another series of rapid creaks sounded through a half-open door off to his left. With a silent prayer he crossed the carpeted boards until he could see a sliver of the room beyond, past the limewashed glow of the door panels. Again, the sound of wood on wood. He strode forward, pistol extended as he pushed into the room.

For just a second the housekeeper was too shocked to scream, gaping up, slack-mouthed, from her rocking chair, at the pistol wavering in her face. Then, as if possessing a life all its own, a thin trilling wail seemed to force itself out of somewhere deep beneath the gaudy quilt that enveloped the elderly woman.

Before the equally horrified Apothecary could so much as lower his gun, a harsh voice from behind him spoke close to his ear.

"Move an inch and I'll kill you where you stand."

(45)

On the Wall of the left hand the Organ: a string of Witch-Stones from the River Wribble (in Lancashire) in great estimation among the common people of that County; a large wooden shoe found under some old buildings at the Bull's Head in Manchester.

It seemed to the soldier that Hepzibah Sharratt's sense of urgency had finally prevailed upon the driver of the Barouche. Once past the polite environs of the city's grammar school and the ranked chimneys of the ancient hospital, the light coach cut the corner of Schoolhouse Lane and set off at speed along the Birmingham Road, scattering a waddling array of ducks in its wake.

As the little city fell away behind them, Copeland saw the hilltop village of Shenstone rising some miles ahead, its church tower lit, briefly, by weak sunlight that shortly gave up the unequal contest with the lowering, wind-driven showers that stung the soldiers face.

Close to eleven, the coach came to a halt outside a low brick house set at some distance from the village proper. Glancing back over his shoulder, Copeland could see no more of the city than the tip of its great steeple above a round-topped hill in the middle distance. His guess had been about right, something approaching an hour's ride.

The soldier watched as the young woman – once more rejecting a helping hand – jumped down from the coach and ran along a garden path to the porch, leaving Blain to tend to the horses. There was no indication that he was about to follow her, so Copeland – noticing the entry to a green lane well-screened from the coach – dismounted, tied his horse to the hedgerow, and ran heavily along its length as it curved towards an orchard at the side of Hepzibah Sharratt's destination.

A broken-backed gate sagged against weed-grown posts, offering scrambled access to the neglected apple trees, branches furred with mould and lichen, twigs black against a pewter sky. His heavy topcoat enabled him to push, imperviously, through chest-high stands of nettle and rank Elder until he came up to a broken rain butt against the backshoot of the house, its downpipe sagging away from untended thatch above. Everywhere a sense of dereliction and neglect, though the coarse grass and bushes growing close about the walls offered ideal cover as Copeland worked his way around to the nearest window.

Just as he'd negotiated the broken carcase of what had once been a dog kennel, he stiffened, as a muffled cry came from somewhere inside the house, and pulled himself as close to the grimy window as the brambles allowed. As the soldier edged his head around the worm-eaten frame and squinted into the room, a flash of white against the gloomy interior drew his eye to a far corner. There in the broken shadows, spread across a strewn table, Hepzibah Sharratt writhed in ecstasy, her legs wrapped around the shoulders of the heavy-set figure who stood, pumping and grinding into her.

The unreasoning agony of bile, of fury and the searing rip of half-healed scars betrayed him for barely an instant, though enough to bring him lurching to his feet, his hand splintering the rotten sill beneath his weight, as he fell heavily against it.

The young woman's head jerked up as her eyes fought for focus, past the thrusting man, bucking now, in spasm, heedless of anything but his fulfilment.

For an instant her eyes lit in shocked recognition and then her mouth, one moment slack and ugly with need, the next forming into a scream of warning, as she made to push the gasping weight from her. Cursing his own clumsiness, Copeland turned and plunged away from the window, knowing his pistols would be worse than useless, fired half-blind through the filthy panes. With what little element of surprise he could still summon, he waded through the brambles, their coils and thorns dragging at him as he fought towards the door.

He knew, numbly, even as he broke free onto the cinder path, that he was too late. With a clear line of sight to the struggling interloper who had suddenly burst into view, Blain was already jumping down from the coach, a short-barrelled gun in his hands. Caught between him and the porch, Copeland lunged desperately for the door handle, stumbling, completely off-balance, as it swung inwards. From the shadowed interior a heavily booted foot arced up. He fell, helplessly, into its vicious swing, and the world broke up around him.

"Again." The shock of water pierced the carapace of pain once more, though this time, the bleeding man choked in response, a red gout spraying from between his torn lips.

The riding boot had caught him squarely between his broken nose and broken teeth, as the molten agony at the centre of his face testified. He spat again, the dank air razoring through raw wounds as he gasped for breath. Before he could register his surroundings, a large shape bent towards him – a faceless silhouette, black against the dreary light.

"So, after all these years you're still sniffing around her, are you, *Harry-Boy*? Just what does it take to teach you a lesson? We're going to have to find that out, don't you think? And a whole parcel more, besides."

Before the soldier could reply, the flushed face of Hepzibah Sharratt seemed to materialise beside his.

"What are you *doing* here, Harry?" she hissed, her expression unreadable.

"Following you, you stupid little bitch," exclaimed the standing man. "Ask the soldier-boy something we don't know, or shut your mouth – you've done enough harm already!"

"Was it you, at the Pool, that saw these two big, brave men off, Harry?" she asked in a parody of sweet enquiry, ignoring the contemptuous dismissal. "It was, wasn't it? I can see it in your eyes."

Through the surging waves of pain that seemed to radiate from his core, Copeland studied the face whose spectral presence had haunted the years. He said nothing, gathering himself for what he knew would come soon. Life had begun to leave its mark in eyes grown a season colder, a mouth turned – almost imperceptibly – sourer, a complexion no longer lit with roses and sunshine. But then the girl he'd loved – as much as life itself – had died and died again in every broken dream and wakeful night for as long as he could remember.

"It means that he's with Greene, somehow, Ned, but I don't see how he can have… ."

The hand descended and twisted into her hair, pushing her violently to one side, her eyes wide with pain.

"You don't see because you don't use your eyes, Girl! Or your brain, half the damn' time," snarled the man. "Why don't you stitch my name on a banner and wave it through the town. You must have left a trail a mile wide for *this* clod to follow it."

He turned back to crouch in front of the bound Engineer: "You should have been a farmer, Harry, that way you might have lived longer. But we'll have our little talk in a short while, so save what's left of your breath till then."

He straightened and for the first time the soldier could see Ned Blanchmayne clearly. He saw a man stripped of any veneer that might have been applied and polished for the small society of the Middle Colonies, for the currying of favours or the easing of deals. The striking likeness to his younger brother began with height, breadth, the same strong features and squared-off jaw, but ended with the eyes and the aura of calculating malevolence that seemed to hover about him like smudged air.

He was leaner, harder, than the Engineer remembered, as if

surplus humanity had been sloughed off, leaving only a vicious *bone* of a man.

Copeland's blood turned to water in his veins as Blanchmayne said harshly to the woman: "I'll need time to work on him, 'Bah, and you've wasted enough of mine as it is." Before she could protest he grabbed her wrist and pulled her into a rough embrace, one hand thrusting into her crotch the other twisting her wrist behind her neck. A gasp of pain, stillborn in her throat, was stifled as he crushed his mouth onto her gaping lips. He broke off, staring at Blain who had stood silent, unmoving, since the soldier had regained consciousness.

"Why are you still here, Sam? You're not getting a taste for forbidden fruit, now, are you? Get out and see to your horses, man, before you find your balls sewn up in your mouth! You'll take Mrs Sharratt to do what she must do, then get straight back."

He turned contemptuously to Copeland, hog-tied to his stool. "I'll be well done with this one by then."

"Let me cut him now," drawled Blain, his eyes never leaving the soldier.

"Y'always did like your steaks tender," quipped Blanchmayne, raising a hand to the stained dressing at his ear. "I owe him, then some."

"Then y'all gonna have to settle for him with a spade when y'all get back," drawled the big man in mocking mimicry. "Now get your bag of bones, and Mr Sharratt's fine Lady out of here. There's a whole lot to be done and a narrow time to do it in."

Hepzibah seemed about to speak, before she was smacked none too gently across the buttocks and propelled towards the door. "*Scoot!* There'll be time a-plenty for gabbing when you're done. Finish it while you still can and let's have done with it."

Even amidst the cold fear that was now numbing his pain, the soldier felt a sudden stab of dread as the door closed on the departing pair, neither sparing so much as a backward glance at the bound man.

Blanchmayne ignored him, crossing to the strewn table and pouring a careless measure from a black bottle. He drank deeply, poured again and then stood, looking at the soldier. "You know I'm going to kill you, *Harry-Boy*, so which way's it going to be? The choice is yours. It'll be the last you ever get to make, so think on it: the long, hard way or a quick knife? Tell me what I need to know and have done with it. It's the best deal on the table."

At that moment Copeland knew that all he could do was try to keep Ned Blanchmayne talking, and to do that he must talk, too. Through swollen lips he croaked: "I can't talk if I can't breathe. Give me a drink first, for pity's sake."

He was gasping for breath already, nostrils blocked with congealing blood.

With a grunt, Blanchmayne fetched the bottle and held it to Copeland's ruined mouth. The soldier choked on a scream as the raw spirit seared him, lightning strikes of agony lancing through his head, his breath reduced to a hiccoughing wheeze.

Looking down, without emotion, on the soldier losing his fight for breath, Blanchmayne began to doubt Copeland's ability to talk even if he could be persuaded to. Reaching behind him, he pulled a short, broad-bladed knife from its sheath on his belt and, ignoring the bonds that lashed the soldier's feet beneath the rough stool, cut the rope around Copeland's hands.

With a feral grin he said: "Really messed you up, didn't I, Harry, and I was scarcely even trying! Clean yourself up."

With that he tossed a handful of soiled rags onto Copeland's lap.

"…Need water," the soldier managed, scarcely able to believe his luck.

Blanchmayne's hunger for information was a weapon that might, somehow, be turned against him – the soldier felt the first tiny prickle of hope.

A chipped pitcher of water was thrust, roughly, into his hands by the American. "You've got as long as it takes for me to piss," he said, assuring himself that the soldier's bindings were firm around legs and feet before striding to the door and unbuttoning himself in the porch. As the sound of prolonged urinating came from the doorway, the heavy-set figure blocking the light, Copeland gingerly rinsed out his mouth and despite the blinding pain did what little he could to clear his nose.

As Blanchmayne hawked loudly and spat before turning back into the house, Copeland bent quickly and hit the lip of the water jug, hard against his stool, knocking a large chip from it.

As the American came back in from the low porch, Copeland managed to replace the jug on the floor to his rear. Striding around him, Blanchmayne ignored it completely, jerking Copeland's arms behind him and retying the wrists with practised ease.

"So, *Harry-Boy*, what's it to be?"

As he appeared to struggle towards a decision, the soldier's fingers found the pitcher's broken lip, its edge sharp against his wrist. He began to rock, almost imperceptibly, to and fro, eyes closed as if in agonising indecision. Then he opened them, and finally addressed the other.

"You know I'd have killed you if I could," he slurred. "I would have called you out, if it hadn't meant exposing … her."

"Expose *her*?" Blanchmayne laughed coarsely. "Why, there's nothing she likes better than exposing *herself*, *Harry-Boy*! If you hadn't been so busy trying to be the proper little suitor then you'd have wised up that you could've been a-gobbling there soon as saying *howdydoo*! When I had her at fourteen she was stickier than a honeypot, even then."

The soldier prayed he would keep talking.

"I wasn't the first to dip in there though, *Harry-Boy*, not by a long chalk." He leered down at the bound man. "But if the lying little bitch is to be believed, you never *did* get to try your luck, did you? Kept your cock in the Commissary did they? Along with all those other ball-less suckers they call *Officers and Gentlemen*? Sure as shit, there ain't ever been a quim worth killing for, *Harry-Boy*;

there's always another coming along, just wet and waiting! Hasn't soldiering taught you even that much?"

Revulsion and a dark, primal fury churned in Copeland's gut, as he looked at his tormentor, rocking, swaying in his agitation. "So, what *is* worth killing for, Blanchmayne?" he wheezed. "*Money?* Even you must have stowed away enough of that, by now. You've been robbing the world – and your own brother – blind, all the years I've known you."

Then, though, before the American could respond, a strange sensation swept over the hurting man, a sense of slowly dawning realisation only made possible by the goad of his pain. He saw in front of him – for the first time – a gaunt, wasted man, homeless and alone, hiding away in a foully ramshackle hovel. In that moment he knew. *There's always another, just wet and waiting.* Hepzibah Sharratt was less than nothing to this debauched husk of a man, so why pursue her to the depths of England if not for some other reason? The words *love* or *affection* were no part of this debased equation.

"That's *it*, isn't it, Ned?" he said slowly, wonderingly, "you need *her* even more than the poor creature craves you! Can you not get your hands on what you've tucked away all these years, without her? Is *that* it? The reason you've slaughtered your way through this poor, bloody, City? She has some kind of hold on *you*, hasn't she?"

Against all odds the soldier was rewarded by the flash of fear in Blanchmayne's eyes, though drunken fury flooded in behind, as he lurched towards the rocking, wide-eyed prisoner, the bottle smashing at his feet. The open-handed slap sent Copeland and his stool flying, only to be yanked upright, the scruff of his collar seized by the maddened attacker, shouting obscenities and brandy fumes into the soldier's quailing face.

Livid and bleeding again from the fresh assault, Copeland reeled back from the spitting abuse. Then, it was over, the American standing, breathing heavily as he looked down on Copeland. Slowly, terrifyingly, a smile began to spread across his wal-nut-brown features and his shoulders began to shake.

"You're *guessing, Harry-Boy,* just guessing, ain't you? Guessing all the way down the line. I can see it now: you've not got a cock-sucking clue in *Hell* what you're talking about!"

Still laughing, he went to a cupboard and pulled out another black bottle.

As he opened it and began to fill the nearest cup, he grinned across at the soldier. "*Slaughtered my way through your poor bloody City? Me?* Oh, *Harry-Boy*, you've picked the wrong Blanchmayne! That job's being wound-up right about now." The stubby knife reappeared in his fist. "Just like this one's going to be."

Above the small mantel: A clumsy oval carving in
Canal Coal, 9 inches by 7, of King Charles the 2d,
on Horfeback, on the oppofite side, his Queen.

The Apothecary turned with infinite care to the source of the command, his pistol lain as instructed, on the floor.

"*You?*" he whispered in bewilderment, staring at the tall, heavy-set figure that covered him, with a horse-pistol grasped in a steady hand.

"Well who in *Perdition* did you expect, Greene?" barked Isiah Blanchmayne.

"This is where I've lived for the past year, ain't it? But *you*, Sir. What in the name of God are *you* doing here, prowling about like some damned housebreaker? Speak up, man, I'm about plumb out of patience!"

"I believed you to be ... I thought you were... ," the Apothecary began, and then, suddenly, he rallied, as molten anger and a terrible urgency overcame him. "If there are any explanations to be made, then *dammit*, Sir, it's *you* who'll be making them! Shall we start the process by addressing you correctly, Mr *Wightman?*"

The heavy pistol wavered for a moment and then dropped, as the big man seemed to deflate in front of the astonished Apothecary. Isiah Blanchmayne slumped back against the balustrade as if winded. "Oh, merciful Christ, *no*! Not that demented claptrap again! Is this what it has all come down to?"

Without thinking, Richard Greene stepped forward and took the pistol from the American's unresisting hand. "And if you must know, Mr *Wightman*, I believed you to be your brother; back from the grave to which I intend to return him."

"*You?* My *Brother?* How can you possibly know any of this? It's not possible! I myself have only just…."

"Have only *just* realised he has been cutting a murderous swathe through my city?" shouted Greene, reaching up and grabbing Isiah by his lapels, careless of anything now other than his own pent-up fury. "Only *just* started to count up the corpses, Mr *Wightman?*"

He shook the ashen man violently, once: "Old Richard Neille, burned in his bed?" Twice: "My good friend Michael Rawlins, dead from a bullet?" Three times: "A wretched thief choked on his sick-bed? Poor vain Pomlett, destroyed by poison? And you only just *what*, Mr *Wightman?*" screamed Greene into the face of the terrified Blanchmayne. "*Just* realised that they almost did for me on Christmas Eve, your bastard brother and his creature Blain? *Just* discovered my wife was sentenced to death because of your lunatic family and its lunatic ancestor?"

The American's mouth was opening and closing but no sound was emerging, as Greene realised that he had pinned the tall figure against the wall, his feet scarcely touching the ground. He released him in sudden disgust with both himself and the gasping man, now struggling to support himself on legs seemingly turned to jelly.

"I must sit," he gasped, pushing himself off the wall and stumbling towards a doorway on the landing, scarcely noticing the petrified housekeeper, still cowering within, as he fell on to a day bed.

"Bring some brandy, and look sharp about it, please," rasped Greene, amazed at his own authority. "There'll be time enough for apologies when this is settled. *Quickly* now!"

The plump woman waddled off as fast as her legs would carry her, returning, perspiring and breathless with a decanter and two glasses, which she made to fill.

"Just the one, for him, to the brim!" he ordered, watching the other man's shrunken form as he sought to compose himself after the Apothecary's furious onslaught. "Now, please wait upon us downstairs. We shall call if you are required." He turned to the American.

"Drink it, *all of it*," ordered Greene, and watched as Isiah gulped down the potent spirit. "Now talk and talk fast. Lives depend on it."

As the brandy flushed colour back beneath the brown cheeks, the American's eyes seemed to swim in and out of focus, as he looked up at the baleful figure of Richard Greene who was re-checking the priming of his retrieved pistol before pocketing it.

"Drink it, I said. *All of it*!

He watched as Isiah drained the spirit, and then, gasping for breath, exclaim: "You cannot possibly believe that I, *we*, have had anything to do with those tragedies you talk of," said the American, heavily, his eyes avoiding the Apothecary.

"I am only going to warn you once, whatever you call yourself," rasped Greene. "You'll answer to me or to the hangman, depend on it."

The big man flinched, visibly, from the lash of Greene's words, before finally meeting the small man's eyes and replying: "But why would we involve ourselves in old family tales used to frighten naughty children. It was all *centuries* ago, whatever dad and his...."

Too late. He tried to stop himself.

"All right," said the Apothecary, a new, dangerous calm in his voice, "perhaps to you it *is* all meaningless history, but there are others – *generations* of others – who felt differently. Am I correct?"

Blanchmayne nodded a head bowed in misery.

"Not being the eldest son, I was spared the burden – there is no other word for it. It was a blasphemous piece of nonsense this family has trailed around since poor, mad Edward decided he was The Baptist – come again, preparing the way for The Final Days. I've prayed to God to have mercy on the wickedness that my ancestors enacted in those many years after his burning. They were mad with grief and anger. Can you imagine what they, *he*, went through?"

He looked pleadingly at the Apothecary, who simply nodded for him to continue.

"Do you know that Edward was actually pulled from the flames by the crowd, the first time, Greene? *Rescued*, spared – or so he was led to believe!"

"It was only afterwards that those murdering cowards cooked up the claim that he'd recanted as the flames were lit – to cover their own guilt and the shame of being seen for the black-hearted dogs they were. Then, when he denied their lies, they dragged him out of prison, weeks later, and sent him back to the flames. There was no reprieve that time."

"And so your ancestors…?"

"Edward's son, and then *his* son, in turn," interjected the broken man, dully.

"…became Judge, Jury and Executioner of all those they could reach from that wretched Court," said Greene, his eyes never leaving the other, "ending only when the *Wightmans*, ironmongers of Burton on Trent, upped sticks to become the *Blanchmaynes*, Traders to the Middle Colonies," continued the Apothecary as if reciting from a lexicon. "But they took more than just their business with them, did they not?" he added.

"There was a letter," the American murmured. "A damnable thing – handed from father to eldest son. I came across it when I was clearing my – Ned's – effects. Not that he had ever given a damn about it, for all I knew. It was the work of a terrified, addled mind, Greene. It charged every generation to swear an oath that they would seek to avenge the murderers of *The Lord's Anointed*. That's how Edward described himself: 'let my blood be upon them and their children', it said. No-one in living memory had paid it any more heed than as some peculiar family rite of passage, just a form of words, without meaning over there. Certainly, no-one could have accused either my father, or grandfather, of believing in *anything* except money. Ned's a proper chip off that block," he added bitterly.

"So, it passes unheeded for generations, until now," said the Apothecary, bleakly, "when, for reasons unknown, your brother decides to resurrect himself and carry out the unfinished business. He started with the cold-blooded burning of an old man tied to a bed. An old man with his tongue cut out. I saw Richard Neille die. It was an act of bestial wickedness."

As he spoke, Greene had unconsciously raised a hand to his scarred brow. Blanchmayne looked at him, aghast. "Dear God in heaven, I swear that I have never made even the connection until this moment. *Neille* was the name of the bishop from that Court, wasn't he? The list was part of the letter."

"*Was?* You keep saying *was*. Where is it now?"

"I destroyed it for the vile object that it was, Greene. It had done too much damage already. I know now that its poison had even reached my own daughter."

"*Your daughter? Hepzibah?* How so?" said Greene urgently.

Blanchmayne hesitated, his misery seeming to grow by the minute. "Hepzi has always been a ... *singular* ... somewhat solitary girl, Mr Greene. She never made many friends and her tomboy nature was the despair of her dear, late mother. There was," he hesitated again, "an *incident* – when she was little more than ten. She burned her dolls, Greene – one by one – each tied to a little stake."

"But how could she have known?" countered the Apothecary, horrified, in spite of himself.

"My wretched brother, it seems, had filled her head with it all, treating it as no more than a joke when I confronted him. *Bedtime stories, no worse than many*, he said. He either didn't know, or simply didn't care, about the damage inflicted on a young mind. Hepzibah became quite hysterical when we tried to speak to her about it, seeming to have mixed up the story and her own actions in her head. We let it drop, out of concern for our daughter's peace of mind, believing it to be the end of a sorry business."

"Until...?" prompted Greene, seeing Blanchmayne's reluctance to continue.

"Until Hepzibah lost her first baby, Mr Greene," he said, finally. "We had hoped that her marriage to young Sharratt would..." – he seemed to search for the word – "*alleviate* the moods and black humours of her adolescence. If anything it made the situation worse. As her parents we could sense that all was not as it should have been between young newlyweds, but," he shrugged, helplessly, "what can one do in such circumstances? Hepzibah was never close to her mother, and I was so often away. I returned from a trip into Canada, a week or so after she lost the child. I shall never forget her words, or the state she was in, when I went to comfort her."

Richard Greene watched dispassionately as Isiah wrestled with his anguish.

"She screamed into my face, Greene. My own daughter. 'His blood is upon us and our children'. She had been shown that damned letter! I know it now – I wish to God I'd known it then. From that time on, she seemed to have nothing but coldness for either her husband, or for us, her own kin."

"And did that include her feelings toward her uncle, your brother, Ned?" said the Apothecary quietly.

Suddenly, Blanchmayne was on his feet, white with fury.

"*Damn you* to Hell you smug little...."

Greene was on his feet before the trembling man could utter another word. "Sit down or I'll *knock* you down, you hopeless, blind fool!" he bellowed.

Isiah Blanchmayne gaped in shock at the incandescent face, inches from his own, and began backing away from the glare of its ferocity.

Greene was not to be stopped now.

"You have stood by whilst your *own* daughter was debauched by your *own* brother and have the gall to damn *me*, you craven turd! The same murdering bastard of a brother who's taken four lives while you've been too busy taking care of business to notice? *What kind of Godforsaken imbecile are you?*"

Blanchmayne was weeping now, his walnut-brown cheeks wet with helpless tears. "I could do nothing, *nothing you hear*! Not to undo the vileness of Ned's actions – it was all too late when I realised…."

"But it's *not* too late to stop the bastard in his tracks before he kills again. Where is he man? Tell me now!"

The big man howled his reply at the Apothecary. "But it wasn't *him*, Greene, don't you see! It can't have been! As God is my witness, I know this – he didn't land at Bristol until a week after old Neille died!"

Greene felt, at that moment, as if the ceiling had collapsed upon him. For an instant his mind seemed to shut down, refusing to even register the implications of the words he'd just heard. He could do no more than stare in stupefaction as Blanchmayne stumbled on.

"The first inkling I got that my brother lived was when I went to draw upon a shipping reserve account we had always kept at Bristol. I found it had been cleaned out, quite legally, by its co-signatory – Ned. I'd know his odd scrawl anywhere. I saw it with my own eyes, the signature of my dead brother, dated April 24th. It was the day he landed – from the brig *Nancy*, out of Boston. His name was on the harbour manifest. It said *Wightman* – he must have thought it a great joke."

"I saw him *here*, with my own eyes, the day he shot Michael Rawlins! I thought it was you!" shouted Greene, a feeling of uncomprehending panic rising in his throat.

"Yes, maybe you did, but that was *months* later, Greene! He must have followed Hepzi here, for whatever reason, but I've seen neither hide nor hair of him. You *must* believe me – the swine has tried to leave me destitute, poor Billy too! He cares for nothing, no-one, but himself! I am ashamed to say it of my own flesh and blood, Greene, but my brother is a Godless, gutless bully.

He would no more lift a finger to settle some ancient score than he would trouble to settle one of his own debts. Unless of course, there was something in it for him. He's worthless. I think I've always known it. Better he'd stayed dead."

"I've no argument with that," said the Apothecary slowly, his gaze directed at something far beyond the American, an almost dreamlike trance seeming to have overcome him, "but wherever we find him, we find your daughter. *Your own daughter*, Hepzibah. Do you understand what I'm saying?"

Uncomprehending, Isiah Blanchmayne stared at the small man until a sudden tremor appeared to jolt through him, his nostrils flaring, his eyes widening in shock, then incredulity.

Before the American could speak, Richard Greene appeared to shake himself free of whatever had gripped him and said without expression: "It is now apparent that your daughter is dangerously ill – infinitely more so than anyone could have imagined. She must be found. We can only pray that wherever he is, she may still be. Kindly summon your housekeeper."

If there was any question forming in Blanchmayne's mouth, it dissolved as he looked into the Apothecary's eyes.

"All I can say is, Sir, that it's not my place to tittle-tattle." The nervous woman looked appealingly at Blanchmayne. "I have my position to think about."

"Mrs Beale, I am responsible for upsetting you grievously," said the Apothecary with what little patience he could summon, "and for that you have my unreserved apology, but I must know – *we* must know – of any clue you have – any clue at all – as to where Mrs Sharratt has been going these many weeks."

Suddenly, the Apothecary saw in her eyes that she knew. Resisting the urge to shake her bodily, he continued, as persuasively as he knew how: "You will be betraying no confidences; there will be no blame for either you or your mistress."

"My *mistress*, Mr Greene? I *don't* think so, Sir," she replied with a spark of indignation. "I'm in Mr Clarke's service, have been for eleven years, and a kind gentleman he's always been." A tear shone in her eye. "I'm not at the beck and call of some little...," she broke off in alarm, staring at the American. "I'm sorry, Sir. I didn't mean to...."

He seemed to become aware of her by degrees then waved a listless hand, saying: "Just tell us Mrs Beale, for the love of God."

"Well, it's not *me* who's seen anything at all," she began, diffident again, "but Dolly's young man," she nodded towards the distant scullery, "his people farm, in a small way, out by Shenstone. *He* reckons he's seen the Barooch out there, stopped like, plenty of times at some old tumbledown, up by the village, but it's not for me to say what...."

Her hands were suddenly grasped by the Apothecary. "That's all we need to know, bless you, Mrs Beale." He swung back to Blanchmayne. "*Shenstone!* We can get there in half an hour! I need a horse."

The American gave all the appearance of a walker in a waking dream as Greene urged him to the stables. Ahead, he glimpsed Blanchmayne's horse, still saddled, tethered by the door. Then, though, as he turned to the figure beside him, two thickset figures rounded the stable yard gate and hurried towards them. He opened his mouth to speak as they came to an abrupt halt. Both ignored the Apothecary completely.

"Blanchmayne? Isiah Blanchmayne?" one enquired.

The American bridled, visibly, at the bluntness of the question. "Yes, but who in perdition are you?"

"Isiah Blanchmayne," came the jaunty response, "I have a warrant for your arrest, sworn out by the Justices at Bristol. On the seventeenth day of this month, March, on behalf of Hoare's Bank. I now intend to enforce said warrant, by the authority vested in me. Shall you come along without a fuss, Sir?"

The speaker's companion had, by now, taken up position behind the American's shoulder.

"This is all a mistake nothing more, but I must remain at liberty to...."

"Yes, Mr Blanchmayne, quite so, Sir. That'll do now. Come along now, no fuss, like a good gentleman." The tall man seemed to diminish between the pair as they closed around him.

With a wild, despairing look at the Apothecary, he called: "Take my horse, Greene, there's nothing to be done here. For God's sake, save what you can!"

The Apothecary was already running to the stable door.

(47)

A piece of Cope worn by Wickliff: an holy Water Cistern in Glass.used by Roman Catholic's to hang in their bedrooms.

The reek of butchery met him even before he could cross the threshold. With his gorge rising, Greene inched forward. In one hand he held his own pistol, in the other the unfamiliar weight of the American's weapon, as he squinted into the gloom. Blood. He could see blood, everywhere. *Too late!* shrieked the voice inside his head.

"*No!*" he bellowed. Then, his voice seething with hatred: "Come out you black-hearted bastard, into the daylight. You craven, murdering filth!"

He was met by a groan from somewhere behind the door. It was worse than anything he'd ever seen. The body sprawled in a sea of its own blood, black in the dirty light. Everywhere, *everything* was sodden with it. Already flies were glistening all across the contorted ruin of a man.

Ned Blanchmayne's throat was ripped from ear to ear, his fingers hooked forever in the rictus of his agony, a great gash torn through breeches into his thigh, his face pulped, barely recognisable.

The Apothecary spun towards the sound of another, shuddering groan. "Harry, *oh sweet Jesus!*" His voice seemed to belong to someone else, as he rushed to the tattered, bleeding soldier who lay, propped against the wall.

Relief swept over him as Copeland's eyes flickered open and the broken lips attempted a smile.

"I did for him Richard," he croaked. Greene wiped a froth of blood away from the corner of the soldier's mouth. "Was him or me. Cut him, bad, before he could… ."

The soldier's head appeared to loll into unconsciousness, a great shard of broken glass dropping from his nerveless hand. Then the eyes wavered back once more. "Stop the bitch, Richard." Copeland whispered between swollen lips. "I'll live. *Go.*"

"But I can't leave you like this! We must… ."

"*Saddler Street*," bloody spittle bubbled between his lips, "Gone for Theo … go quick … 'm all right." With that Copeland raised a trembling arm and pushed weakly against Greene. "*Go!*" His head fell back.

"I'll send help, Harry, trust me!" panted the Apothecary, reassuring himself with a lightning assessment of the soldier's injuries, before jumping to his feet. "Old Clarke's housekeeper will have alerted the constables well before now. I would expect them to be already on their way."

The soldier managed a nod, still gesturing urgently with his hand.

"Say as little as possible, though; no one will expect more of you."

When he saw that Copeland had registered all he'd said he ran from the shambles to his tethered horse. *At least,* he thought, mind racing ahead of panting breath, *Theo will have Tillett and the boy with her. She'll be down in the shop, in the public eye. What harm can come to her there?* It was as he hauled himself into the saddle that the realisation struck: *Today, Wednesday, was half-day closing. The streets would be empty.*

Sick dread flooded into every crevice of his being.

He swayed and jolted away down the muddy track, clinging fiercely to the mane of Blanchmayne's stallion, as it picked a sure-footed way towards the turnpike road below.

ITEM:

A portable Barrel Organ, which by means of Clock-
work plays sixteen tunes; a small human Faetus dried,
a starved Swallow both covered in Glass.

An unremarkable morning had given way to one of the busiest noontides since Christmas. An hour earlier, Theodosia had decided that now was as good a time as any to oversee a thorough dusting of the topmost shelves, one of the few remaining chores to be seen to before the widely broadcast departure due that coming Saturday.

One by one, the Delft jars and glass bottles were handed down to join the japanned canisters, in ranks marching down the wrapping counter. The acids and poisons were brought under her personal scrutiny by the cash box – though handled a sight too nonchalantly, to her mind, by the apprentice. Richard would have to speak to him about his attitude, she decided, particularly in view of their forthcoming absence for such a protracted... She caught her thoughts as they were already well-advanced along the imagined road to Bath, and Tillett was surprised to hear Mrs Greene exclaim *'Nonsense!'* to no-one in particular, shaking her head and glaring into the middle distance. He knew better than to notice.

Then, though – as if a queue had been forming somewhere out of sight and was now beginning an orderly shuffle forward – the shop began to fill. It was well past their accustomed early-closing time that the last of the throng was seen off the premises, and Theodosia was aware that both the staff had been casting covert glances at the clock behind her.

"If you'll finish up, James? I'll be above for ten minutes with the takings. Leave the door latched and I'll lock up. Make sure you are both here in good time tomorrow, and we'll get this sorted out before opening." She closed the door to the stairs behind her.

"Go on, you get straight off," said Tillett, not unsympathetically, to the fidgeting apprentice. "Though if she's not waited, she's not worth the chasing. Mark my words."

With a grimace the youth hurried away.

Five minutes later, after a last glance to see that everything had been left to his satisfaction, the shop-man turned to leave. As he reached for the handle, a shape – distorted, multicoloured, through the leaded panes – suddenly filled the glass in front of him, waving urgently through the closed door. With an inward sigh he opened up, revealing the flushed cheeks of a black-haired woman he'd admired on each of her visits to the floors above.

"It's Mrs … *Sharratt* … I believe? Can I be of assistance, Madam?"

"Oh, you have been already," she cooed, "just by still *being* here!"

He began to imagine losing himself in the fathomless eyes.

"I'd *so* hoped to catch you before you closed. I wanted to surprise your mistress!" Then, seeing the quizzical look forming on the shop-man's face, she bestowed a radiant smile. In a most confiding manner, requiring a lean towards an ear growing pinker by the minute, she continued: "We, too, shortly take our leave of Lichfield. It is my *fondest* wish to thank *dear* Mrs Greene for all her good offices during our stay in your charming town."

"Pray, enter then, Mrs Sharratt. I'll be pleased to announce you," said Tillett with heavy-handed gallantry.

"No, no. Thank you!" she whispered, stepping briskly into the shop. "You're most kind, but that would spoil the surprise! We've not seen each other for several weeks, so I declare I shall creep up those stairs and say 'boo!'"

Tillett, by now the compleat co-conspirator, could only grin, foolishly.

"I'm quite familiar with the way up, so, please, don't let me detain you further. I've kept you quite long enough, but you've been *so* kind."

With reluctance, he detached himself from the feather-light hand laid on his arm, and, bowing awkwardly, whispered: "Please remind Mrs Greene that she has still to lock up, then, Mrs Sharratt."

He hesitated just a moment more, before murmuring: "I'll be off, then... ," and letting himself out. "...If you could just drop the latch behind me, Mrs Sharratt?"

"Oh, most assuredly," the young woman replied, putting down her canvas bag.

As the redbrick spindles of the Almshouse chimneys came into view, the Apothecary redoubled his pace. The Roan had gone lame half a mile back, and glancing over his shoulder, he could see that she was barely able to keep the pace he'd been setting. With a murmured apology, he continued to lead her urgently on, reins taut around his wrist as the corner approached. Sweat flicked from his face as he shook his head violently from side to side, to no effect. Nothing could dislodge the images of nightmare that looped through his mind. *A black figure mounting his stairs; a figure bearing a bag of blades and rope and tinder.*

ITEM:

A Lock of Hair in a Locket of Queen Mary of France,
daughter to Henry 7th of England found in her tomb in
St Edmondsbury in Suffolk, she was interred in the Year
1535. In another Locker, a Lock of Queen Ann's Hair.

As she'd finished separating the coins, she first felt the draught;
frowning in annoyance as it stirred the papers on the open bureau.
She was certain she'd closed the shop door. Pausing to scoop small
change back into the cashbox, Theodosia Greene did some brief
calculations in her ledger and closed it with a nod of satisfaction.
Then it came again. She shivered as a tingling chill rose from her
fingertips. It was as she made to stand up that she knew she was
not alone, even before she turned.

"Know this, Theodosia Webb. I shall kill you here and now,
unless you obey me."

"Oh, so it's you," Theodosia said quietly, unmoving, as she
fought to keep the dread, the shock, from rising in her voice.
"I suppose I shouldn't be surprised. You worked so hard to scorn
my friendship, I should have been warned."

"Be quiet," said the young woman without expression. She was
about to continue when the sound of cutlery came rattling up
from the scullery in the yard below. "*Upstairs,*" she said, gesturing
with the small two-barrelled pistol in her hand, "Don't doubt I'll
use this."

Hepzibah Sharratt stepped back onto the landing, putting distance between them. One hand held the gun, unwaveringly, never
leaving Theodosia Greene's back, as they climbed the stairs; the

other hefted the canvas bag above the treads. Ahead of them, on the top landing, a large, ornately carved chair stood beneath a painted model.

"*That*," said the voice behind Theodosia. "The chair. Push it inside."

Theodosia Greene braced herself against it, and, making much of its weight, gradually manoeuvred it into the first of the Museum rooms. Hepzibah Sharratt watched dispassionately then glanced around the cluttered display until her eyes fell on a pair of ornate oil lamps standing in their niche beside the passage door.

"Over there. Turn its back to me."

"Can you not bear to look me in the eye, Hepzibah?" said the Apothecary's wife, straightening. "It's to be the coward's way to the end, is it?"

"What does Mrs *Shopkeeper* know about *bravery*, I wonder?" said the other, as if to herself, her mouth suddenly ugly with scorn. Then, as if in answer: "Well, *here's* our chance to find out." Striding forward she raised the pistol level with the grey-green eyes. "*Sit!*"

Fighting the urge to lunge her hand down into her apron pocket, Theodosia Greene lowered herself into the throne-like seat. Stark terror began to grip her, as her now-invisible assailant was reduced to formless sounds behind her. Then, before she knew what was happening, a lariat was dropped, expertly, over her shoulders, and yanked tight with a vicious tug that almost dragged her from the chair. Once, twice it was wound around her, pinioning her torso and upper arms to the chairback. She could feel her pistol's smooth hardness directly beneath a hand spread across her thigh. *Please God, no more ropes*, she mutely beseeched. *Give me that one chance, at least.* Her fingers felt frozen into a claw of panic as she tried, imperceptibly, to feel for the aperture of the apron pocket. She knew, then, that it was beyond her reach, unless she could gather the coarse linen and somehow lift it.

"Now, about looking you in the eye, Mrs Shopkeeper Webb," said a conversational voice close to her ear. The heavy chair was dragged around to face the door, the young woman walking back round it to look down on its occupant.

"I'd hate for you to miss my preparations. I've been to so much trouble."

"You *nasty* little trollop," rasped the bound woman, fury soaring up through her fear. "It's not enough that you've committed foulness upon foulness, is it? You cannot resist *mocking* and *demeaning*, as well! Is that what you think they did to poor, mad Edward out in the Marketplace? Mocked him? Spat on his dignity, his faith? Is that why you hate us *all* so much? Is that what all of this lunatic quest for vengeance has been about? Getting *even*?"

"Don't patronise me with your sweet reason," hissed the soured mouth. "Do you think for one *minute* that either you and your randy little excuse for a husband even *begin* to understand?"

She gave the most mirthless laugh Theodosia had ever heard.

Then, gazing up into the empty, sky-blue eyes, the older woman murmured: "It's all about the child, isn't it? Losing Ned's child?"

Hepzibah Sharratt flinched back as if she'd been lashed, the orbs of sky suddenly shot through with cold fire. With a spastic jerk she straightened, her chin lifting, her nostrils flaring with passion. Then, in a patient, lilting voice, she spoke the most awful words that Theodosia Greene would ever hear.

"No, Mrs Shopkeeper. What it's all *about* is The Coming." She paused, as if expecting some response from her prisoner. "The Coming of *The Liberator* – are you not familiar with that name?" she continued, "It is the Embodiment I was born to bear."

The Apothecary's wife could only gape. This was a blasphemy born of utter madness.

"Ned is the Conduit," continued Hepzibah Sharratt, quietly, reasonably, "just as I shall be the Vessel. He is the Seventh Son. Seventh after the first who came to prepare the Way, and I am that Woman whose seed shall break the Serpent's head. Mankind will be released from thrall. It's all written down, there can be no mistake. It's all been revealed to me."

'*The Cathedral, and all it represents, has long had its day, Mr Hoare, if, indeed, it ever had a purpose*', the words from that far-off dinner party returned to mock the terrified Theodosia. *Sweet Lord, how did we miss it?* she asked herself, cringing inwardly. *How could we have failed to recognise this utter aberration in our midst?*

"So, you see," continued the black-haired woman, "that for all the fuss they've made about him, *Mother Mary's* little Nazarene was neither here nor there."

Then, she smirked, mouth twisting in disdain. "So what a waste all those draughty old shit-heaps of churches have been, when it's been *my* baby that's been awaited, all this time!"

"But, Hepzibah," whispered the Apothecary's wife, "You *lost* your child, and then another … don't you remember?"

"Not *remember?*" shrieked the woman with a violence that possessed her in an instant. "Not *remember* them? Leaking out of me? While my half-wit husband blubbed and wailed for what he thought was *his?* Oh, I *remember* them, you stupid cow, better than you'll ever know!"

Then, abruptly, her mood seemed to swing, again; corrosive anger replaced by a look of such malevolence that Theodosia thought her heart would freeze. "But neither of *those* babbies was the One, were they, Mrs Shopkeeper? Even *you* must see that now? Couldn't have been, could they, poor little blobs? Not with you and that old bastard Neille still unpunished."

"*Unpunished?* Oh, for the love of God, Hepzibah, what punishment could still be due for something done so long ago?" She was pleading now, attempting to grasp any shred of reason that might remain in the young woman's head.

"It was a vile, senseless crime, an act of barbarity carried out in the names of God and Justice! But how can *I* be held responsible for it? What purpose can my death serve?"

Suddenly, Hepzibah Sharratt was in her face, nails raking into her plaited hair, spittle spraying Theodosia's features as the pinioned woman shrank back in revulsion.

"*Let my blood be upon them and their children!*" she shrieked. "My child will *live* when the last of you has gone to the flames, when the last debt is paid! *Only then!*"

"But, Hepzibah," the desperate woman cried into the demented face above her, "You can never *bear* another child! You *know* that!" As the words left her mouth, she knew she was a dead woman.

Hepzibah Sharratt sat back on her heels for a moment, apparently lost in thought, before jumping to her feet and looking enquiringly about the Museum, as if for the first time. "Ah yes, there you are," she said brightly, lifting the first of the lamps and listening, appreciatively to the slosh of oil within it. Removing the glass chimney and laying it carefully to one side, she set the lamp down again and walked to her bag.

The bound woman could only watch in horrified fascination.

"First things first," Hepzibah said, removing a small stoppered bottle and a cloth. Even before she uncorked it, Theodosia knew what it contained. She tried to pray, but no words would come, as the colourless liquid was upended onto a wadded cloth and the choking stench of ether filled the air.

"I told him once – your husband – that I was in his debt. This is quittance. You'll feel no pain."

They were the last words.

(50)

In the little Cabinet next the passage: the Eggs of a
Land Snail lately discovered in Tobago, the tail and
claws of the Bever, the Tatowing Instrument.

The barouche stood, like the sentinel it was, close to the ramshackle stable gate at the rear of Saddler Street. Panting, dishevelled, the
Apothecary had rounded the corner of Bore Street, before pulling
his limping mount into the first yard he encountered, as soon as
he'd caught sight of the coach. One glimpse of the empty street
had been enough; the horses were tethered to the garden wall,
muzzles bowed in nosebags, but Blain was nowhere to be seen.
Inside the stable, watching the back gate to the garden – that was
where Greene guessed he'd be. How, then, to draw him out without squandering precious minutes, if his guess was right?

As the Apothecary looked down to check the priming of his
pistol, he saw the scatter of wind-blown fir cones at his feet. He
had his answer. Gathering several handfuls of the dry husks he
pocketed them hurriedly before emerging from the yard, leaving the roan tethered to a scruffy conifer. Keeping close against
the walls and yards to his left hand, he approached his own gate
along the broken footway. As he came up to the bleached planks,
repaired and bodged a score of times in the years since they'd
taken up residence, he thanked Providence for their decrepitude.
Through the roughly boarded gaps, a tendril of pipe smoke drifted, the Apothecary catching just a whiff of its fragrance before the
breeze tugged it away. Standing hard against the heavy gatepost,
he cocked the pistol in one hand. With the other he pitched the

(247)

first of the cones at the withers of the nearest carriage horse. With a whinny of alarm, it bucked in its traces, head tugging at its halter as it tried to turn, shying now, in alarm as the second and third of the small missiles struck home. Both began to paw noisily, hooves clattering against the paving, the light coach swaying alarmingly behind them.

The Stable gate screeched open, as Blain, cursing, hurried out to the source of the commotion. As he emerged, the Apothecary's booted foot tripped him – Blain's own impetus sending him sprawling headlong, a short-barrelled gun flying from his hands as he tried to break his fall.

He rolled as he struck a wheel, blood blossoming from his cheek, his face twisted with shock and a wild fury. Even before he spoke he was grappling at his belt. "You're dogmeat, cunt!" he snarled, his blade, free of its sheath, already arcing back for its throw. Unwittingly, the sprawled man's hand and knife struck heavily at the fetlock of the horse behind him, and, even before Greene could react to the threat, the frightened animal did so. Spooked already by the cones and the turmoil that had erupted from the stable gate, it kicked wildly against the fresh attack, both its rear hooves smashing against the carriage and whatever else they met.

The Apothecary shrank back, the barouche threatening to topple towards him, as both horses trampled and reared in fright, Blain already motionless beneath their hooves. Greene took one look at the twisted, bloodied head, lolling at each fresh strike of the iron shoes. *Enough.* He ran for the gate.

Heedless of the blurred face glimpsed through the scullery window, its mouth opened in surprise, the Apothecary wrenched open the passage door and ran for the stairs. The rank stench met him as he climbed.

She heard the doors and the boots upon the stairs, as she backed away from the candle stub, its little dance of flame now bright against the dark boards on which it stood. A little less than half an inch of life remained for the unmoving woman, mirrored in the lamp oil pooled around her and soaking her skirts.

Let him watch, then, the other thought, placid, now. Picking up her canvas bag she stepped quietly behind the door and looked to her pistol. The boots reached the first landing, pausing, irresolute. She read the silence with a small smile touching her lips. The boots began to climb again; slower, more guarded, now. *No, he shan't watch*, she decided. *I shall kill him as he comes through the door. He'll only try to spoil everything.*

As he reached the landing, the tableau that met his eyes seemed to suck what little air remained from his lungs, the chemical stench searing his eyes and nose with its bite. Aghast, he took in the sight through the open door: Theodosia, slumped against her bonds, her head sunk, her face unreadable beneath a tangle of disordered hair; the oil, the flame. *A black wing, beating, beating, against the dying light.*

With a bellow of rage he threw his pistol aside and launched himself through the low doorway, diving, both hands stretched out, towards the tiny stub and its shimmer of incandescence.

It was the dive that saved him.

The pistol shot exploded above him as he hit the sopping boards, its ball shattering the window leads where his head should have been. A splinter lanced into his thigh but his cry was lost as he cannoned into his wife's legs, smashing the candle aside in a wild, flailing sweep that sent it across to roll, extinguished instantly, into the passageway ahead. With agility born of desperation, he was back on his feet in an instant, hauling himself up against the heavy chair, spinning to face the black-haired woman, crouched now, behind the open door. He stepped, urgently, in front of the inert form of his wife, putting himself between the two women. As he did, a faint groan escaped Theodosia's lips and his heart soared. *She was alive.* Scarcely able to breathe in the miasmic air, his eyes blurred with tears, he stood, panting, wheezing, and tried to focus on the figure of the young woman.

She seemed diminished, somehow, shrunken and feral, as she crouched at bay.

"It's finished, Hepzibah. He's dead."

She straightened, looking puzzled, her head tilted to one side, black hair tumbling over her shoulder.

"Ned's dead. Blain, too. It's all over. Give me your gun."

Her body jerked and she straightened, though her eyes seemed focused on another place, another man. Her hand dropped to her side, as she began to shake her head from side to side.

"No, no, can't be so," she began, in a sing-song whisper, which gradually built in its intensity as she repeated the words like some nightmare rhyme. Abruptly she stopped, the sky-blue marvel of her eyes suddenly flaring with recognition as she took in the figure of Richard Greene. She raised the pistol and fired its second barrel.

As the gun came up the Apothecary threw himself back, shielding his wife as he tumbled, heavily, against her knees. The bullet cut a slash of agony across his shoulder, missing Theodosia by a hairsbreadth as Greene sprawled across her.

With a howl of frustrated malice, Hepzibah Sharratt hurled the useless weapon at them and ran for the door.

Greene fell to his knees beside the moaning woman who was beginning to struggle weakly against her ropes and raised her chin in his cupped hand. The grey-green eyes flickered in recognition.

Jumping to his feet, skidding, sliding, across the treacherous floor to a wall-mounted display, the Apothecary pulled down a tomahawk. He hacked through the ropes with frantic urgency, careless of the blood already staining his chest and arm. As the last coil fell free, he gripped both her arms and gasped: "I'll be back, my love! Back in an *instant!* Don't try to move."

She could only whimper in response, and Greene felt the fury course back into him.

Stooping to pick up the pistol he'd thrown aside, the Apothecary scrambled down the familiar stairs. He was guided, half way down, by the sound of breaking glass from the shop below. Heedless, now, of anything but the rage that drove him, Richard Greene burst into the shop to see the wild-eyed woman clawing at the street door.

She turned, groping blindly on the counter at her side, and hurled a pestle at his head. As it smashed against the cabinet behind him, the first cries of alarm sounded from the street outside, shapes bobbing and weaving beyond the coloured glass.

Greene ducked, as a brass mortar hurtled towards him, protected only by the countertop as it slammed past. As he rose, Hepzibah Sharratt ran back towards the cash desk, away from the urgent shouts and knocking sounding at the door and windows.

"There's nowhere left to go. Stop now, Hepzibah, for the love of God!" He raised the pistol. "I'm as prepared to use this as you ever were."

"*Love? God?*" she shrieked. "You don't know what the words mean, you little streak of piss!"

She backed away in a crouch, cornered, as he began to approach, across the floor. Looking desperately about her, her eyes suddenly fixed on the array of bottles left beside Theodosia's desk. Grabbing the first to hand, she turned, smirking in momentary triumph as the Apothecary stopped dead, frozen by the sight of what she held.

It was one of the acids, the ribbed green glass of its jar half full of liquid.

Frowning with concentration, she seemed to read: *Aqua Fortis*, her lips forming the words, though no sound came out.

As the Apothecary watched with sickened fascination, she appeared to conduct a brief, unintelligible conversation with herself, before carefully easing out the glass stopper.

Greene began to back away, but the black-haired woman no longer seemed to see him. She first peered at the stopper in her hand and then lifted the bottle in a single motion to her mouth.

Instinct erupted within the small man and he leapt towards her.

"*No!*" he screamed, revulsion tearing at his throat.

The perfect lips closed around the rim, and the bottle tipped back, all in the blink of an eye.

The effect was instantaneous. The vocal chords seared away before she could scream; a vomiting gout of blood and burning mucus spewing from the blistering wound where her mouth had been, her tongue a charring worm in a smoking crater. In deranged agony, as her body spasmed and thrashed on the floor and the nauseating sweetness of burning flesh fouled the air, Hepzibah Sharratt was consumed.

As the clamour outside rose to uproar, Richard Greene dropped to his knees and wept.

51

ITEM:

In a lofty glass case are these articles brought from Otaheita and
O-why-ye: A Formee or Military Gorget worn by the Warriors,
composed of Feathers of the Tropic Bird, Teeth of the Shark
and fringed with the Hair of a White Dog in a curious manner;
a shield of twisted Cordage coiled up in an artful manner.

As in so many other things, Theodosia Greene had been proved
right. The cost was prohibitive, the waters were noisome and
the company was proving little better – especially out of season,
though neither of her companions seemed, at all, to mind.

Whilst not actually discouraging company, the somewhat odd
trio were seen all around Bath, taking chocolate here, sipping a
cordial there, but always seeming so *complete* in each other's company, one sensed it would have been an impertinence to intrude.

The Officer of Engineers, gap-toothed, resplendent in redcoat
and nose-splint, cut a well-mannered dash on Milsom Street as he
handed the fine-looking woman in and out of coaches and chairs.
She, though – opinion noted – seemed prey to the damp vapours
of the city, needing frequent recourse to a cambric handkerchief
into which she coughed discreetly.

The small, scarred man, arm bound up – so *mysteriously* – in
its sling, limped at their side. He appeared to be recovering from
a long illness. He was seen rather less about the *Emporia*, even
though, one gathered, *his* was the pocket book providing the mil-
linery and *objets bijoux* that so delighted the pale lady. He would
gravely settle in cash for everything, whenever there was a delivery
to the pretty house in Rivers Street.

All in all, Trade decided, these were visitors of a most *satis-factory* stamp for early spring. *Le Beau Monde* – at this time of year absent in its elegant entirety – would scarcely have deigned to notice.

Returning before the early dusk to a house already bright with candle-lamps, Colonel Henry Copeland and Mrs Theodosia Greene had spent a most engaging afternoon at *Piquet* in the nearby Assembly Rooms. They'd ensconced themselves at a baize-covered table near one of the fireplaces, enjoying a steady succession of *amuse-bouches* and bowls of tea as they played. The white-gloved attendants, only too pleased to receive paying custom on a leaden afternoon, were most attentive.

"It really is rather like having the whole place to one's self," enthused Theodosia, kissing her husband lightly on his brow.

"How has your afternoon gone, Richard?" she enquired, adding: "Should you not be wearing your spectacles, my dear?" before he could respond.

The owner of the tired eyes smiled up at the woman in his life. "Really rather well, Theodosia. Would you care to read it?"

Passing the sheet to his wife, he stood, rubbing his hands together. "It must be about that time, don't you think, Harry?"

As the men moved away to the decanters set out on a highly polished dresser, she sat and read the well-loved hand, its curlicues and quirks set neatly on the page.

An Organ; built originally by Father Smith for the uſe of the Catholic Church of Lichfield, after its deſtruction by the Fanatics during the Oliverian Uſurpation, when no part of that goodly fabric fit for the celebration of Divine Service was left, but the Chapter Houſe: thiſ inſtrument at the reſtoration of the Church by Bishop Hacket was removed and placed in a loft of the Lady Choir, where it stood for many years, no uſe being made of it.
In the year 1740 it was taken down and placed in the Vicars Hall.

In the year 1745, at the late Rebellion, a large number of his Majesty's soldiers being quartered in that room, it was taken and broken open and the pipes (mostly of wood) were burnt; in this condition it was taken by the late Dean Penny, given to Mr John Alcock, then the Organist; who having for some time made use of it as a cloaths press or cupboard, in the year 1746 sold it to the present owner, who by the assistance of the recently deceased Mr Adcock of Leicester Fields, London, has restored it. It has a stopped Diapafon and principal of Wood, a twelfth and fifteenth of Metal.

It was only when she'd finished reading that Theodosia Greene began to realise just how much her husband must be missing his business and his Museum.

It had been the day after the unspeakable, as all three of them sat nursing their wounds, that the Apothecary seemed struck by a sudden thought.

"Our supposed departure was due two days hence, was it not? On Saturday? Everything is booked and organised down to the smallest detail, the better to lend conviction to our subterfuge? Why, even Tillett and the boy believe it, still! *I* believe we should turn fancy into fact. In fact, I am *convinced* of it!"

The others had regarded him with exhausted indifference until his words began to sink in.

"What, up-sticks? Now of all times?" the soldier had mumbled through swollen lips, seeming about to reject the notion out of hand. Then he'd paused, looking across to Theodosia wrapped in several shawls and looking drained of all her colour and vitality.

"Although… ," he'd continued, thoughtfully, "perhaps it *is* the way we can begin to put the monstrosity behind us. Once you've made your report to the Coroner, and I've said my piece, there would be nothing to detain us."

"*Exactly!*" said Richard Greene, with distressing brightness, "My *very* thought!"

He had taken his wife's limp hand. "Will you trust me in this, my dear?" he'd said, gently. "I know it to be the right prescription!"

Six weeks on, the Apothecary's wife sat in their modestly elegant accommodation warming to the memory. She gazed across at the two men, standing against the heavy drapes of the bay window engaged in animated conversation as they watched the world pass by. A woman would be grateful to have even one such in her life, she thought. "Richard, I do believe we should be thinking of home before too long."

The night before their departure, a theatre party was determined upon as their final foray into city society. They arrived in some style, their coach drawing up outside the newly built playhouse in good time for the promenade and refreshments.

Through a rank of flambeaux, they left the ebb and flow of traffic and entered the gilded foyer, already a-buzz with chatter and laughter, the milling crowd lit to perfection by spectacular chandeliers.

As Theodosia surveyed the powdered, glittering throng, a voice called out and a strikingly angular woman could be seen waving a fan, imperiously, in their direction. An equally sharp-featured man materialised at her side, looking hard across the foyer's jostle.

"Why, it's Lizzie *Hoare*, Richard!" exclaimed Theodosia, "Her husband, too! I'd recognise that yellow dress anywhere."

Greene could only grunt in reply, deriving conspicuously little pleasure from the prospect of renewing that particular acquaintance, though it was obviously too late to avoid it.

"How d'you do, Sir," the banker said, his features registering scarcely more enthusiasm when introductions were made. "Hardly expected to see you here, Greene, such a long way from home."

"No further than it was for you, Sir, when we shared the hospitality of William Clarke – and of course, the Blanchmaynes."

Looking hard at the Apothecary before he replied, Hoare

lowered his voice to reply. "Look, I was as sorry as the next man about Billy Clarke, but I'll be *damned* if I'll have his death laid at my door. I know your game, Sir!" He glanced, edgily, around him. "This is neither the time nor the place for it."

The women were already absorbed in chatter and were paying not the slightest heed as the Apothecary replied: "What *game* might that be, Sir? And why should I bother to play one at all? I have the great good fortune to be my own man – beholden to neither *your* good offices nor the goodwill of your bank – a double blessing as both commodities would appear to be in such short supply."

"*Dammit!*"

Heads began to turn around them.

"The writ against Blanchmayne was a business matter. Our ... *acquaintance* ... didn't come into it."

"Of that, at least, I am assured," Greene said evenly, "for what type of man would subject even something as slight as *acquaintance* to the odium of a debtors' prison if it could be avoided? It was merely *business*, of course, though surely not of any great acuity? For how might a man make restitution – for another's fraud – when he's behind bars, pray?"

White with annoyance, Hoare hissed: "You'll be blaming me for that poor, mad girl's death too, no doubt?"

By now, both wives had stopped and were staring in concern at what was rapidly becoming a public spectacle.

"For *that*, Sir, no, I do not, though can you be certain that the *next* loan you call in so readily, the *next* luckless family you ruin – in, of course, the name of *business* – does not end in just such extremity? It seems to me that you are only too *pleased* to welcome the bearers of bulging purses and pocketbooks to your club and a damn' sight too *ready* to throw them to the wolves when their wallets are empty."

"Blanchmayne has been *released*, damn you!" The banker was, by now, spluttering with anger. "Young Sharratt stood surety for him when his late wife's monies were discovered. I saw to it without delay, even though it means waiting for probate!"

"I imagine Isiah's gratitude for such selfless action knew no bounds," said Greene, turning then to his wife. "I fear that I've lost my taste for further entertainment, this evening, Theodosia, but at least we can take comfort in the knowledge that the profits of Hoare's Bank are no longer in jeopardy."

"Then I'll keep you company, Mr Greene," said Theodosia, linking his arm.

"Much as I should enjoy hearing even more about the wonders of Bristol, we've an early start in the morning – back to our little *Island of Tranquillity*."

52

ITEM:

Over the Closet Door: of exceding antiquity, the Horns of an Oroch, red-stained by the Irish Peat in which they were found.

His companions' capacity for sleep continued to amaze Richard Greene: neither lurch, sway, rattle nor jolt seeming to intrude on their noisy repose as they joined the coach's other occupants in snoring away the interminable miles.

The past weeks, the Apothecary reflected, had done more to restore all three of them than he could have imagined, and they were returning home like different beings to the spent and tattered invalids who had set out from Lichfield only weeks earlier.

They'd left behind them the hubbub of plasterers, glaziers, joiners and well-wishers – let alone the usual gawpers and ghouls – that had descended on the shop in Saddler Street over the days before their departure.

What could not be left behind, though, were the images, the sights and sounds, of the several waking nightmares each had endured. And yet – Greene marvelled – somewhere along the way, perhaps in the sulphurous fog of the ancient Baths or perhaps in the third bottle shared around a dinner table, *somewhere* the healing had begun.

That they'd been so damaged could come as no surprise, the Apothecary decided. The fact that they'd managed to come through it as they had, though – *that* was little short of miraculous.

As for those others, though – whether any such miracle could be wrought for a husband widowed in such grotesque circumstances, or a father paralysed with grief – these were not matters that the Apothecary could bear to dwell upon. Neither could have been spared the complete revelation of Hepzibah's dementia, though knowledge of even a part of it would have been enough to test most men.

Liquor and pillow talk had given the girl the means to bind her uncle, threatening to divulge his embezzlement unless it could be made to serve them both.

She could steal from a father she loathed, just as well as Ned Blanchmayne could rob a brother he despised. Perhaps, mused Greene, that was how they'd found one another.

The identity – or lack of one – of a corpse carted in from Shenstone was never about to be confused with that of a dead man in Connecticut. This one though, in life, had come close to murdering a Colonel of Engineers, who may well have succumbed to his wounds but for the timely arrival of the Lichfield Constables.

It had been revealed to the hastily convened Civic officers, that Colonel Copeland – by merest chance – believed he had recognised a colonial deserter and felon and had decided to confront him in the proper manner. It was only thus that he had managed to intervene in such timely fashion in his subsequent defence of Mrs Sharratt.

The Coroner's Court heard how this brute he had happened upon was preying on the trust and sensibilities of a young, emotionally disturbed compatriot and had doubtlessly gained access to her by means of her wretched servant. He and the man Blain had been seen drinking together on various occasions in a low Inn at Wall, the Court learned. The manservant, now a hopeless, drooling cripple, since being trampled beneath his own horses, would never speak again – if, indeed, he survived his injuries.

The Coroner learned how the Officer of Engineers had surprised the first blackguard in the very act of forcing himself upon his unsuspecting and terrified victim – and set upon him, in her defence. She, in turn, had fled the scene in shame and horror, the brutal assault – as it would later emerge – having served to unbalance her reason utterly.

Now in fear for his position, her manservant had rushed his near-hysterical mistress back to Lichfield, to that source of ministration that had already, once before, been her salvation: Apothecary Greene. The Court had been invited to imagine the callous disregard Blain would have shown for his hapless horses on that drive and – once having delivered Mrs Sharratt to her destination – how it would have been in a belated move to calm the frenzied animals that he had fallen foul of his own cruelty.

To round off the catalogue of horrors, the post-mortem report on the self-immolation of Richard Greene's lunatic patient – within the Apothecary's own premises at Saddler Street – proved to be more than most in the stuffy Guild Chamber could stomach.

In the face of such grotesqueries, the wafer-thin rationale woven behind them had been grasped with a fervour that surprised neither Apothecary nor Officer of Engineers. *For this or any other Court to have been presented with even a fraction of the actualities would have taken it into realms unimagined; realms so utterly beyond its comprehension or redress that nothing but unending misery and impotent recrimination could have come of it. Better that a father and a husband, might, at least, be given a chance to limp away with what little was left to them.*

This was what they'd determined upon, the Apothecary, his wife, and the soldier – for better or worse – in the certainty that there exists more than one species of truth. They were left to mourn the victims of a pitiless delusion, it being the price they had agreed upon.

Their final change of horses, at *The Star* in Birmingham, meant that for his travelling companions, Lichfield was little more than a snooze away. For the Apothecary, though, the familiar miles that passed allowed a final, sombre, reverie before life caught up with them all once more.

One twisted, rat-tail of a question had been answered when

he'd least expected it, in the shop, of all places, on the morning of their departure. Although officially closed, and with the worst of the cleaning-up barely completed, he'd looked up from the last prescription left to fill, to see Frederick Vale fidgeting in the doorway – to the obvious annoyance of the glazier at work there. Before he could be discouraged, the whey-faced bookman had called out: "May I have a brief word with you Mr Greene? I shan't detain you more than a moment, Sir."

There had been little the Apothecary could do, but invite him in.

Once there, in the shop's low-ceilinged intimacy, the man's embarrassment became almost palpable.

"Mr Vale, how can I be of assistance? Forgive me, but my time is at a premium this morning. I must hurry you."

"I felt I should, well, somehow, pay my respects, Mr Greene."

"Your *respects*? Forgive me, I don't follow you," said Greene, failing to keep the impatience from his voice.

"Well, it's just that with there being no answer at the Prebendary House – with it all locked up – I didn't know where else to come. This is where she ... where it *happened*, after all, so, I thought... ," he tailed off in embarrassment.

"Pay your respects to the late Mrs Sharratt, d'you mean?" said Greene. "Now I understand. If you'll forgive me for saying so, I'm surprised you knew the lady, Mr Vale. She was a very *private* person."

"Oh yes, Mr Greene. She came in to the Library any number of times, always content to rummage about – not like *some*," he added, with his habitual sniff of disapproval.

"She was always a proper lady and must have made her poor father proud. Even borrowed books for him – how's that for thoughtful? A good daughter, without a doubt – and a beautiful wife for poor Mr Sharratt."

"I can see how much you admired her, Mr Vale. I can't say I'm surprised – there was, indeed, something singular about her.

Apropos her borrowings, did she, by any chance, sign herself as Blanchmayne? I believe I saw that name, though not Sharratt, when last I borrowed from you?"

"I *do* believe she did," mused Vale, then he brightened. "Why yes, I'm *certain* of it! She was borrowing for her father, after all. Though why do you ask, Mr Greene?"

"Oh, who knows where our minds lead us, at times, Mr Vale. It is of no import, I assure you." He moved, pointedly, towards the door.

"I shall be certain that your respects are passed on, Mr Vale. Both Mr Blanchmayne and Mr Sharratt will need all the comfort that can be afforded in the weeks to come. Thank you for your visit. It has meant more than you know."

With a shriek of springs the coach lurched into a deep pothole, all the passengers thrown in unison to one side.

"Are we there yet," yawned the Apothecary's wife, her eyes still closed.

"Not quite yet, my Dear. We've just passed Bassett's Pole," he said, refraining from any mention of the gibbet, seen silhouetted against the afternoon sky.

"Bassett's *Hole* more-like," grumbled Copeland. "I'll settle for manoeuvres any day."

"I swear I'll sleep for a week when I climb into my own bed," murmured Theodosia.

Unbidden, as the gallows dwindled behind them, Greene's mind drifted back to the pathetic dupe who'd have filled just such a cage. *Reckon you could fix it for me walk to the 'angman, do you, Mister?* Ned Blanchmayne had denied Jack Davey that walk.

Copeland had told Greene of the American's drunken laughter as he boasted of the cold-blooded killing. Fortunately, the Apothecary had been spared the sound of it.

"Can do it when the fancy takes me, Harry-Boy – but left the rest of 'em to your sweetheart! She never stops fancying it! I've got you all to myself, though."

He'd not been ready for Copeland's move, hands burst free, hurling himself and the stool which still held him, away from the slashing blade. The broken bottle opened Blanchmayne's thigh first, then finished him as they'd rolled amidst the shards. The soldier would never talk of it again.

As the City finally came into view, the Apothecary gazed expansively at the familiar skyline. Over to the left, the Ladies of the Vale, the twin spires standing in the shadow of the great steeple, to the centre – St Mary's – rising above the Marketplace. To the left, on its wooded eminence, St Michael, up on Greenhill.

Shortly, once the Grammar School was past, The Friary would be coming up on the left.

By the time she was ten, the girl could shoot the eye from a pheasant, or so Isiah used to boast. She must have still been up there, in the darkness behind the swinging pane, with one of Ned's rifles. The walnut-skinned man, hat pulled low had been nothing more than a sentinel.

"You know nothing, Mrs Greene! Do not suppose otherwise, or I shall disappoint you more!"

She would have stood, upstairs, on the darkened landing at Dam Street, too, gazing; purloined medication in one hand, canvas bag in another, through to an old man napping on his bed. There'd been medication for Pomlett, too, smeared onto barbs and left to hook him.

Again, as so often in the past weeks, the Apothecary silently begged for forgiveness – so many missed promptings, so many instances of the fingerpost overlooked. *So much death.*

The arrival of the coach in the bustling yard of The George shook Greene from his mood. The questions – or at least those that could be formed – were answered now.

53

ITEM:

On a board with a antique frame, gilded, a painting by Leonard di Vinci, of our Saviour; a front Face, the two fore Fingers of his right Hand erect, as giving his benediction, in his left, a Crystal Mound; the height of this Picture within the Frame measures twelve inches, breadth, ten inches. A Landfcape in Nun's Work.

As the last of the baggage was delivered to Saddler Street, the heavy, canvas-wrapped roll was manhandled up to the topmost floor. Richard Greene had refused to divulge its contents when it had arrived at the elegant door of the house in Rivers Street, prepared, infuriatingly, to say no more than: "You will approve, Theodosia, never fear."

He followed its passage into the first of his Museum rooms, directing the porters to leave it against a wall of displays.

"My wife will see that you're looked after, lads. Many thanks."

Left alone, he stood back to examine the expanse of floor ahead. Just as he'd expected, no amount of bleaching and re-staining had removed the lamp-oil stain – its shadow spread like some dark continent, mapped across the old oak boards. He strode to the stand of blades against the wall and selected one, returning to carefully slit the long sack-wrapped roll open. He'd barely spread the richly coloured carpet when he heard her footsteps on the stairs.

She found him standing in the doorway, his back to her as he gazed across the floor. As she came up behind him, placing her arms around his waist, he said: "It's from a people called the

Balooch, I was informed. D'you see the blues in the weave? They're almost black. It's very old."

She stood close against him, looking across the covered boards. "You were correct, Husband, I *do* approve."

As they came down later, they were met at every turn by the lingering tang of paint and varnish, overlaid with notes of lavender and fresh polish. Down below, a cross-section of the City's artisans had left pristine shop premises, still redolent of new wood and plaster, where Tillett and the boy had reigned supreme these past weeks.

The shop-man, almost jellied with apprehension, had hardly believed his own ears when informed that his position was secure despite his role in the tragedy. His loyalty and diligence during the Apothecary's absence had been little short of exemplary, opinion agreed. The boy had seemed especially delighted at his master's return.

Richard and Theodosia Greene were settling to a high tea when the commotion erupted below, and they stared at each other in sudden apprehension.

"Dead? I'll show the Dog who's dead! Greene! Greene, I say! Come down, Sir, and explain yourself, if y'can!"

A beam of relief spread across the Apothecary's unremarkable features.

"Don't be alarmed my dear, I do believe it's Sir Eldon Pagnell. I seem to recall that, recently, we may have taken his name in vain – so to speak."

As the small man hurried to the landing, he turned back to his wife.

"At times such as this, thanks should be offered that we are not the proprietors of a china shop."

f i n i s

Acknowledgements

My particular thanks go to Joanne Wilson, Museum & Heritage Officer at the Samuel Johnson Birthplace Museum, for her unstinting help in providing access to the prized copy of Greene's 1786 Museum Catalogue, items from which feature as chapter headings in each of the Apothecary Greene novels. In addition, the original catalogue frontis appears as an insert in the opening text.

The image of The Friary grave slab (p.11) was recorded by Richard Greene in 1746 and appeared as a woodcut later that year in The Gentleman's Magazine. It was subsequently reproduced in Stebbing-Shaw's *History and Antiquities of Staffordshire* in 1798. The original slab, now much eroded, can still be seen, built in to the back wall of The Friary – now part of the Lichfield campus of South Staffordshire College.

The design/typographic expertise of Steph Thelwell and Noel Robson has made a sterling contribution in the solving of typographic conundrums arising from coping with 250-year-old text, whilst Tom O'Reilly at Page d'Or has demonstrated near-saintly patience and fortitude in his editing skills, coordination and encouragement.

Thanks also to photographers Barry Slemmings and to Bob Yeatman of Eastern Lightcraft.

Finally, to Ralph James, MBE, Chevalier dans L'Ordre des Palmes Academiques. MBE. Erstwhile bookseller of Lichfield, early fount of much advice and encouragement.

The Bishop's Grimoire

Whilst visiting Eccleshall Castle, palatial country residence of Lichfield's perennially absent bishop, Richard Greene witnesses the chance discovery of an ancient iron box, secreted in the ruins of a medieval gatehouse. Glimpsing its contents, the Apothecary mystifies his companions by insisting that the book revealed within must be approached with great caution. An arcane symbol partially visible on its cover identifying it as a work of ritual magic: A Grimoire.

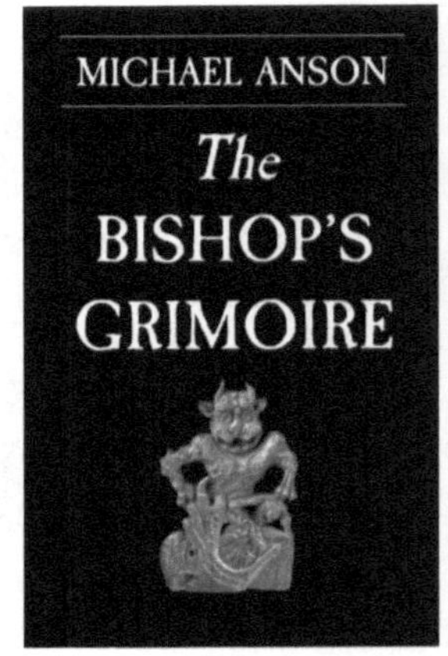

Now begins a series of malign coincidences, frighteningly inexplicable occurrences and the unwelcome realisation that the book is now actively being sought; a fact confirmed by attempted burglary and aggressive confrontations with the intimidating agent of an unknown principal. The provenance and authenticity of the age-old book identify it as an incredibly rare survival – a 'Black Legend', stolen five centuries earlier from the Vatican library, owned – and hidden – by Walter de Langton, a bishop of Lichfield who had stood trial for witchcraft around the year 1200 in Rome.

No one can envisage the approaching cataclysm: the collision of a demonic, stygian past with the presence of the prophet of Reason and the Nobility of untainted Mankind. In Greene's desperation that the book must somehow be destroyed, he unwittingly sets that scene.

As demented obsession turns to poisoning and murderous abduction, Greene must fight for more than life itself, burdened with the terrifying knowledge of what 'The Bishop's Grimoire' contains ... and seeks.

The Ashmole Box

Providential chance brings Apothecary Richard Greene to the aid of a terribly injured man – the victim of a mantrap on a nearby estate. An encounter that will ultimately reveal the survival of an astonishing Roman artefact – and with appalling symmetry – bring about not only the deaths of all who seek to gain from its discovery but also force Greene into questioning the passions and principles that have been the touchstones of his life.

Beside that unravelling strand of sadistic cruelty, deprivation and corrosive greed, another narrative begins – a story close-on a century and a half in the making – when The Ashmole Box (and the deathless mystery it conceals) arrive at Greene's Museum door.

Somehow, then, as if the veil of time itself is pierced, a revenant, a memory so real in both its power to mystify, to terrify, is summoned by the opening of the long-forgotten bequest. A half-seen presence in a tower consigned to memory, a pointing figure glimpsed in a flag-draped aisle, a nightmare vision of a dance of death.

With every passing day the years that separate the long-dead Ashmole and the hapless inheritors of his legacy seem to dissolve and intertwine, as first one and then another of the cryptic pointers yield their secrets and point the way to a discovery beyond the Apothecary's wildest imagining.

To a place of ancient wonder whose guardian is Death.

An extract from

The Bishop's Grimoire
by Michael Anson

(1)

A Knot and Crucifix in Silver, richly ornamented with Jewelry
Work, fuppofed to have been worn by a Cardinal at Rome, on
his Cloak or Mantle An ancient Crucifix in Silver, fuspended
by a Chain, compofed of three hollow filver Beads;the back part
may be opened, in which are feperate Cells for Relics, &c.

Eccleshall Castle, Staffordshire. Spring 1766. The tour was
going from bad to worse. The regrettable fact that a perennially absent bishop had, reportedly, waved a ringed hand in lordly
acquiescence to the proposal that 'visitors of quality' be admitted
in order to admire his rural palace was one thing, the *actuality*
of these over-educated *gawpers* quite another – as a thoroughly
disgruntled Steward was rapidly deciding. The realisation that he
had greeted the visitors' wholly unexpected arrival with a mis-but-
toned waistcoat and recent egg stains on a brocaded lapel would
only become apparent to him when such incidental mishaps had
long paled into insignificance in the face of the day's calamities.

The first of what were to become the afternoon's legion problems was the weather: a perfect blue sky with a proper comple-
ment of fluffy clouds and the most unseasonal warmth in living
memory. Warmth perfectly acceptable in and of itself, but considerably less so in conjunction with the second week of a drainage

(270)

programme intended to clear a noisome, centuries-old moat and the castle's attendant marshes. The stench, even he had to admit, was so bad as to be almost visible, a miasma hanging across formal gardens, topiary and classical terrace alike. A stench that had met today's visitors as they were confronted by the occasion's second problem: the transit of the moat's residual ooze across an alarmingly makeshift bridge erected beside its sturdy medieval counterpart (access to the latter now being blocked by a rubble-filled cart half-emerged from the scaffolded ruin of a gatehouse apparently in the process of demolition by the dozens of labourers swarming about its ivied walls). Instead of the anticipated rapid transit between their coach and the elegant portal of the great house itself, the passengers were forced to negotiate the alarmingly unsteady span, clinging to grimy, roped balustrades whilst attempting to avoid any downward glances at what lay beneath the rough planking. In various degrees of disarray, the visitors regrouped on the perfect lawn, to be met by the stiffly liveried figure who hurried towards them, attempting – without success – to disguise his perplexity.

"We are expected, I believe?" said the older of two clergymen, clearly aware, already, that they were not but stepping forward from his companions with what appeared to be a folded letter extended to the nonplussed Steward.

"His Grace, your master, assured us of our welcome, today... ," he glanced briefly at a pocket watch drawn from his waistcoat and continued, pleasantly: "...at two o'clock in the afternoon. So, here we are."

There was nothing to be done other than a mumbled assent to a visitor obviously not prepared to debate the point, so with all the dignity the Steward could muster they were ushered into the mercifully cool welcome of a spacious hall, redolent of lavender, beeswax and the memories of winter logs consumed in the stately fireplace.

The smallest member of the foursome, now gazing with

interest about them, was a quietly dressed, unremarkable figure obviously relieved to be free of the confining vehicle and the unexpected rite of passage, fanning himself with a slim pamphlet. While a cordial was being summoned for his fellow visitors, he left the group to examine a display of blue and white china on a pair of consoles set against the panelled wall. Failing to notice a rug spread on the tiled floor, he was suddenly reduced to a flailing, ungainly welter of arms and legs, as it slipped from beneath him, and he fought desperately for balance. It was only the intervention of his nearest companion that averted disaster, though not before a foot had connected with a table-edge and come within a heartbeat of dislodging a pair of lidded pots that tottered and slid towards disaster.

In a mixture of apparent solicitude and proprietorial panic, the Steward rushed forward, showing, the now-stable figure realised, a far greater concern for the china than for him.

"They're *armorials*, Sir, specially commissioned, only recently arrived from China and three years in the making," their red-faced host blurted by way of what might have been intended as explanation, but which emerged as petulant accusation. "My Lord would've had my head if they'd been... ." He seemed suddenly to remember his appointed role. "That is, I'm sorry if... ." Before he could compound his outburst, the clerical figure that had been standing beside a straight-backed, self-possessed young woman hurried forward as if to defuse the misfortune of the moment, exclaiming:

"Richard, you really must curb your enthusiasms or we shall be declared *personae non-grata* before we can even begin to take in the wonders of My Lord's Treasure House! I'm sure even Lionel will agree."

With a wan smile, the small man disengaged himself from the providential arm that had saved the situation and having adjusted a comically skewed wig turned, disarmingly, to the mortified Steward.

"Thankfully, it would appear that both your head and your master's pots are safe for the present. I must apologise for my clumsiness, as my wife is forever insisting. I shall proceed with caution, be assured."

Richard Greene and the grinning figure of his companion rejoined Cannon Seward and his daughter beside the hall's centrepiece, an elegant circular table displaying a large bronze of a roman charioteer in headlong gallop.

With a visible gulp of relief, the Bishop's Steward embarked upon what was obviously a well-practised introduction to the tour itinerary.

"In the absence of His Grace, Bishop Cornwallis, I am instructed to welcome you on his behalf to his rural seat and to express his Grace's regret that you find us in the throes of refurbishment and beautification of this ancient castle."

Greene couldn't help himself: "And would one be correct in assuming that an integral part of His Grace's scheme of beautification necessitates the demolition of Bishop Langton's ancient gatehouse to his equally ancient castle?"

The Steward stiffened and sniffed audibly before responding in an unsuccessful attempt to disguise his annoyance at the interruption: "I am not privy to His Grace's purposes, Sir, though I can attest to the dangerous condition of that old... ."

Lionel Blomefield laid a quietly restraining hand on his companion's arm, speaking for the first time: "I believe we are interrupting your flow, as it were, my good man – though I must share Mr Greene's disquiet at the sight that met our... ."

"What we are all saying, of course... ," Seward interposed, expertly, "... is pray continue; we can scarcely wait to see the wonders you are about to reveal."

At least partially mollified, the Steward attempted to regain his theme. "Built in 1305, by the Bishop Walter Langton as the rural seat of his Diocese of Lichfield... ."

"Our very own. He also built our... ," murmured Blomefield,

only to be silenced by a sharp glance from the Canon.

"Responsible also for the construction of the fortification of Lichfield's Cathedral Close," continued the Steward stiffly, "and the great bridge across the city's Vivarium."

"Whose draining we have resisted thus far…," added Lionel Blomefield, sotto voce to a companion who tried to ignore him.

"…and all these labours executed at a time when his Grace was also Chancellor of England to King Edward the First," the Steward continued manfully.

"Much as your master, our own dear Bishop, is burdened with The Deanery of Windsor and that of St Paul's simultaneously, in addition to the onerous responsibility of this, his own diocese," said the young woman, with smiling composure, linking arms with her parent as she spoke. "Where do these blessed men find the time and energy, one must wonder? It must surely be to do with what can only be described as little short of a *genius* for delegation – and the uncounted broad backs, such as yours, gentlemen… ." She embraced them all in a guileless gaze. "…prepared to shoulder ever-greater burdens in the cause of such elevated servants of the church."

The Steward knew that whatever was going on here, he didn't much care for it, so hurried on, staring hard into the middle distance.

"Bishop Langton's castle suffered such violence on behalf of the Royal cause during the Great Rebellion that, fifty years on, Bishop Lloyd had little choice but to demolish most of the ruins remaining and build this fine… ."

"A process that continues to this day, apparently," said Greene to no-one in particular.

"…House," the Steward managed, "with the gardens as we see them today laid down by his successor Bishop Hough."

"Gardens whose delights we shall have to forego, in the circumstances," added Canon Seward, unconsciously wrinkling his aquiline nose. "Had we but been forewarned of the inconvenience to which we are putting His Grace by such an untimely intrusion, we would have postponed a visit long anticipated."

Seeing the expression on the hopelessly wrong-footed Steward, the Canon took mercy and said breezily: "…But lead on, pray."

As one grand room led to another, with the party conducted through what appeared to be an ever-more costly gamut of elegance ranging from Chinoiserie to Roccoco, from Heppelwhite to Rubens, the Steward, – now obviously at ease with his role – read from brief notes pointing out Bishop Cornwaliss's additions to the collection. It became rapidly apparent, though, that any works pertaining to classical themes would be immediately claimed by an impossibly erudite young woman, determined to expound – at length – upon their mythology and everything else that sprang into an over-active mind.

As they were completing the tour, now returned to a grand salon overlooking the manicured lawns, the Canon's daughter paused beside a spectacular prospect of the Roman Forum set in a gargantuan gilded frame. After a moment's contemplation of the tumbled grandeur she turned to her companions: "Confronted with even the noblest ruins of antiquity, am I alone in wondering why there appears never to be sufficient funds, or will, to look to our own?"

"Anna…," her father began, a note of reproof in his voice.

"No Papa, dearest, forgive me, pray, but there must surely be a time when the nurture of our own dear old places, and, not least, the good folk who treasure them as much as we shall ever do, must be taken into account. Why, the Chapter House of our own Cathedral, His Grace's *own* cathedral, is as sorry a wreck as the estate cottages we passed not a mile from Eccleshall's gates."

"As is my porch at St. Mary's," said Blomefield with feeling. "Even the swifts have fled from it."

"And apparently Eccleshall's venerable gatehouse," added Greene, with a smile of pure mischief, "though that is more in the nature of a rookery one would imagine; while it still stands."

The Steward could no longer contain himself: "We are instructed on its dismantling following the unfortunate damage caused to His Grace's coach at the time of his last visit…."

"Would that have been early last year or was it in '64?" enquired Seward mildly, "time does so fly by."

Ignoring the implication, the Steward blustered on in an injured tone: "A chunk of masonry the size of my hand fell and broke one of the coach lamps, Sir, as my master's coach drove beneath. It could have been a grave accident…."

"Indeed, it could have scratched the paintwork," added Greene helpfully. "So what alternative was left to his Grace but to obliterate the offending monument?"

"Just so, Mr … Greene, just so," came the grateful response.

"Well. On that happy note I believe we should take our leave," Seward interposed briskly. "We have a long and dusty road ahead of us."

As they stood in the grand doorway once more, the Canon dug into a coat pocket, producing a small purse from which he extracted several coins, pressing them into the Steward's ready hand.

Just as he was about to make their farewells, a rumbling crash, shouts of alarm and a blood-curdling scream carried across the lawn from the wreckage of the gatehouse by the bridge. A complete corner of dressed stonework had collapsed, and a bloodied, half-buried figure could be discerned struggling weakly amidst the choking dust-cloud of rubble.

Greene was already running towards the scene, shouting back to the astonished Steward: "Boiling water, cloth for bandages, brandy! Quick! For pity's sake."

Blomefield turned to the dumbstruck Steward: "Mr Greene is a surgeon-apothecary – quickly, do as he says!"

Seeming to awaken from a stupor, the Steward turned, wordlessly, and hurried back into the house, shouting instructions.

Though moved as little as possible beyond the danger of further collapse, the injured man now lay, propped against the balustrade of the terrace with head, shoulder and both hands bandaged in torn bed sheets, his breath coming in hoarse wheezes, his eyes wild with shock. With propriety cast aside, Anna Seward, careless of grass-stains on her silken skirts, knelt beside him gently dabbing at the pallid skin with vinegar-dampened cloths.

He bent sideways, suddenly, gasping with pain, before vomiting onto the mown grass.

"Concussion," said the Apothecary with complete authority, turning to the concerned group gathered around them. "Does he live locally?"

"Less than a mile, Sir," a voice responded. "Us can get 'im 'ome on a barrow, like."

"Well, gently does it, if you do. Avoid jolting him. He must rest completely for several days, and drink plenty of well-boiled water."

"That'll be the day," another voice volunteered, met with relieved laughter from the assembled work gang.

Greene turned to the hovering presence of the Steward: "I would normally have my bag of tricks to hand, but not today. I suggest that your master would encourage you to send to Stafford for medical opinion once we have left. Fatalities on one's premises, engaged on one's business, do have a tendency to create much … inconvenience, as I'm sure you will appreciate. I feel sure His Grace will not begrudge the cost of comfrey balm and poultices for this poor fellow."

"No, Mr Greene. Certainly Mr Greene. I'm sure my master will be most…."

A shout interrupted him.

A dust-smeared figure, eyes bright in his filthy face, was coming towards them, stepping from the last of the strewn rubble. It held a sizeable object across spread hands.

Obviously recognising the approaching man, the Steward said: "It's Lowe, Tom Lowe," he gestured around the assembled workmen. "He's the Gaffer here."

"Found this, Sir," said the dust-caked man to the Steward,

"Right behind where all that sh … stonework fell on our Will. In some sort of cupboard, like. Old as the 'ills, I reckon. Like this… ." He held out the dull metal object, a box by the look of it, its surface pitted with rust and black with spider webs.

"Treasure, or what, d'ye reckon then, Sir? Something in it for poor old Will and us lads, then?"

As if a veil dropped upon him, the Steward – within an instant – was all haughtiness and cold authority: "Whatever might be contained within, if indeed there is anything but spiders – it is His Grace's property and, most importantly, His Grace's *business*! Send two men off with your fellow and put the rest back to work. Quickly now, His Grace has not employed you to idle and gossip."

With barely concealed disgust, the foreman turned to his men, nodding them back to the ruin then walked away without another word. Two remained to gingerly lift the prone figure into a barrow, before carefully picking their way back through the broken arches.

With some care, the Steward placed the box on the stone parapet before turning to the visitors: "Well, I must not detain you, Gentleman and Miss Seward. I shall… ." He got no further.

"What we shall do now is to return to a degree of privacy, the better to examine the discovery," said Canon Seward with quiet authority. "As a churchman of some seniority I have not the slightest hesitation in acting *in loco Cornwallissis*, so to speak. By happy coincidence you have the double blessing of not only an excellent medical man in our Mr Greene, but also an antiquarian of equal note. Your master would have it no other way."

Before anyone could disagree, he placed the box in the Steward's unresisting hands and led the way back into the Castle.

With the charioteer carefully set aside and the box now standing upon a hastily laid cloth, the Canon spread his hands, saying: "Well, Mr Museum Keeper, what do we make of this?"

Richard Greene was already absorbed. Just as Seward had assumed command of the situation out on the lawn, now his own moment had arrived: "We shall need a blade of some sort to free-up the lid, and perhaps a drop of lamp oil to loosen the hasp and the hinges – if they will shift at all, that is."

Within moments the box, now brushed clear, stood amidst a scattering of rust-flakes and crawling things seeking another refuge. Greene peered closely at the lid, before requesting a lit candle be held for him.

"There's a faint scratch-carving, clogged-up at present; an armorial, from what one can discern. It will be better revealed with some polishing. So now... ."

The lid, now freed, opened with little difficulty, and – as one – their noses caught a whiff compounded of great age, mildew and some faint, unguessable scent. None of it pleasant.

A book, its cover limp and dulled with antiquity filled the space as if made for it. Loosely knotted thongs of hide, or possibly cloth, wrapped the bindings, partially concealing a lone symbol burned, or engraved, into the stuff of its covering.

With a murmur of fascination, Seward, standing at the Apothecary's shoulder, bent forward and reached to untie them, only to be stopped, forcefully, by Greene.

Seeing the surprise in his old friend's face, Greene raised a hand in apology and said quietly: "Forgive me, but I rather think it would be better not to touch this lightly – if at all. That... ," he pointed to the partially obscured symbol "... tells me so. If I am reading it correctly, this really is most peculiar; most peculiar indeed."

****

Artist, academic and sometimes bluesman, Michael Anson lives in Norfolk, England.

9 781916 129719